NO ROOM FOR RAGE

In the dim light of the closed carriage, Susannah saw the flash of Connor's smile, then saw the shadow that was his hand reach up to cup her chin. She might have pulled away, but by then Connor had caught her lips with his.

It was the gentlest of kisses, featherlight, promising more than it gave. It was tantalizing, his mouth warm, teasing on hers. Suddenly Susannah was no longer stiff or holding herself away. Her mouth opened to him, and instantly his kiss intensified, his mouth firming, demanding more, giving more.

As always Connor O'Neill was not acting in the least like a gentleman. But how could Susannah be angry when she was not reacting remotely like a lady . . . ?

EMMA LANGE is a graduate of the University of California at Berkeley, where she studied European History. She and her husband live in the Midwest and pursue, as they are able, interests in traveling and sailing.

Irish Earl's Ruse

by

Emma Lange

A SIGNET BOOK

SIGNET
Published by the Penguin Group
Penguin Books USA Inc., 375 Hudson Street,
New York, New York, 10014, U.S.A.
Penguin Books Ltd, 27 Wrights Lane, London W8 5TZ, England
Penguin Books Australia Ltd, Ringwood, Victoria, Australia
Penguin Books Canada Ltd, 10 Alcorn Avenue, Toronto, Ontario, Canada M4V 3B2
Penguin Books (N.Z.) Ltd, 182-190 Wairau Road,
Auckland 10, New Zealand

Penguin Books Ltd, Registered Offices:
Harmondsworth, Middlesex, England

First published by Signet, an imprint of New American Library,
a division of Penguin Books USA Inc.

First Printing, June, 1992

10 9 8 7 6 5 4 3 2 1

1

THE COACHMAN did not need to blow his horn to have the gates to Ridley Stud opened. Half a dozen children raced to do the honors almost before he'd begun to slow his team of matched chestnuts.

As the crested carriage passed them, the children dangled from the gates, straining to see inside, but they were too low. One or two received an impression of a plume, nothing more.

All was not lost, however. They knew there was the faintest possibility the carriage would stop at the gatehouse. Half-holding their breaths, the opened gates forgotten for the moment, they waited, poised.

"Hurry!"

It was the cry of the eldest, Will. He'd realized a moment late that the coachman had not used his whip. The others leapt to obey, and were pulling upon the gates, when they heard the coachman cry, "Whoa, there!"

If that were not enough, as they scrambled to shut the heavy gates, they could hear their grandmother exclaim, "Lady Susannah! Why! Fancy you're getting down here just as you used to do," quite as if she had not spent the previous week debating with them whether Lady Susannah Somerset would keep to her old custom of walking the last mile through the woods to her grandmother's house.

The gates fastened, the children ran up the drive toward the carriage, keeping silent as they could, lest they miss hearing Lady Susannah's reply. It came low and pleasant in the next moment.

"Two years may have passed since my last visit to Ridley, Mrs. Barnes, but my tolerance for bouncing about in a prison has not changed, it would seem."

The children quite failed to mark the faint amusement lacing Lady Susannah's voice. As one they stared directly before them at the Duke of Beaufort's newest and most elegant carriage. A gleaming black with gold trim, it looked a fairy-tale conveyance to them.

Agog to see the lady who could find fault with such an equipage, they trotted hurriedly around the carriage just as their grandmother exclaimed, "Well! But look at you, my lady!" Pleased to follow the plump, rosy-cheeked woman's directive for once, the children found themselves staring as a slender lady with a willowy yet feminine figure was handed down from the carriage by a liveried footman. "Why 'tis the finest lady you've grown to be!"

Mrs. Barnes's grandchildren were incurious how Lady Susannah had looked before. They could not imagine that she had ever looked very different than she did then, in the most elegant carriage dress they'd ever seen. Of light blue crepe, its long, flowing skirt seemed made for her, a woman who was taller than they had expected. Neat dark brown kid half-boots peeped out from its hem, and on her head she wore a bonnet of matching blue crepe that sported a dashing sable plume.

Kate, the second eldest of the children, remarked how the color of Lady Susannah's plume matched her eyes, but the other, younger children were too overcome by their visitor's general appearance to analyze the particulars of the beauty of the lady before them. As children do, they simply accepted the clear, faintly gold-tinted complexion, the high, defined line of her cheekbones, the exotic slant of her dark eyes, and the contrast those eyes made with the little of Susannah's honey-gold hair they could see beneath her bonnet.

Then, just as they accepted that Lady Susannah Somerset was the most beautiful, even the most elegant lady they could ever hope to see, she smiled. Too young to know the words "aloof" and "reserved," or even "cool," they had thought her expression merely what one ought to expect of a duke's daughter. Now they saw how wrong they had been. Lady Susannah's face had been masklike in comparison to the way it came alive when she smiled at their grandmother.

"Surely two years have not made such a difference, Mrs. Barnes."

"Go on with you, my lady!" Mrs. Barnes beamed. " 'Twas a girl ye were the last time ye came for yer summer here at Ridley. Now 'tis said ye'll soon be a wife."

Susannah turned away, ignoring the curiosity plainly sparkling in Mrs. Barnes's eyes, and waved up to her father's coachman. "That will be all, John. Pleasant journey."

He lifted his whip with a grin. "God willin', we'll make the stables withou' mishap, m'lady."

As Susannah smiled again, the children giggled, for John's destination was only a mile or so further along the curving drive, and, reminded of them, Susannah looked back to Mrs. Barnes. "These are not all Ronald's children, are they?" she asked, referring to Mrs. Barnes's eldest son.

"The eldest two are Ronald's. The others are Anne's. She lives over to Bury Saint Edmunds now. The children only stayed over to meet you, my lady."

Susannah took the hint and allowed Mrs. Barnes to present her five grandchildren. The peonies in Mrs. Barnes's garden were in full flower. Bees buzzed about them, creating a lazy hum in the background as the children, giggling, jostled forward to be singled out. Little by little, Susannah felt herself relax, felt the constriction of the carriage ease from her limbs, felt the restrictions of London and two Seasons lift.

"I am very pleased to meet you," she addressed the children, when Mrs. Barnes had done. "You remind me of myself when I came to Ridley in the summer with my brother, Sebastian."

The children looked amazed, for they could not imagine Lady Susannah had ever resembled them, but Mrs. Barnes laughed. "And what scamps you were, my lady! I trust Lord Sebastian is well?"

"We get precious few letters, Mrs. Barnes, but in his last,

Sebastian reported being very well. He is enjoying the work he does for Wellesley, and I suppose that is the most important thing.''

"Aye, 'tis, and good for England too. God willing, we shall defeat that Boney soon! And how was Mrs. Mimpriss, my lady? The same, I suppose?''

Susannah smiled. She had almost forgotten in two years how inquisitive her grandmother's retainers could be. No servant of her father's would have asked, however delicately, whether she had thought to provide herself with her usual companion for her trip from London to Newmarket.

"Exactly the same," Susannah allowed wryly. Everyone knew Mrs. Mimpriss for a chatterbox, but Susannah had found the good widow's rattling particularly bothersome that day, as a good bit of it had revolved around Susannah's future. "I left her off at her house in Newmarket, though, to spare her the journey out to Ridley and back." And to spare myself listening to her another moment.

"I hope Mr. Barnes is well?" Susannah inquired of the gatekeeper's wife. When Mrs. Barnes said her husband was ever so well and would be delighted to see what a ''lovely'' thing ''their'' Lady Susannah had grown into, Susannah took her leave.

"Tell him I shall come to see him tomorrow and to have a well-remembered taste of your famous strawberry preserves, Mrs. Barnes.''

"Well! Fancy ye should remember such a thing as my preserves, though 'tis true you and Master Sebastian ate yer fill many a time! I shall have a pot ready for ye, my lady.''

The children followed along with her, until Susannah came to a path that entered the woods just a little further on. A shortcut to her grandmother's home, its green shadows looked particularly cool and inviting that warm June afternoon.

Like good fairies, they watched her, waving, until she disappeared around a bend. Gradually, as the sound of their high, piping voices receded, Susannah's steps slowed, and she began to look about her with something of a smile.

Just as Mrs. Barnes had not changed, so the woods at

Ridley were achingly familiar. The same tall hawthorns and stately oaks shaded patches of larkspur and columbine. When she came to the stream, she found along the bank the frothy ferns she expected, and in the water, thick-leaved water lilies.

It was a landscape Susannah knew as well as her hand, having explored it every summer with Sebastian. Indeed, she considered Suffolk the scene of her childhood. At Deerbourne, her father's estate in Surrey, she and her brother had lived a miniature adulthood, for the Duke of Beaufort had expected his children to exhibit the manners and airs of well-bred adults from the time they were able to walk, and he had been careful to hire governesses of like mind.

Only at Ridley had the reins been loosened. Susannah paused by the stream to untie the ribbons of her fashionable bonnet. In fact, the reins at Ridley had often been nonexistent. The dowager Duchess of Beaufort, having never reined herself in, had made no effort to curb her grandchildren. Oh, there had been limits. Susannah and Sebastian could not have created mayhem. Short of anything so dire, however, they had done as they pleased. Gussie only required that they amuse her, and they had both striven assiduously to do so.

Beaufort knew, of course. Susannah and Sebastian never doubted it, for their father's omniscience was an article of faith. Why he had allowed them to escape annually to his mother's golden, lazy, lax world had never been entirely clear. Likely it had been a combination of interests: Gussie's determination to see them, and Beaufort's desire to have Deerbourne to himself for a few months.

Susannah tossed her head then. She did not wish to think of her father, nor even of Sebastian. She would miss her brother greatly, but she was determined to enjoy this particular summer. Her last one. No! She would not think of the future. She would only spoil the reprieve she'd managed to wrest from Beaufort if she did. She'd one more carefree summer at Ridley, and she meant to savor it fully.

An especial warmth lit Susannah's dark eyes as she stepped out of the woods. Framed by the trees stood Ridley itself, all mellow rosy brick and stacks of chimneys. There were twenty-one, she knew, having counted them dozens of times.

Across the drive, smooth, rolling lawns stretched down to a lake, and beyond to denser woods. A secret place awaited her within them, but just then Susannah's interests lay behind the house.

Walking slowly, she approached Ridley's heart, the stables where her grandmother's thoroughbreds were housed. Of course they were the same! Six long thatch-roofed buildings, of the same brick as the house, stood before her. As each was divided in the center by a breezeway, she could look through to the paddocks, where Ridley's proud, sleek, blood racehorses grazed.

"Cor!" Rounding the corner into the breezeway, a young stableboy drew up with such surprise that the water in the pails he carried sloshed out. Only a little older than Mrs. Barnes's grandchildren, he flushed, abashed to find himself confronted with such a vision.

"Do you know where John Mulcahey is, young man?" Susannah did her grandmother no impoliteness to seek Ridley's head trainer first. For all Lady Augusta's free ways, she kept to a consistent schedule, and at that hour of the afternoon she napped.

Somewhat to Susannah's surprise, the boy shook his head. "N-n-nay, m-miss!"

"Lady Danu, then?" she asked, taking pity on the lad and not pursuing the matter of where Ridley's head trainer could possibly be.

"The Lady? Sh-she be in sixteen, m-miss."

Susannah frowned, thinking it odd the mare was confined on such a day, but she despaired of getting more out of the bedazzled boy, and so started off to investigate for herself.

From behind her the boy blurted, "B-b-but ye cannot go there!"

"It's all right," she called back offhandly over her shoulder. "Lady Danu knows me."

At the stable door Susannah paused, an almost painful sense of homecoming welling up in her. There was the familiar gloomy, filtered quality of the light and the churchlike hush. The air was earthy as ever, though. A mixture of thatch, and straw, and feed, and generations of horses, the pungent odor brought back a rush of memories.

In particular, she recalled her first sight of Lady Danu as a foal struggling to stand on spindly legs that seemed to have no more strength than noodles. She and Sebastian had immediately disputed who would have especial claim to the filly, and at John Mulcahey's suggestion, they had tossed a coin to decide the issue. Susannah had won. She grinned suddenly, recalling how grudgingly Sebastian had accepted his loss. "Well, after all, I can't say I mind," he'd lied ever so loftily. "I don't believe she'll have any speed."

How wrong Lady Danu had proved him! In her six years, she had won every race she had entered.

Still smiling, Susannah found the stall numbered sixteen, but before she could even look over its half-door, an authoritative male voice called out curtly, "Hold, there! The mare's skittish."

The light was behind the man as he strode through the stable door, but though she could not see his face, Susannah knew him to be a stranger. She recognized neither his voice nor his tall, lean figure.

"You needn't worry," she assured the stranger coolly. "John knows me, as does the mare."

Susannah turned back to Lady Danu's stall. She had no more than touched the latch, however, when the man caught her arm, stilling it in midair.

"I said hold," he repeated as firmly as he gripped her.

Susannah stared in astonishment at the strong hand presuming to restrain her. "Let go of my arm!" Unbelievably, his hold tightened. "I said unhand me!" she ordered, flinging up her head.

It was some consolation to Susannah that she could see she took the stranger by surprise. His brow lifted when their eyes met, but it was a small consolation, for she felt her own eyes widen, and she was not at all accustomed to betraying her reactions so obviously.

He was no stablehand, as she had assumed. He'd too much authority in his bearing. She registerred the thought only fleetingly, however. It was his looks that had caught her so off-guard.

He was a schoolgirl's fantasy, if the girl were the sort to dream of rogues or pirates or dark Irishmen. He'd hair black as soot, a straight nose, strong chin, a firm, well-formed mouth, and eyes that would have startled had he been a fair-haired Norseman. Surrounded as they were by absurdly thick sooty lashes, however, their pure sky blue made her blink.

Susannah fought an instictive desire to try to break free of him. She would not engage in a pulling match she was certain to lose.

"Release me." Her voice conveyed her displeasure no less for being low and clear and distinct. "I am Lady Susannah Somerset, Lady Augusta's granddaughter, and I do not care to be manhandled."

A gleam lit his eyes. The certain knowledge that she had amused him infuriated Susannah, but he did release her and give her a slight bow. If he meant the latter gesture to mollify her, it did not. Susannah judged its lazy quality to be more mocking than respectful.

"And I am Connor O'Neill, my lady, at your service."

"The greatest service you may do to me, Mr. O'Neill, is to step out of my way."

"Ah, now, that I cannot do, my lady."

"Are you paralyzed?"

He laughed.

Her eyes flashed. She had not meant to amuse him, as he well knew. And she was quite able to ignore the power of his smile, though he did have, in all, a very appealing strong white smile.

"I am pleased I amuse you, Mr. O'Neill, but that was not my intent. My intention was and is to visit an old friend."

"Ah, but that is precisely why young Tom Dawkins came after me posthaste, my lady." The slightest suggestion of a lilt colored his voice, giving it a musical quality. "Lady Danu is a friend to no one at the moment. She's in foal for the first time, and skittish as the devil. I'll not risk her, her foal, or you, with all due respect, my lady, by allowing you to approach her while she is confined in her stall."

Susannah thought the "with all due respect" insulting. Tall for a woman, she still had to arch her neck to meet his gaze directly. The brown eyes she held upon him sparkled with displeasure. "Where is John Mulcahey?"

Connor did not miss her flashing eyes, but the effect upon him was not what Susannah would have wished. That angry gleam had brought their deep rich sable to life. Connor so appreciated the effect, and their unusual slant, that he absorbed her question a moment late.

"Mulcahey? Ah, John's in Ireland. I am his replacement."

"No!"

Susannah stared, her anger forgotten temporarily. She had looked forward immeasurably to seeing John Mulcahey again. He had been at Ridley since before she'd been born. It was he who had taught her and Sebastian to ride, and he who had with a ready smile revealed all the secrets of the stables. A man in his fifties, John had had a craggy face reddened and seamed by the days he had spent in the open with his horses.

This man, for all that he was more . . . masculine than Mulcahey, was not half so weathered or earthy or familiar as her old friend.

Something of her disappointment showed in her expression, and Connor said not without sympathy, "It is only a temporary arrangement. John will return. But until then, I am the head trainer at Ridley."

They both knew that as the head trainer, he'd the ruling of the stableyard. Mulcahey had been the most indulgent of despots. Susannah could not recall a time she had not gotten her way with him. But this man stood regarding her with a half-smile that hinted far more at a challenge than at indulgence.

Susannah's jaw tightened as she took in that look. Who was he, anyway, to look at her so?

Connor's smile deepened. "I do believe you doubt my credentials, Lady Susannah."

Susannah knew instantly he'd adequate credentials. He would not have been half-laughing otherwise. Likely better-than-adequate ones, even, for now that she considered it, she knew John Mulcahey would never have left the stables to anyone incapable of managing them. Still, Susannah saw an opening and she took it, allowing her eyes to sweep him with a glance she made certain was dismissive.

"On the contrary, Mr. O'Neill, your credentials are quite obvious—to anyone who knows my grandmother." She watched him to be certain he understood her meaning, and felt a surge of pleasure when his eyes narrowed suddenly. "As for me, whatever your credentials, it is at the meet I'll measure your worth."

With that thrust, Susannah swept about, conceding defeat on the subject of Lady Danu, but nothing else. "I shan't take up any more of your time, Mr. O'Neill. You must have duties that need your attention. As for Lady Danu, I shall see her tomorrow when she is let out in the paddock."

Another man, also a stranger, stood by the door. Not so tall as O'Neill, he was broader, squarer. Susannah did not know what he had heard of her exchange with his fellow, nor did she care. In passing, she accorded him only the faintest of nods.

Liam O'Flaherty watched Susannah swish by him with an appreciative look in his eyes. She was beautiful, and because it was summer, her traveling costume was of light enough material to display more than hide her long legs and slender figure.

But when he turned to look up at Connor, who had come to join him at the door, Liam's smile faded abruptly. "Och, now, an' I cannot like the look in yer eye, Connor! 'Tis trouble, for certain. Who is she?"

"Lady Susannah Somerset, Lady Gussie's grand-daughter."

Liam's rugged brow creased the more. "The one that's to be here for the summer?"

"All three months of it."

"Blast! Just listen to you! She's Sassenach!"

"As Sassenach as they come," Connor agreed amiably. "And as beautiful. I don't plan to make her my wife, Liam."

"Bless me!" Liam looked up to the heavens beseechingly. "She's not only Sassenach, but gentry. You'd best make no plans a'tall with her."

"I can entertain myself, surely," Connor protested too blandly. "Only a little kiss, when she thaws. Surely she will thaw. No woman with legs that long can be cool forever, do you think?"

Liam gave a grunt of frustration. "She'll divert you!"

"Oh, aye, I do hope so." Connor grinned, but when Liam cursed again, his manner changed. "Don't fash yourself, Liam," he admonished abruptly, no laughter at all lingering in his eyes. "I'll not be forgetting what it is we're about here in bonny England. How could I, when it's so cursedly serious? And that reminds me, is it not time you departed to look about Norwich Castle and its county jail?"

"Aye, 'tis," Liam replied with an abrupt nod. "I'll return when I've some word on Seamus."

"Go with God, Liam."

"And you, Connor O'Neill"—Liam shook a thick gnarled finger at the younger man—"keep away from the devil!"

2

SUSANNAH'S half-boots tapped out a brisk, emphatic rhythm as she mounted Ridley's front steps. Her pleasant, comfortable sense of homecoming having evaporated, she failed to remark she was crossing Ridley's threshold for the first time in two summers until the door opened and her grandmother's ancient butler, Soames, greeted her with eyes that were suspiciously bright.

Susannah spoke as fondly to the old man as she had to Mrs. Barnes, but she had to school herself to patience when the old dear went on about how lovely she was, how much the lady she'd become, and how glad he knew Lady Augusta would be to see her.

All the while Susannah smiled graciously and bent to kiss his old cheeks, she wanted to fly up the stairs to Gussie's rooms to demand to know who the devil O'Neill was. She had never heard of a temporary head trainer. As she had implied to the Irishman, she had no illusions about her grandmother. Gussie delighted in proclaiming her enthusiasm for an attractive male, but Susannah was determined to learn what recommendations he possessed other than his obvious physical ones.

He had ruffled her. She admitted it, though the admission did not please her. She had never before been ruffled, a state she associated with empty-headed hens.

"Ah, here is Stubbs now, my lady," Soames announced

in his grave way. "She will know precisely how her ladyship is."

Thin and wiry, with sharp eyes and a manner to match, Agatha Stubbs, Lady Augusta's dresser, was unapologetically abrupt in her manner. "Pleased to see you, my lady."

"And I am pleased to see you again, Stubbs. Are you going up?" Stubbs's reply was a single decisive nod. "Then I'll accompany you, and you can tell me how Gussie is as we go."

"My lady is very well," Stubbs reported, falling in beside Susannah. "She was delighted to hear you arrived safely, and looks forward to welcoming you at dinner."

"Not before? I had wanted to say at least hello now."

"Lady Augusta is not prepared, my lady."

Susannah understood. A renowned beauty in her day, Lady Augusta never appeared before anyone but Stubbs before she had undergone a lengthy ritualistic toilette. "Ah, well, it won't be long to dinner. Is anyone in particular coming tonight, do you know, Stubbs?"

"I do not know if you are aware of it, Lady Susannah, but your cousin Mr. James Somerset is staying at Ridley just now. He will join you this evening, I believe."

Susannah had not known her cousin would be on hand, though she was not surprised. He had often joined her and Sebastian at Ridley in the summers. "Does James intend a long stay, do you know?"

"I have not been advised of Mr. Somerset's plans, my lady. But I can say he brought three trunks with him."

Susannah chuckled. "I stand so advised, Stubbs, and will conclude, as you no doubt have, that James does not plan a short sojourn at Ridley."

"As you say, my lady," Stubbs murmured, the sparest of smiles curving her thin lips.

Before dinner, upon entering the Queen's Saloon, where it was the custom for the company at Ridley to gather, Susannah smiled to herself. The first to arrive, she could give herself up to the pleasure of the view. It was one of her favorites in the house, as it was framed by a thick clematis vine bearing impossible large papery flowers of deep rich purple. In the far distance rose Warren Hill, up which she and Sebastian had used to race their mounts. Nearer, between the green woods and the house, the lake shimmered silver and mauve in the twilight. Recalling the time she and Sebastian and James had overturned their boat in the middle of it, Susannah smiled outright.

Held by the view and the pleasant memories, she missed the man standing to the side of the windows. His black evening clothes blended with the shadows, but he heard her, and when he turned, the light caught on the white of his cravat.

Assuming he was James, Susannah opened her mouth to greet her cousin; then he stepped forward into the last of the sunlight, and Susannah exclaimed in astounded tones, ''O'Neill!''

''Lady Susannah.'' The Irishman inclined his head, taking the time as he did so to sweep her with a more frankly assessing look than Susannah had received in all her two years on the town in London. She scarcely noticed. Or she did notice, and knew, insensibly, a spurt of relief that she'd chosen a flattering silk of dull gold to wear. But her own appearance was not uppermost in Susannah's mind as she took in the black-haired Irishman.

Nor even did she dwell overlong upon his handsomeness, though at the first sight of him she had received a little jolt, almost as if she had forgotten in the few hours since she'd seen him the particulars of his looks: his straight nose, his strong jaw and determined chin, his well-defined mouth, and, finally, his singularly blue eyes.

What struck Susannah the most powerfully just then was how at ease he appeared standing there in Ridley's most elegant gathering room. His evening clothes were modest but unexceptionable. And far more important than his dress, he held himself without any of the stiffness common to men who found themselves on unfamiliar, intimidating ground.

She had stared too long. Susannah knew it when she saw his mouth lift at the corner. ''I think I have taken you by surprise again, Lady Susannah.''

Susannah allowed a single arched eyebrow to lift slightly. "Yes, Mr. O'Neill, you have taken me by surprise. I did not see you at first, you blended so well with the curtains."

Having sought to elicit indignation, Susannah was annoyed to see a spark of amusement in his eyes again. If his reaction intrigued her as well, she'd not the time to consider it, for her grandmother swept into the room then, crying grandly, "Susannah! Susannah! Susannah!"

"Gussie!" Susannah loved few people, really, but those few she loved, she loved fiercely. "Gussie," she repeated, a smile few were privileged to see, and even fewer to receive, lighting her face. Connor, observing it, was surprised by its power. The cool arrogant beauty who had attempted to put him in his lowly place had vanished. "You look marvelous, my love!"

Lady Augusta was, indeed, a marvel. Almost as tall as her granddaughter, her full figure corseted ruthlessly into the curves of an hourglass, she did not look above . . . well, she did not look her seventy-and-five years. Certainly there was not a line to be seen upon her meticulously powdered face. And if her hair was not so lustrous a honey-gold as Susannah's, still it was very thick and full.

Lady Augusta's only concession to age was the silver-headed cane she leaned upon somewhat heavily as she held out her arm to her granddaughter. "Susannah! My dear child, you have grown up while I was not on hand to approve. Dear heaven, but I do think you may be as beautiful as I was!"

Susannah grinned. "I am flattered, ma'am, as I know from your own lips you were the most beautiful girl of your time."

"And quick, too—as I still am!" Lady Augusta laughed gustily as she held out a cheek Susannah knew not to actually touch with her lips. Real kisses ran the hazard of disturbing her powder. When Susannah had saluted the air, Lady Augusta swept her about to face her guest.

"My granddaughter, Connor. A beauty, is she not?"

To Susannah's vexation, the Irishman took shameless advantage of the situation, subjecting her to another raking look before he turned his rogue's blue eyes to Lady Augusta.

''As Lady Susannah is your image, ma'am, how could she be less than ravishing?''

''Darling boy!'' Lady Augusta shrieked with delight. ''Because I adore your flattery so, I shall discount entirely that you have only echoed my own remarks.'' She turned her surprisingly vigorous smile upon her granddaughter. ''O'Neill has come to us as a replacement for Mulcahey, Susannah. Though only a temporary arrangement, I must say it is a most satisfactory one!''

O'Neill, Susannah observed, showed not the least embarrassment at Gussie's approval of him. If he suspected Lady Augusta had taken him on for his looks, not his merits, he either did not care or was not concerned, for he returned her a smile that seemed genuinely fond. ''I assure you, my lady, the satisfaction is entirely mutual.''

Lady Augusta chuckled hugely again and flung out her hand, that the Irishman might lead her to her favorite chair. Susannah took a place upon a settee, while Connor went to stand with his shoulders propped casually against the chimneypiece.

''Actually, I knew of Mr. O'Neill's coming to Ridley, Gussie,'' Susannah addressed her grandmother. ''But not the reason for it. I hope John has not taken ill?''

''You needn't look anxious, my dear. You will only develop wrinkles for naught. Your old friend is quite well. It is his father who is on his deathbed, which can be little surprise. John himself is no gosling. But let me feast my eyes on you, my dear! Lud, I was afraid Beaufort might press the life right out of you in the two years he had you entirely to himself.''

There was a pause as Soames entered bearing a tray with sherry and port, but if Susannah hoped her grandmother might, in the interlude, think better of remarking further upon Beaufort before the Irishman, she was to be disappointed. Even before old Soames had creaked out of the room, Lady Augusta rolled her eyes at her head trainer.

''I can't think how Beaufort came to be my son, O'Neill. I declare he is the coolest man alive! I'd have disowned him, said he was not mine at all, but he's the image of his father. Sebastian got out from under him, thank God! Went off to Portugal, though Beaufort nearly disowned him for his patriotism. It's harder for a girl to escape, though." She swung back to look approvingly at Susannah. "I was afraid for you, gel, but I can see you've your spark, still. Can't imagine what I'd have done had you turned into the merely pleasant sort of person James is. He's a sweet boy, of course, but he does take after his mother's people, the Darnsworths, and I never thought them very amusing. Ah! I shall have to desist, for here he comes now."

Actually two gentlemen entered the room from the terrace, one Susannah's cousin, James Somerset, the other Major Hornbeck, a longtime devotee of Lady Augusta's.

A bluff, ruddy-faced man of unfailing good humor, Major Hornbeck greeted his hostess with fond gusto while James welcomed Susannah to Ridley with a kiss upon her cheek. Changing places, Major Hornbeck lifted Susannah's slender hand to his lips and took his turn remarking what a beauty she had grown to be. "You take my breath, my dear. And that, though I was forewarned. We are not so horse-mad here in Newmarket that we did not hear what a figure you cut in town! From everyone's account, you ran away with the field."

Susannah laughed. "You've not lost your gallant tongue, I see, Major Becky, and it is such a great pleasure to be flattered in track cant, I'll forgive you mentioning London, when all I want to hear is Newmarket's news. Come, tell me everything the patrons of the Rutland Arms have to say of the coming meet."

"Thank you, my boy." Major Hornbeck accepted a glass of port from James and subsided onto the settee beside Susannah. "The Arms is in an uproar, my dear, and all on account of a horse here at Ridley." He smiled, delighted to see he had taken Susannah by surprise. "The talk of all Newmarket is the black that O'Neill here took it into his head to acquire. James and I strolled out to see him, lad." The major turned his smile upon O'Neill. "Lord, he's a rogue! Do you truly think you can tame him in time?''

The Irishman shrugged noncommittally. "I've the notion to try, at any rate."

Had he blustered, Susannah would have doubted him instantly. That he did quite the opposite gave her to believe he thought he could tame his horse. The major evidently shared Susannah's reasoning, for he slapped his knee enthusiastically. "Stap me if I don't think you'll do it! You see, my dear"—he turned to enlighten Susannah—"no one would touch the rogue when he was put up for sale in Newmarket. No point in it. He couldn't be ridden. Then O'Neill saw him, and taking pity on him for the way he was treated, bought him."

"Pity!" The derisive cry was Lady Augusta's. "You'd make O'Neill a sentimental fool, Becky, when the truth is he's a smooth-talking rogue. Don't forget he's convinced me to underwrite the colt's food and board."

Susannah looked on, amazed and amused all at once. Surely there was never such a place as Ridley. At her grandmother's stud, the head trainer not only was invited to dinner and treated as a boon companion, but he actually owned one of the horses in the stables.

She had been away from Ridley too long and forgotten what was held most important there. James reminded her when he raised his glass in eager salute. "To Saracen!" he exclaimed, "And to winning! I hope you know, O'Neill, that I've a side wager with Bunny Townshend on this roguish colt of yours. And that I can ill afford to lose it."

The Irishman regarded the younger man with a faint smile. "Losing generally sits ill with us all, Somerset. I can only promise to do my best."

"Hmmm." James considered a moment, then grinned cheerfully. "I shall just have to hope your best bests! I can't undo my wager, after all."

Susannah smothered a laugh as Lady Augusta exclaimed aghast, "Undo a wager!" and proceeded to read her grandson a lecture on the merits of risking as much as possible on long, long odds. "Gets the blood flowing, my boy! Keeps you young."

She might have declaimed a great deal further on the subject, for it was one of the tenets upon which she had based her quite satisfactory life, but Soames crept in to announce dinner.

The Irishman looked no more out of place in Ridley's formal dining room than he had in the salon where Queen Anne had once been entertained, but Susannah suspected carrying off dinner would be a great deal more difficult than sipping port flawlessly had been. Looking through her lashes, she waited to see if he had any notion which of the four forks beside his plate was the correct one for buttered prawns. To her surprise, he did not hesitate. The prawn fork in his hand, he looked up and caught her gaze upon him.

Even from across the table she had no difficulty discerning the gleam that sprang to life in his eyes. "Not hungry, Lady Susannah?" he inquired, an ironic tilt to his mouth.

"On the contrary, Mr. O'Neill," Susannah replied, quite up to the challenge in his eyes. "I am famished. We'd only a light luncheon on the trip from town."

Her grandmother, overhearing, would know where Susannah had stopped for luncheon, and the conversation became general, touching on the abominable state of the roads, the blessedly fair weather they'd enjoyed, and, finally, the news from town.

Susannah had known her grandmother would wish to hear the *on-dits*, but she had hoped Lady Augusta might wait until they were alone to raise a particular subject. Lady Augusta had never been one to cultivate discretion, however.

After the first two courses had come and gone, she shot her granddaughter a considering look. "Well, Susannah. As you do not seem inclined to say, I am forced to ask. Do you come to us betrothed? Did you decline the invitation to stay with Philip and the Mountjoys in Brighton this summer because you'd no need to go, or because you are putting Lord Bland off?"

"I say, Grandmama!" The reprimand burst from James. " 'Tis no way to speak of Sunderly! He's one of the most-sought-after catches in town!"

"Is he?" Lady Augusta eyed her grandson consideringly.

"I'm not surprised, I suppose. He has impeccable manners no doubt, is plump in the pocket certainly, and will be the Earl of Grafton when his father obliges everyone by sticking his spoon in the wall. You and Becky and everyone else are welcome to see him as the perfect match for Susannah. For my part, I cannot imagine that any son of Grafton could possess even a *soupçon* of spirit, and therefore I shall maintain that this Sunderly is not even fit to touch Susannah's shoe."

Susannah laughed, no mean feat, given how annoyingly aware she was that her future, perhaps even her husband, were being discussed with the greatest frankness before an audience she did not consider friendly.

"I shall make a note of that, Gussie, and reprimand the viscount next time he leans down to give such offense. As to why I am here: I was growing dull as a dog. You will not countenance it, but after two years away from you, I was close to accepting that all dowagers, by nature, behave themselves. I am relieved to see how ill my memory served me."

"She's got you, Gussie!" Major Hornbeck, smiling broadly, saluted Susannah with his glass. "Bless me, but I'm glad you're home, my dear! 'Tis time someone took her to task."

"Hmpf! What she's done is avoid answering. As if I would accept such pap in lieu of an answer. What I want to know, Susannah, is are you betrothed or no?"

"I do believe you ought to join Sebastian in Portugal, Gussie. He's mentioned interrogating prisoners in one or two of his letters." When her grandmother made a threatening gesture, Susannah protested mildly, "I have no clearer answer, truly. Sunderly and I are on the best of terms. I have not come to Ridley to avoid him, but to see you, my dearest Gussie, and your horses. It has been two years, I shall remind you. And now you know as much as I do, I hope you will concede we've discussed family affairs overlong. Surely we are boring poor Mr. O'Neill to tears."

Susannah was not at all, even on such short acquaintance with him, surprised to find the Irishman amused. But she did not care that he'd recognized her diversion. She had wanted to change the subject, and as well, had decided it was time he took his turn upon center stage.

"Tell me, Mr. O'Neill. I am curious. Have you trained horses elsewhere?"

Susannah had not expected O'Neill to be deceived by the idleness of her tone, and he was not. His mouth curved as he gave her a look that was, for all the lazy-lidded quality of it, entirely penetrating.

Aware of a certain leaping of her pulses as she faced him, Susannah was equally aware of a feeling of anticlimax when Lady Augusta did not allow him a rejoinder, but exclaimed triumphantly, "O'Neill has trained for the Earl of Iveagh, my dear. You remember the Irishman who did not deign to come to England himself, but did condescend to send his bay colt to win a very heavy purse for him four years ago? You did train the bay, did you not, O'Neill?"

"I did."

"I met him once, you know."

"Who is that, my lady?"

"Iveagh."

Because she was looking at him, Susannah plainly saw the Irishman start, then catch himself. "The earl?" he asked, his voice quite neutral.

"Surely there is not a Duke of Iveagh!" Lady Augusta retorted with a laugh. "Did you know him, O'Neill? The old earl?"

"Ah, the old earl." Susannah thought she heard a note of relief in the Irishman's voice, but could not tell from his expression if she only imagined it. "No, I did not know him. He was before my time."

"I thought so." The reply mystified Susannah, and earned Lady Augusta a close look from O'Neill, but the older woman seemed to forget what she had said as soon as the words left her mouth, for her expression became rather dreamy and she said, "Iveagh was a little before my time, as well, unfortunately. He was such a good deal older than I, in fact, I never knew him nearly so well as I'd have liked."

A footman appeared at her side with a large platter of roast grouse, interrupting, likely for the better, Lady Augusta's reminiscences. Into the momentary lull Susannah heard herself say, "Where in Ireland are you from, Mr. O'Neill?"

She could have bitten her tongue the moment the words were out, for when he looked to her, there was something dancing in his eyes that told her her display of interest had gratified him. "Connacht, my lady. On the far side of Ireland, where the hills rise misty blue above clear, deep loughs."

"And the grass is emerald green, doubtless?"

"Well, to be sure, my lady, Ireland is called the Emerald Isle."

Truly he was a devil to bend so teasing a look upon her when he must know she had been trying to goad him. And, Susannah admitted, he had nearly won a smile. The only reason he had not, she allowed, was that the footman with the grouse arrived at her side, giving her a much-needed excuse to look away from the infectious light dancing in his brilliant blue eyes.

3

SUSANNAH pulled at the hem of her riding jacket; eyed the effect, then pulled again, only to achieve the same negligible result. Her jacket rode up again the moment she released it.

Her mouth tightened. She was dressed as she had always dressed for the exercise gallops. The grooms would think nothing of her breeches. A racehorse was too powerful to be galloped riding sidesaddle, as they knew better than any, and she fully intended to take up her old custom of riding out with them at dawn. It was one of her favorite treats at Ridley.

Damn the Irishman. He was the reason she had dithered in her room, though the day had dawned brilliantly fresh and clear. Imagining the look he'd give her had made her hesitate, and she resented that he'd affected her so. She was not in the habit of concerning herself with the opinions of others. Nor would she be now; she was determined upon it.

Whatever her determination, Susannah was relieved when she reached the stableyard to encounter an old friend first. Head groom at Ridley as well as its most capable jockey, Jeffrey Murdoch greeted her with a pleasure untinged by even a suggestion of disapproval.

"Bless me! Lady Susannah! Good day to you!" He stood back, shaking his head. "I was told you'd got home safe again to Ridley, but no one thought to warn me what a beauty you'd become while you were up in London.''

Susannah returned him a smile that proved there was yet a little of the old Lady Susannah about. ''You've a tongue as smooth as any London dandy, Murdoch, as I don't doubt the serving lasses at the Rutland Arms have had occasion to tell you. As to what I've become, I must say I am more concerned over what I was. Everyone has remarked with such approval how changed I am, I've begun to fear I must have been as homely as a duckling two years ago.''

Murdoch laughed outright. ''Nay, my lady, you were a bonny lass, but only a child, you understand? Now, 'tis a fine—''

''Murdoch!'' A deep, authoritative voice interrupted them. Susannah recognized it instantly and took a long breath as, following Murdoch's lead, she turned to face the breezeway behind them.

''There are horses to be ridden, man!'' Connor O'Neill strode into the sunlight, a smile on his face. ''Ruin today or . . . What the devil?''

She was Lady Susannah Somerset, daughter of a duke, and still her cheeks heated. How dare he subject her to such a slow, derisive appraisal!

''The devil is this, Mr. O'Neill.'' Susannah regarded the Irishman through dangerously narrowed eyes. ''I have helped exercise the horses at Ridley since I was twelve years old, and I mean to do so this summer. Because I've less control over a racehorse when I ride sidesaddle, it has been my habit to ride astride. Now, I would appreciate it greatly if you would cease staring at me as if I were . . . a freak and assign me a horse for the morning. If you've not given Barley Boy to another, I would like him.''

''And do you always order things to your liking regardless, Lady Susannah?''

Susannah lifted her chin a notch and raised her sweetly arched eyebrows, so that she looked, though she was unaware of it, very imperious indeed.

''Regardless of what, Mr. O'Neill? I can ride any horse in the stable—but for your rogue, perhaps,'' she conceded before he taunted her with the real possibility that she could not handle such a brute. "You may ask Murdoch, here, if you doubt my word. And anyway, it is only myself I shall hurt, if I cannot. I came to have my summer at Ridley, and as my summers have long included riding out every morning, I fully intend to ride out today."

Susannah was a beauty, truly she was, and it was not so much that Connor lost sight of that fact as that his own not-inconsiderable temper flared. The position of hireling being new to him, he was not accustomed to taking orders from anyone, and particularly not from an arrogant girl, however lovely.

A black eyebrow winging upward, he flicked his gaze to the breeches that did nothing to obscure either the length or the curve of her legs. "Your ability to control a racehorse aside, do you seriously believe your grandmother would approve this . . . costume you intend to wear among a pack of grooms?"

It was the wrong question, given Lady Augusta's love of the unorthodox, and Susannah leapt upon Connor's ill-considered argument with pleasure. "And do you, Mr. O'Neill, seriously believe my grandmother would object, given that I have known her 'pack of grooms' since I was a child? Or do you suspect her reservations might extend only to the new men in the stableyard, of whose manners she cannot be certain?"

Susannah had all but forgotten Jeffrey Murdoch until Connor shifted his gaze from her to their rapt audience. "And what are you grinning at, Murdoch? Do you mean to tell me you do not think this is mad?" He waved his hand in Susannah's direction, leaving unclear whether he thought her desire to ride mad, or her costume, or both.

"Ah, but 'tis true the lass can ride," Murdoch, still grinning, vouched for Susannah. "I promise you that, O'Neill. Let her have a go and see for yourself."

Connor's decision did not come immediately. Susannah was made to wait a long moment before the appearance of a new gleam in his eye forewarned her he did not intend to capitulate gracefully.

"Very well, then, my lady. As you wish, so be it. We will take the measure of your seat upon a horse."

And if that insultingly suggestive concession were not enough to make her fume, O'Neill called out for three horses. He would not take Susannah's word—or Murdoch's—that she could ride well enough to match the grooms.

There was no question, of course, whether he was capable of controlling the large muscular colt brought for him. While Susannah exchanged greetings with all her old friends in the stableyard, Connor mounted his horse. The colt was restive after a night confined in his stall, but the Irishman sat the thoroughbred with ease.

Barbarian, Susannah muttered entirely to herself. And entirely unfairly, as she knew. True, the Irishman was tall, and broad-shouldered, with long, well-formed legs that filled out his buckskin breeches rather better than Susannah had ever seen the tight-fitting garment filled out, but she knew very well no gentleman of her acquaintance, regardless of title, would have spurned the Irishman's athletic figure had it been offered to him.

Barbarian, she growled again, unable to think of a better epithet as they proceeded single file down the lane that led to the heath. He rode behind her, and hard as Susannah tried, she could not relax. Sitting stiffly upon Barley Boy, she could feel the man's blue eyes examining her as no gentleman's would have been.

Through the silvery leaves of the birches that lined the lane, Susannah caught sight of her old nurse's cottage. Nan was part Irish. The thought made Susannah roll her eyes. The old woman was nothing like the man behind her. He was outrageous and insolent.

A flock of geese flying high overhead, their wedge pointing toward Suffolk's coastal fens, honked noisily, drawing her attention. She would like to fly as high as they did. She would be free up there. It took Susannah a moment to realize it was not of the Irishman she'd thought then. And little wonder. She could leave him anytime she wished. The Viscount Sunderly and his imminent proposal of marriage, however, was a different matter.

And then, ah, then, Susannah quite forgot even Sunderly.
They had come to the end of the lane, and suddenly there
was no beseeching suitor, no demanding father, nor even
a disturbing Irishman. It was summer in Suffolk, and the
heath lay open before her.

When Murdoch spurred his mount, Susannah did the same.
Barley Boy responded instantly, stretching his long, powerful
legs. And they were off, pounding across the low, smooth,
limitless turf of the heath.

Susannah passed Murdoch soon enough. He was mounted
upon a smaller filly, but she was aware that another set of
hooves stayed with her. Ruin, O'Neill's horse, was older
than Barley Boy, but strong. It would be a race.

The blood in Susannah's veins leapt, and she laughed aloud
as she leaned down low by Barley Boy's neck, urging him
on. "Come on, Boy! Let's show that blasted Irishman how
we run!"

Susannah's laugh floated back to Connor, buoyant and
joyful and challenging too. A chagrined smile curved his
mouth at the sound. She'd every reason to laugh.

She had proved him wrong on all counts. Not one of the
grooms had leered at her in her breeches. She might have
been one of their own returning to the fold, the way they
had welcomed her. Or almost, Connor corrected himself,
for he did not think they'd have greeted another groom with
quite the pride they obviously had in "their" Lady Susannah.

It was a not-unjustified pride, particularly as far as her
ability to ride a horse went. Barley Boy was no easy rascal
to manage. Connor had thought the lady boasted when she
declared she would ride him.

It was those long legs, no doubt. Connor's smile changed.
At least he'd consolation. Every morning he would have the
pleasure of appreciating her in those breeches. And certainly
she was a greater pleasure to follow across the heath than
Murdoch. Even tamed into a long thick braid, her honey-
gold tresses made a far more enjoyable flag than the jockey's
grizzled head ever had.

A large outcropping of stone marked the end of the distance
Mulcahey liked to run his horses. Susannah had forgotten

to ask if O'Neill stopped there as well, but she pulled up anyway, and turned, slowing Barley Boy by degrees.

Connor performed the same maneuver a few moments later, and when he had slowed Ruin to a walk, he pulled in beside Susannah. She awaited him, dark eyes sparkling, head tilted, and looking, in all, very, very smug.

He grinned. "Your point, my lady. I stand corrected, rolled up, and converted. You may ride any mount in Ridley's stable you choose, any morning."

Susannah had not expected such an unreserved concession. It was her experience that males begrudged being bested.

"Well!" She was too surprised to say anything but the truth. "You are gracious to say so."

"I could scarcely say otherwise." Connor's laugh was undeniably, and somehow thereby attractively, rueful. "You not only managed the Boy very nicely, indeed, you reached the rocks before I."

Susannah's eyes warmed at that, and she chuckled as she leaned to pat Barley Boy's neck. "The Boy's a good horse."

"You are a superb rider."

The flat statement pleased her. Indeed, Susannah felt such a spark of pleasure, she flushed. And looked away at once, unsettled. "Thank you, Mr. O'Neill. Ah, look." She waved as a horseman trotted up to them, quite as relieved as she was pleased to see him. "Here's Murdoch."

"How can you put such faith in an Irishman, James?" Bunny Townshend, the speaker and James's friend, was one of several guests Lady Augusta had invited to dinner. "Jove! The man can be little better than a heathen."

"He don't have to be civilized to ride a horse, Bunny!" James protested with quite adequate logic. "And he can do that, can't he, Susannah?"

"Yes. He's a horse trainer."

Neither young man registered the irony in Susannah's voice. James looked triumphantly at Bunny, and Bunny looked miffed. "You may apply to Susannah all you want, James, but she cannot assure you the Irishman will win the Two Thousand Guineas with his rogue! I still say he can't!"

The fourth member of the quartet of younger people, a nubile girl with wide, thickly lashed doe's eyes, tossed her head, causing the fat sausage curls she wore pinned high on one side of her head to tremble warningly. "I wish the both of you would stop wrangling over this horse! You've made your wagers. Why must you go on? I am bored to tears."

Susannah watched James color and turn at once to placate the girl, who was Bunny's cousin and staying with his family for the summer. "I beg your pardon, Miss Limley! We are remiss. Tell me what you would prefer to speak of instead, and I shall make amends."

Phoebe Limley had long ago formed the habit of calling attention to her dimples by allowing her finger to linger just beside them when she smiled. "Let us discuss how we shall entertain ourselves this summer." She dimpled prettily for James. "I've one notion. Do you know, sir, that I have never been on a picnic?"

"A picnic?" Bunny wrinkled his rather long, narrow nose. "Do you really wish to take luncheon outside in the heat of the day with a lot of loathsome bugs and dust? Have a heart, Phoebe! Think of something else to entertain us."

Miss Limley did not, Susannah observed, like to be crossed. Her wide eyes narrowed rather precipitately. "You needn't come along, Bunny. James will not need your assistance to entertain Lady Susannah and me. You will come, Lady Susannah?" Phoebe turned to cast a cajoling look at Susannah. "I know from James that you are fond of outdoor excursions. Do say you agree we ought to have a picnic, if the weather remains fair."

"If the weather remains fair . . ." Susannah chanced to meet James's eyes, and she found herself wishing she did not have a soft spot for her cousin. Mutely but eloquently he begged her to respond cordially to Miss Limley. Though an imperceptible sigh escaped her, Susannah did, therefore, finish pleasantly, " . . . a, ah, picnic would be most enjoyable."

Miss Limley squealed happily. "There, Bunny! If you wish to be in Lady Susannah's good graces, you will have to come along. It will be the greatest fun."

Instantly Susannah regretted succumbing to James. She'd given Phoebe Limley the opportunity to retaliate against Bunny by artlessly announcing his interest in Susannah.

Susannah did not know Miss Limley well. Their circles overlapped only occasionally, but she knew enough of the girl to know Phoebe attracted men easily, for she was an heiress, pretty in a conquettish way, and though small, enticingly rounded. It did not hurt either that she had long since mastered the art of flirtation. James, for one, looked positively bemused by the fluttery looks and dimpled smiles he had received in considerable number.

There had been some rumor or other about Phoebe at the end of the Season. Susannah could not recall what had been said. She'd not cared much, and had been distracted besides. Doubtless the girl's difficulty had involved a man, though. Phoebe would not stumble on any other account, and just as certainly, whatever had occurred was the reason she had been sent from town to stay with Bunny's parents.

Her presence explained James's decision to while away the summer at Ridley. Since he had taken rooms in town, he had not been accustomed to visiting Gussie for so long a time. Susannah doubted his taste, but not his interest. But for an occasional exchange with Bunny, he'd hung on every giggle Phoebe threw his way.

Even then Susannah heard him say with the greatest earnestness, "If we do make such an excursion, Miss Limley, I will permit it to take place only on the mildest of days. Your skin is too delicate to risk exposure to the elements."

Which would eliminate the dress Miss Limley was wearing that night, Susannah remarked to herself. Exposure was the aim of its cut.

Unbidden, Susannah thought of the Irishman. Did his taste run to low décolletage? She'd have been surprised if it did not. He . . . No, she'd been about to say he was a low character, but that was too unfair. He'd behaved nobly, in fact, when he had conceded defeat that morning. Bunny had called him uncivilized, but Susannah rather imagined that the pettish dandy would have reacted a great deal less civilly had he received the undoubtedly smug look she'd given O'Neill. A faint smile curved Susannah's mouth as she recalled the Irishman's response. He'd a remarkably irresistible grin.

4

SUSANNAH swung up lightly on the fence, a carrot for Lady Danu in her hand. She had forgotten to bring a treat on her first visit the day before, and the chestnut mare had kept a wary distance, for she was quite as skittish as O'Neill had warned.

Susannah slipped down from the fence, though Lady Danu tossed her head nervously and snorted. "Easy, Lady, easy." She spoke in a low, soothing voice. "You are undone by this new experience, are you not? I cannot blame you. I think I should be too."

Slowly, Susannah moved forward one careful step at a time. "Will your foal be a filly, Lady, as lovely and proud as you? Or a colt to race that Saracen and beat him soundly?"

The mare whinnied, and Susannah smiled. "You'd like that, eh? And this carrot, what of it? You've not lost your taste for treats, have you?"

A little over an arm's length away, Susannah stopped and held out the carrot, leaving it to the mare to choose whether to close the distance between them. Prepared to wait all day if need be, Susannah continued speaking. "You are thinking I have been away too long—and are right, of course. But it is the way of the world that one must grow up. Look what's happened to you."

Lady Danu snorted, bringing her head down sharply. "Yes, I know," Susannah continued, wryly now. "They want to marry me off and get me breeding too. It is the lot of a female, they say. Ah, but come. Let us make the most of this last summer of freedom I've won for myself.''

Beguiled by the soothing, tantalizingly familiar voice, Lady Danu took a wary step forward, then another, and another. Once she shook her head, seeming unsettled, but Susannah remained very still, holding out the carrot. It proved an irresistible lure. Extending her neck suddenly, the mare plucked the carrot from Susannah's hand. She disposed of it rapidly, keeping a close eye upon Susannah, and when she was done, she tossed her head again.

Susannah held still, waiting to see what the mare would do. The issue hung in the balance a long moment; then the mare stepped forward, lowering her head to her pleased mistress.

''Ah, now you believe it is time I scratched you, I see.'' The mare's glossy chestnut coat rippled as Susannah stroked her behind her ears. ''Have you missed this, Lady? You shall have all you want of such attention this summer, I promise.''

Completely won, the mare not only allowed Susannah to stroke her fill but even protested when her mistress made to go. ''Off with you.'' Susannah laughed and pushed at the sleek head nudging her shoulder. ''I've not had my breakfast yet. I shall bring you another carrot later.''

Susannah turned to go, only to miss a step. Lady Danu saw the man by the fence at the same time, and with a sharp snort retreated to the far side of the paddock.

Susannah registered the mare's desertion only vaguely. Her attention was on the Irishman standing with one booted foot on a lower board of the fence while his arms rested on the top one. He had watched her when she was unaware, and she felt exposed, though she had done nothing she would rather he not see.

By the time she reached the fench, Susannah's heartbeat had slowed to something near its normal pace, and she managed to greet Connor with a crisp nod. ''Mr. O'Neill.''

He was dressed as he had been for the exercise gallops from which they had returned only a little before. As it was a warm morning, he wore no coat, only a white shirt that lay open at the throat. As had been the case earlier, Susannah had to exert an effort of will to keep herself from staring. She could not have said what her fascination was. The V did reveal curling dark hair, true, and the thin material of the shirt did cling to his powerful shoulders as a coat did not, but she'd seen men dressed as casually before.

Connor did not return Susannah's greeting as she swung up and over the fence. When she stood beside him, he nodded in the direction of Lady Danu, now regarding them warily from the far side of the paddock.

"You've a remarkable touch with horses, Lady Susannah." There was a pause before he turned to impale her with a gaze so flinty and at odds with his laudatory words, Susannah stiffened in surprise. "And you may count yourself lucky I witnessed the effect of that touch for myself. Had I not, I promise you, I'd have administered a dressing-down severe enough to flay your delicate ears."

"Would you, Mr. O'Neill?" Susannah's dark eyes flashed. "Well, then, I am glad you came along to see you'd no need to exercise yourself unduly!"

"Lady Susannah." The tauntness in Connor's voice suggested a man holding to patience only with an effort. "I can and will do without the unpleasant surprise of finding you unattended in the paddock with a mare who has bitten, and wickedly, too, every groom here, including one as sure with her as Murdoch. The next time you take it into your head to do anything so freakish, you will consult me first."

"Pray how much consultation do you require, sir?" Susannah snapped in turn. "I believe I told you only two days ago I would see Lady Danu when she was let out into the paddock."

"Damn it!" Susannah flinched. It was useless to tell herself he would not dare to lift a hand against her. From his expression she suspected it would be his greatest pleasure to swing her over his knee and flay, not her ears, but her backside. "You know very well I'd no notion you meant to approach so near to her! I am responsible for that mare, her foal—and you as well, when you are in the stableyard."

"Would you have believed me if I'd told you I could bring her around as I did?" Susannah demanded, certain he would not have.

"I'd have doubted you," Connor admitted frankly. "She's been mean-tempered with everyone, no matter how long she's known them. But I'd have come to see what you could, in fact, do with her."

"How reasonable of you." Despite a considerable desire not to, Susannah believed him. After a moment she shot him a grudging look. "All right, then. I'll not pull any freakish pranks unless you or a minion is on hand to supervise."

"No minions," he objected flatly, but there was a softer look about his eyes. "You've all the minions wrapped around your finger."

Susannah opened her mouth to protest, but Connor forestalled her. "I am not blind, Lady Susannah. It has not escaped me you are the darling of the stableyard. You will come to me, and no other, with your plans."

Their eyes clashed a long moment, but for Susannah it was a losing battle. He'd the right to forbid her the stables altogether, if he wished. The angle of her chin indicated clearly how little it pleased her to submit.

"Very well, I will come to you, Mr. O'Neill, but only because you have agreed to trust me in return."

Susannah had not noticed before how the lines radiating out from the corners of Connor's eyes creased attractively when he smiled. Perhaps she did then because his smile came so suddenly. "There must be Levant trader blood in you, my lady, you bargain so."

Susannah laughed. Only a moment before, she'd been furious with him, and might be again if she thought of the arrogant way he had dealt with her, but an image of Beaufort seated on a carpet bargaining for . . . anything, was irresistible.

Connor had not expected to make her laugh, and now he stared almost bemused by what he'd wrought. She took his breath, or at least a little of it, with that smile in her eyes.

Taking advantage of her good humor, he said, "To

celebrate our agreement, shall I introduce you to Saracen, my lady? He has just been let out into the paddock.''

She was going in that direction anyway, Susannah told herself, and there could be no harm in maintaining some degree of ease with the Irishman. She would spend her summer with him, after all. ''I should be pleased to be introduced. I admit I am curious about him.'' They strolled off toward a paddock that lay nearer the stables. ''Is Saracen truly such a rogue?'' she asked as they went.

Connor allowed that the colt possessed a truly wicked temper. ''But in his place I should have a far worse one. There are some very ugly scars on his neck and flank.''

''And we call him the brute,'' Susannah murmured in complete sympathy with the colt. ''A pity his former master cannot be treated similarly. Ah!''

Her first glimpse of Connor's stallion was a magnificent one. His black, glossy coat reflecting the sunlight, Saracen was running for the pleasure of it, his long mane whipping out like a triumphal banner behind him.

''He is nice, is he not?''

Susannah chuckled. ''An understatement, and you know it, Mr. O'Neill. He's beautiful. As fast as he looks?''

''If he can behave, he'll show them a thing or two at the meet, I'm thinking.''

That his lilt had suddenly become more pronounced was not lost upon Susannah. '' 'Them' being all the tame, spiritless English horses he'll run against?''

''Sure and I did not say that, Lady Susannah,'' he protested, but he grinned and a twinkle lit his eye.

Susannah thought he looked like a young, very roguish boy at that moment. ''Who will ride him, though? Surely you are too heavy.''

His grin deepened. ''Not, I hope, applying for the position, are you, Lady Susannah? Have a pity! Think of the blow to my reputation if it were seen that my infamous rogue could be mastered by a lady.''

Susannah allowed her gaze to slide away from his teasing look, and answered with perfect truth. ''I should like to ride him, but not in a race.''

"No. You are right to fear the noise will not suit him greatly. But to answer you, racing Saracen will fall to Murdoch's lot. He has the surest hands in the yard."

As if in echo, they heard the sound of Murdoch's name drift to them through the breezeway. "Murdoch! Murdoch!" It was James calling to the groom. "Have you seen Lady Susannah? Mr. Townshend and I thought to ride out with her."

"Mornin', sirs. As to Lady Susannah, the last I saw of her, she was off by the paddocks."

Following soon upon the exchange came the sound of booted feet in the breezeway connecting the stableyard and the paddocks. Connor turned in anticipation of James Somerset's appearance, only to realize as he did so that he had been deserted. Looking around in surprise, he was just in time to watch Susannah's honey-gold head disappear into the nearest empty stall.

No sooner had she made herself invisible than Somerset appeared, accompanied by a slim, pale dandy who looked as if he had spent more time upon his toilette than he ever had upon a horse.

"O'Neill!" James called out amiably. "Have you seen Susannah? Bunny has come in hopes of riding out with her, but I'd no notion to warn him she rises near dawn."

Bunny Townshend flushed, reacting in part to being made to seem as if he were dangling fruitlessly after Susannah Somerset, but also to the frankly assessing glance the tall, well-built horse trainer gave him. "I wish to speak with Lady Susannah," he attempted to correct the impression James had made, addressing the rather unnerving man as loftily as he could. "Direct us to her, if you please."

"Alas, Lady Susannah did not inform me of her plans either." Connor smiled. "Young ladies are so independent these days, are they not?"

"Now, that's the honest truth, stap me if it ain't!" James exclaimed, thinking not of Susannah but of Phoebe Limley, who seemed to beckon him with one hand and to push him off with the other. "Well, we shall look for her on the heath. It's the only place she can be, if she's not here or in the breakfast room. Tell her we were by, if you see her, would you?''

''Assuredly I will.''

They strolled away, James gesturing boastfully to Saracen while Bunny Townshend shrugged his sloping shoulders dismissively.

Connor waited until they were well out of sight. ''You may come out now, Lady Susannah. They're gone.''

When Susannah emerged, she glanced first in the direction the pair of young men had gone, and was relieved to see no sign of them. The thought of having Bunny hang around her all morning, after she had had a healthy dose of him the night before, had sent her scurrying for cover.

She did not regret her cowardice, only having O'Neill observe it. Slowly she turned, to find him watching her, shoulders propped against the fence and a smile she did not care for glinting in his eyes.

''Thank you, Mr. O'Neill.'' She felt stiff again with him, and though there was no reason at all Susannah should account for her actions to him, she found herself saying as offhandly as possible, ''It is early yet and I am not dressed for company. I did not mean to put you in such an odd position, however.''

''It was an odd position,'' he'd the ill grace to agree, his dratted smile seeming to intensify by perceptible degrees. ''I do not often lie.''

''I said thank you.''

''You did indeed. And I do appreciate your thanks, my lady.'' She stared. The nerve of him. It was not only his words, but his tone. And there was more to come. ''You needn't be so stiff, however. You may be in my debt, but I don't doubt you will find the perfect means with which to repay me.''

''Repay you, Mr. O'Neill? And I thought all Irishmen were by reputation gallant! I see I shall have to revise my opinion.''

He was in no way abashed, no way at all. ''We are a gallant race, my lady. It was your conscience concerned me. I could see it worried you to be in my debt, and I wanted to reassure you that I was confident you would, in your own good time, find some quite delightful way to pay up.''

''I won't tax myself unduly, Mr. O'Neill.''

Susannah had the last word in their little confrontation. She tossed off the line and turned smartly on her heel, but she'd the certain sinking knowledge that she had not taken herself from his overbold company in time. His amused eyes would not have missed the color that had crept into her cheeks when her mind made an unbidden leap and imagined what the impudent devil might consider delightful repayment.

Connor had seen the color and knew its cause, He laughed to himself, even as he appreciated how lovely she looked with her cheeks flushed. And he appreciated her departure. Even angry, she moved gracefully. Her long legs again, of course. Absorbed with watching Susannah stalk off, Connor did not notice Liam approaching until the large man was nearly upon him.

''Now, and didn't I say she was trouble? You did not even hear me comin', for lookin' at her.''

Connor took the reproof without rancor. ''And you've grown into an old woman, Liam. I pray the day never comes that I look for you before I look after a pretty lass.''

''Sure an' she's no pretty lass, man! She's—''

''A rare beauty, I know, I know.'' Connor grinned when Liam swore. ''Lady Danu ate from her hand,'' he went on after a moment in a different, half-musing tone. ''Yes,'' he answered Liam's lifted brow. ''And she has as good a seat as any groom. No, better than most.''

There was a moment's silence as the two men considered how a girl of Lady Susannah's station and looks could have such a touch with horses. The moment ended when Connor shrugged. ''Enough of the lass, Liam. What did you learn in Norwich?''

They were conversing in Gaelic, but nonetheless Liam glanced about, and only when he was satisfied that no eavesdropper lurked nearby did he speak. ''The castle, wherein the country jail is housed, seems quiet enough, Iv . . .

O'Neill.'' Connor did not seem to notice Liam's stumble. He watched Saracen sprint across the paddock, and waited for his companion to continue. "Luckily I found a talkative mistress in an ale house. Her name is Mrs. Dade now, but I learned, after a look at her red hair, it was Molly O'Brien before she married.''

At the news, Connor laughed aloud. "What luck! Tell me she's not comely too?''

"Very comely,'' Liam acknowledged with a grin. "I'd only to ask a question or two to learn they've recently added men to the militia garrisoned at the castle. Molly says she's never seen so many redcoats.''

Connor scowled. "So. They are there and waiting. Is there any talk of an unusual prisoner in the county jail?''

"Aye. 'Twas on every tongue, not only Molly's, that they'd an Irish rebel inside. He's to be taken elsewhere, though no one knows where, sometime, no one seemed to know when.''

"Had anyone actually seen the man brought in?''

"Nay. And puttin' on my best Yorkshire voice, I asked a good many people, especially those with shops nearby.''

Connor cracked his fist down upon the fence. "It's a bloody trap! I'll wager you, Liam, Seamus Fitzgerald was never taken near the Norwich county jail, as rumor would have it.''

"You think they hanged him, then?''

Connor lifted a face as harsh and grim as it was handsome to his friend. "Aye, Liam, he's dead in a fool's cause. The Greenboys! Nipping at Sassenach heels and winning naught but useless deaths. 'Tis through Parliament and the courts we must work.''

"When you were Seamus' age and your brother Rory's—''

"Aye.'' Connor nodded sharply. "I was not so wise then. I'd not yet watched one good man after another killed for naught. And there was some hope in both ninety-six and ninety-eight that with the French . . . Och! There was no hope then either. We've fought them for six hundred years and only managed to cut short the lives of our best and bravest. Well, I mean that profligate, fruitless waste to stop, in my family at least, Liam. I'll find Rory before he can walk into that trap in Norwich, and if I must crack his head to get him home safely to Glendalough Castle, by the bloody rood, I shall!''

5

"I QUITE admire the marvelous excuses you've invented to avoid Miss Limley and Bunny, my dear, but have pity!" Lady Augusta, swathed in layers of diaphanous pink silk, eyed her granddaughter over the rim of a delicate Meissen teacup. "James cannot bring off a picnic by himself."

"He would do better to concentrate instead upon bringing himself off Miss Limley." Susannah made an impatient gesture with her hand. "I cannot understand why James is so smitten with Phoebe. She'll be unfaithful to him before he can get her out of the church."

"Not so soon, surely!" Lady Augusta protested, quite unperturbed. "She will wait until she's given James a son, which is all one can ask, particularly as she brings such a tidy fortune."

"You think Phoebe's fortune will be compensation enough for James?"

Lady Augusta's reply was characteristically decisive. "Of course it will. You cannot imagine James intends to be constant, after all. And she does strike a spark off him. That is more than most husbands have with their wives. Eventually they will go their own ways, true, but everyone does." Lady Augusta shrugged at the mores of the world. "Your difficulty, Susannah, is that you've devilish high standards. It is possible, in the end, you'll have the strength to live up to them—I cannot say—but I doubt James will. Help him plan his picnic and please his lady love! Who knows but that upon greater acquaintance, he may see Miss Limley for what she is.''

Susannah regarded her grandmother wryly. ''You said that last because you know it is the only bait I will take. Very well, then. I will plan a picnic with James, hoping all the while familiarity will breed a deserved contempt.''

''I am glad I persuaded you, my dear. James has been floundering so, I could not bear it. But now we've settled him nicely, let us move on to a far more interesting topic. As you've been at Ridley a week, Susannah, I confess I am wild to know what you've come to think of my Irishman.''

''Your Irishman?'' Susannah put the emphasis on ''your'' and succeeded in sounding amused.

''O'Neill,'' Lady Augusta said, ignoring Susannah's diversion in favor of eyeing the slight flush rising to tint her granddaughter's lovely face. ''Did you know, Susannah, that the O'Neill's were the high kings of Tara long ago, while our ancestors, even your so-very-august Somerset ones, my love, were . . . well, I haven't the faintest notion what they were doing, but I suppose that is my point.''

Susannah's laugh came unforced. ''You are the strangest mixture, Gussie! In relation to James, you play the most pragmatic cynic, but now, in relation to O'Neill, you sound outrageously romantic. Do you think the man a king?''

''Kingly,'' Lady Augusta replied at once. ''You must agree, he has the air, the manners, and the looks of an aristocrat, his position at the moment notwithstanding.''

An image flashed in Susannah's mind of the Irishman seated at her grandmother's table, where he had joined them several times in the past week. She tried to apply the word ''common'' to him, but failed.

Not only were his manners gracious and as natural to him as breathing, but he displayed, unfailingly, a broad well-schooled intelligence. Major Hornbeck's greatest passion next to horses was the Elizabethan age. No matter. O'Neill could discuss Marlowe or Shakespeare as readily as he could debate whether it was more important to breed a racehorse for stamina or speed. And with Gussie, it did not matter what line Susannah's grandmother cast out, the Irishman invariably returned it with amused ease.

As to her . . . he was not the same two moments in a row with her. She exaggerated, of course, but only a little. There had been the day he'd first barked at her with such authority over Lady Danu, only to finish by teasing her about being a trader and extending an amiable invitation to meet his horse. Then, not a quarter of an hour later, he roguishly presumed to suggest she would find some ''delightful'' means to repay him for the lie he'd told on her behalf. As if it had been so difficult for him to lie. She was certain he could lie with ease.

Jove, he did presume! And why did she not simply put him in his place or walk away, cool and untouched? Susannah did not eagerly admit she failed to react so because she couldn't quite. She suggested, instead, that she'd have felt a coward had she not taken up his challenge. And perhaps that was true, too.

Whatever, he was an infuriating man who invaded her thoughts frequently, and she did not care to have her thoughts overtaken even infrequently. At that moment she'd almost forgotten Gussie awaiting her answer.

''What do I think of your Irishman?'' Susannah repeated, trying to make her mind a soothing blank. ''Well,'' she shrugged offhandedly, ''I suppose he rides well.''

At that, Lady Augusta unexpectedly threw back her head to laugh unroariously. ''I don't doubt it! But what a pity I shall never know for certain.''

''Gussie!'' The reproof, intended to be stern, emerged as a gurgle of laughter, proving Susannah was little proof against her grandmother. ''I would tell you you are outrageous, but I would only delight you if I did. You know very well I meant to say he is an excellent horseman. And I shall even grant O'Neill is a better trainer than I expected him to be. The horses are in excellent condition.''

Lady Augusta was successfully diverted. For the remainder of their tea, they discussed the horses in Ridley's stables without reference to Ridley's trainer.

After an hour or so, Lady Augusta retired for her afternoon rest, leaving Susannah at loose ends to drift down the stairs.

It was the first rainy day they had had that week. Ordinarily in the afternoons she pottered in Nan's garden or went to the woods to visit the secret place she and Sebastian had found there. Reached by a circuitous, overgrown path, it was a sunny, secluded dell carpeted by thick green grass and a profusion of wildflowers. A stream meandered through it and, dammed by the roots of an enormous oak, formed a wide, deep pool perfect for swimming.

With the day a misty blur, however, the library held more attraction than her pool. After choosing a book, Susannah curled up on a settee, confident she would not be disturbed, for just as the rain started, James had raced off to Bascom Lodge, the Townshends' home, in hopes of catching Phoebe indoors.

Susannah was not interrupted for an hour or so. Even then, when the door opened, she did not hear it. She only realized she had been joined when the door clicked closed. Looking up, she felt her heart leap uncomfortably in her breast.

They were alone. It was Susannah's first thought. Her second, and she suppressed it immediately, was that there was no one about to disturb them, should she choose to pay up on the debt she did admit she owed him.

He had not come to the library to catch her alone. Tall and lean, a presence in the spacious room, he stood still and abstracted, staring out the window at the rain. O'Neill was quite unaware of her.

On his walk to the house, he had gotten wet. His black hair was damp and as a result curled more than usual at the back onto the collar of the coat he'd donned to come to the house. He turned, still absorbed in thought, registered Susannah's presence with obvious surprise, and finally smiled.

It was a friendly enough smile. Perhaps there was in it a suggestion of the contest of wills between them, but there was certainly nothing in his smile to indicate he had thought of her debt.

Susannah resented that, somehow. While she sat tensed by his presence, he stood entirely unruffled by hers, and if his smile held a hint of rakishness, he was only rendered the more handsome. She could feel her mood deteriorate by not so gradual degrees. Even his looks annoyed her just then. It was unfair that any man, but particularly a man as ineligible as O'Neill, should look like he did when he smiled.

"Mr. O'Neill." Susannah allowed a touch of surprise to color her tone. "Did you want something?"

She succeeed at routing his smile. "Not surprisingly I came to the library for a book, my lady." Connor's eyebrow lifted ironically. "Are you concerned that I am presuming? You needn't be. Your grandmother accorded me the privilege of the library when I first came to Ridley."

Connor gave Susannah no opportunity to reply, only accorded her a slight, dismissive inclination of the head before he went on with his business, crossing the room to the far bookcase and leaving her to eye his strong back with disfavor. He really was the most infuriating man. She had only intended to maintain a little distance between them—as was her right! But what had happened, instead? Though he was the one who had interrupted her, he'd succeeded at making her feel unbearably arrogant. Beastly man.

Into the silence Susannah said after a time, somewhat curtly, "I did not mean to imply I thought you unworthy of the library, Mr. O'Neill."

"No?" Connor did not bother to turn and address her directly, but continued searching the shelves.

"No."

Still he did not turn. Her brow arching, Susannah chided herself for being absurdly concerned with a servant's feelings; then she admitted it was difficult, as Gussie had suggested, to think of him as a hireling. And either way, he had a pride she could not but respect.

"Can I help you find what you are looking for?"

"No." He found the book he wanted and turned before she could rise. "Thank you."

Never had there been a cooler expression of thanks. He meant to leave, Susannah knew, and heard herself say pleasantly, conversationally, "What book did you choose?"

Connor hesitated a moment, as if he debated answering, then with half a shrug allowed, "Ruin needs a poultice for a strained tendon. Lady Gus advised me there would be a recipe for one here.''

"Ah." She could think of nothing more to say. And was displeased, really, to find she wanted to say something. The discovery, and the veiled look in his eyes, made Susannah restless. She shifted, unthinking, causing her book to slip from her lap. Connor politely retrieved it for her. Susannah thought he pounced upon the book like a cat, but she was prejudiced, for she particularly wished him not to see what she'd been reading.

The hope that Connor might not interest himself in her book lived a very brief life. As he lifted it, he glanced at the spine. All Lady Augusta's books were leather-bound, with their titles embossed in bright, highly visible gold.

Even before he glanced up, Connor's mouth was curving. "A history of Ireland, Lady Susannah?" His eyes were guarded no longer. All the light in the room seemed to be glinting in them. "I didn't realize English ladies interested themselves in history, particularly Irish history. Ought I to be flattered?"

"I am sure you will be precisely what you please, Mr. O'Neill."

Connor smiled outright. "Ah. Then I please to be curious as to what you read about my country's history."

He really did possess an infectious smile. Susannah could feel a responding warmth steal into her eyes.

"Often enough I read the name O'Neill."

Her tone was casual, almost bland, but Connor caught the quick look Susannah slanted at him. "Then you must have begun reading at the first of your book, my lady."

"I did, in fact, begin relatively early," Susannah admitted, giving up on the struggle not to smile, but she did not go so far as to confess she had, spurred by her grandmother's remark, looked up Tara in the index and begun her reading at its first mention. "Have there always been O'Neills in Ireland, then?"

"No." He shook his head. "The O'Neills came with the Celts. The first people in Ireland were the Tuatha De Danann."

"Danann?" Susannah tried to remember where she had heard the word. "It has to do with Lady Danu somehow, does it not?"

Connor was half surprised, half amused. "You know more than I suspected. Danu was the goddess of the dawn, and the Tuatha De Danann her people."

"Yes, now I remember! John Mulcahey told me they are the pixies. Do . . . But forgive my manners, Mr. O'Neill. I did not mean to keep you standing. Please be seated."

Connor chuckled as Susannah indicated a nearby chair with the imperious graciousness of an empress. "I feel as if I've been approved to dance the waltz at Almack's," he told her when she looked up, clearly puzzled by his amusement.

She studied him a moment as he seated himself casually upon the arm of the chair, stretching his long legs out before him. "I believe you think me very toplofty, Mr. O'Neill."

If Susannah meant to elicit a disavowal, she failed. Connor agreed, though with a smile. "I do, indeed, my lady. You are as naturally arrogant as you are beautiful."

"Ah." Her breath seemed to rush out all at once. Rogue. He had meant to discompose her with that unexpected compliment. She knew it, because his mouth was tilting at the corner in the beginnings of that grin. "Thank you, Mr. O'Neill." Susannah treated him to a mildly arched brow. "It gives me the greatest comfort to know my assets are as remarkable as my faults."

When he laughed aloud, Susannah was disconcertingly pleased, and because she could feel her own smile growing, she thought it time to return the discussion to Irish folklore.

"I was on the point of asking if you, like John Mulcahey, believe in the pixies, or the little people, as he called them?"

"To be sure," Connor allowed, a smile lingering in his eyes. "I even saw a wee elder gentleman once. He was reclining against the stem of a comfortable toadstool, enjoying his pipe, and when I came upon him, he nodded and bade me a 'verra good dae.' "

With a pleasure that was the greater for having been anticipated, Connor watched Susannah's dark eyes light with laughter. "I am surprised he did not play a trick on you, Mr. O'Neill. John said the wee people could be mischievous."

He nodded with mock solemnity. "They can, indeed. One must always be careful, for the Tuatha De Danann wish to take revenge upon the Celts for winning Ireland from them long ago."

"It would seem there have been many contests for Ireland." Susannah gestured to the book in her lap. "I was just reading about Cromwell when you came."

"Ah, the Protector of the Faith."

All the relaxed good humor that had lit Connor's eyes vanished, and oddly Susannah was reminded of how her grandmother had thought him kingly. Thus, she thought, would a king look when his enemies were mentioned: grave and harsh and set.

"I see you've little affection for the Puritans," Susannah said slowly. "Given what I've read, I am not surprised. In truth, I found myself wondering as I read, that you do not seem to hold all English people in disfavor."

Something flashed in the depths of Connor's eyes. Susannah saw it plainly and was so startled, she did not think to hide her dismay as she exclaimed softly, "You do!"

Abruptly, before Susannah could mark the odd feeling in the pit of her stomach, Connor shook his head. "No. I don't hold every Englishman or woman in disfavor, though I did once. It is no easy thing to endure one's land being harshly occupied and ruled exclusively for the benefit of the conquerors."

He looked at once very grim and very proud, and she knew from her reading he had reason to look so. The English had often been brutal in Ireland.

"No. I cannot imagine it would be an easy thing. If I am surprised," she went on, feeling her way, "I think, it is because, were I in your position, I would be less reasonable —more bitter if you will—than you are."

He weighed her in the moment of silence that followed. Susannah sensed it, sensed he measured her seriousness, and was innexplicably pleased when, after a moment, he responded honestly.

"It took some time, but eventually I realized that nurturing such bitterness as I harbored accomplished precious little. Though I flung myself into one fruitless endeavor after another, all I did was to concede most of my waking thoughts and actions to those I held my enemies." Connor shrugged, the suggestion of a smile that was directed entirely at himself in the depths of his eyes. "In the end, I was too proud to concede so much."

Susannah could well believe he'd that much pride and smiled too. "I think I can understand how pride might counteract such bitterness."

The lines radiating from Connor's eyes creased. "I am not astonished to hear it, my lady."

They had come back to her pride by way of his. As they exchanged looks of understanding and amusement, Connor's smile altered, becoming lazier and more indulgent.

In response, Susannah felt something inside her expand. I am glad you do not harbor bitterness toward every Englishman or woman. The thought formed in her mind, but before she expressed it, the library door swung open and James breezed into the room.

James. Susannah blinked at her cousin. As he nodded at her and made the Irishman some sort of greeting, she felt a spurt of irritation.

Why ever had he returned just when she was having an interesting exchange with someone? She did not think she had been so fully engaged in a conversation since Sebastian left. Certainly none of the men who had paid her court over the last two years had gotten much past praising her eyes. Except for Sunderly, of course. The viscount had been shrewd enough to tell her stories of his school days with Sebastian. But a discussion on the disadvantages of harboring a quite justified bitterness?

Susannah's attention shifted to O'Neill. He was smiling at something James said, and she was reminded of the last few moments of their *tête-à-tête*. He had not been discussing a weighty issue then. Nor had she. She'd been on the point of murmuring something to the effect that she was glad he did not hate all English people—herself necessarily included.

Perhaps it was just as well James had returned, Susannah decided abruptly. She did not regret her conversation with the Irishman. He had been both amusing and thoughtful by turns, and he had not once been overbold. Still, taking pleasure in an interesting conversation on a rainy day was one thing: Allowing herself to be swept up by the novelty—and charm—of the moment and say more than she really need say was quite another.

6

AFTER CONNOR departed, Susannah told her cousin she would help him to plan his picnic, if he still wished her assistance. Delighted, James asked at once for her approval of the place he'd in mind.

"It is quite a perfect spot! You know it, Susannah. Beneath the grove of limes just off the road to Ely? The trees are in flower now, and there is a stream. We can fish if we like!" he added with a boyish enthusiasm that made Susannah smile, even as she wondered how much Phoebe, town-born and raised, cared for fishing.

Susannah suggested they include some old friends: Mary Wardley and her brother, Drew, whose father owned a small, respectable stud farm nearby. Mary was a fine, reserved girl who had been James's especial friend when they were young. Susannah hoped he would compare Phoebe to Mary to Phoebe's detriment. But even if he did not, Susannah enjoyed Mary's company.

James was so pleased with the notion, he went a step further. "Well, if we are inviting the Wardleys, we ought to have O'Neill come! Drew will be wild to discuss the meet with him. You know how Drew is before the races. He can talk of nothing but horses."

It was a most thoughtful suggestion, and not one that ought to have aroused an immediately negative feeling in Susannah.

Indeed, her reluctance to have O'Neill attend surprised her. She could not think of one reason he should be excluded, except for Phoebe. And she could scarcely protest to James that Phoebe was likely to be drawn to the man. That would be a little too much honest speaking. There was the point, too, Susannah reminded herself rather sternly, that she wanted James to see Phoebe for the flirt she was.

And so Connor was invited to the picnic, joining the group some little time after they had arrived at their spot. The young men were fishing, or rather James and Drew fished. Bunny languished in the shade alternately extolling the joys of town and complaining over the discomforts of an outdoor luncheon.

Susannah attended with only half an ear. With the other half she listened to Phoebe discuss fashions with Mary, a surprisingly diverting entertainment, as the two girls' tastes were diametrically opposed, and Mary was not so reserved she did not gasp when Phoebe confided she had once gone out with her underclothes dampened, as was the style with a very fast set in town.

Mary was saying, with surprising backbone, she did not think a lady would display herself so, when Susannah heard the approach of a rider. She knew it must be O'Neill, but for some reason, she was content to allow him to arrive unheralded. She remained as she was, reclining against the trunk of a fragrant lime tree, her flat-crowned, wide-brimmed straw bonnet beside her and her eyes half-closed.

A little taken aback by Mary's uncertainty, Phoebe had rushed to protest that she had not gone far in her dampened undergarments, but she broke off abruptly in midsentence. A half moment of silence reigned and then she said in an entirely different tone, "Is this the O'Neill Bunny and James are forever speaking of?"

No one but Susannah heard her, for James was shouting an excited greeting to Connor. "Just look! I've caught a fish to mark your coming!"

Susannah opened her eyes. James's fish was of respectable size, and he held it up proudly while a servant rushed over

with a basket. Mary and the others congratulated him, but
Phoebe did not seem aware there was a silvery trout wiggling
on a hook only a little distance from her.

Susannah faulted the girl, but knew she was being unfair.
O'Neill looked strikingly handsome that afternoon. The
masculinity of his strong, chiseled features was intriguingly
at odds with the lock of black hair that fell boyishly onto
his brow as a result of his ride. That ride or the exercise
he'd had also made his blue eyes gleam brilliantly. Or
perhaps it was the color of his coat emphasized them so, for
it was sky blue. Of superfine, it was cut well, too, fitting
over his wide shoulders without a crease.

When Connor strolled over to applaud James's catch, the
other men seemed to pale at least a little. Of course, he was
older, and therefore it was not unnatural, Susannah supposed,
that the Irishman would appear more arresting than they.
He'd filled out as they had not quite, and he'd a grown man's
assurance.

Within the space of a half moment, Susannah had thought
of a half a dozen men of O'Neill's approximate age, surely
late twenties or thereabouts, who would have quite failed
to make James and his friends appear so tame. It was not
age alone that worked to O'Neill's advantage, Susannah
conceded. Nor even that he was so very handsome. There
was the intelligence his face reflected, the keenness gleaming
in his eyes and in all, the general impression he gave of
alertness, of energy, of being a man who would dare a great
deal.

Little wonder then, that Phoebe, while James was distracted with his fish, gazed upon O'Neill as a child would
a large, heavily frosted, thoroughly chocolate cake.

The fish safely deposited, everyone gathered upon the large
blanket the servants had laid out. Susannah still did not rouse
herself, only waited in her comfortable position. If she wished
to see whether Connor would look to her of his own accord,
and she did not admit any such thing, then she learned he
was quite prepared to seek her out with a glance. When their
eyes met, Connor might have inclined his head, Susannah
was not certain. She did know she made no like gesture. Yet

she knew they had exchanged greetings with that single mute look.

It was an exceedingly comfortable feeling to speak like that, without words. Susannah marked the feeling, then told herself it was a perfectly natural one. She had had a significant exchange with the man only two days before. They could say hello without needing to wave or shout at one another.

"I hope I have not kept you waiting for your luncheon," O'Neill said to James.

"Not at all!" James laughed. "I'd not have caught the winning fish, had you come any sooner. Egad! The truth is, I'd not have had any fish at all. But I hope it was nothing serious kept you?"

"No." Connor shrugged negligently. "Something always seems to need attention."

"My father has the deuce of a time getting away!" Drew Wardley commiserated. James, reminded of his manners, made introductions all around, then Drew was eager to know more of Saracen. "Is your colt the devil Father says he is, Mr. O'Neill?"

"Yes, Mr. O'Neill." It was Phoebe who spoke, the words coming out almost as a purr. "Do tell us of your stallion. Bunny and James say he is very dangerous."

There was no need for Susannah to wonder if O'Neill saw the interest sparkling so plainly in Phoebe's eyes. James might be distracted, giving directions for luncheon to be served, but the Irishman was looking directly at the heiress. And there was a flicker in his own eyes. Susannah noted it, and that his mouth curved up at one corner.

"Any horse that is mishandled is dangerous, Miss Limley," Connor replied in tones Susannah only acknowledged after a little were quite acceptably neutral. "But with proper handling most such animals recover their natural civility. Saracen is no different."

"You have mastered him then, Mr. O'Neill?"

The desire to shake Phoebe unaccountably grew upon Susannah with every breathless syllable the girl uttered. And where was James? she wished to know. His fish be damned.

He ought to be observing the quickened gleam in his beloved's eyes.

"Master Saracen?" Connor smiled. It might have been the thought that amused him, or he might have been smiling upon the heiress. Susannah found it impossible to tell, only to see that Phoebe dimpled coyly up at him. "In truth, Miss Limley, I don't think anyone masters a horse as strong-willed as he. As with any rogue, one merely reaches an accommodation that suits the both of you. What do you think, Lady Susannah?"

If Connor thought to catch her off-stride with the sudden question, he did not. Susannah met his gaze levelly. "I think you are the expert on rogues, Mr. O'Neill."

Those intriguing lines about his eyes creased deeply on the instant. Unrepentant—and he did know full well what had prompted her remark, Susannah could see the knowledge gleaming in his eyes—Connor laughed. What other response he might have made she was not to know. Drew spoke up, drawing her attention. "You know a thing or two about rogues yourself, Susannah. Don't you remember the time Sebastian wagered you couldn't ride that roan fiend of Lord Markham's?"

"I remember!" James exclaimed, having finished with his host's duties and taken a seat by Phoebe. "I won a tidy sum on you that day, Susannah."

"I was lucky to stay on the roan long enough for you to make your wager, much less win it." Susannah made a rueful face. "What I remember most clearly was the arc I made through the air after he threw me. It took forever, or so it seemed, to get that landing over."

She had amused O'Neill. He chuckled. Susannah found it easy to distinguish his laugh from the others. It was deeper, more thoroughly amused, too, for of course he'd suffered a fall or two in his time. She could not keep from glancing at him. Again, it was not necessary to say anything. There wasn't time anyway. The others clamored for attention, each with a story of a fall to tell; then the servants served luncheon.

Only Phoebe had remained quiet as riding stories were traded. She rode as little as possible, and then only on the gentlest nag. Most certainly she had never suffered a fall. Even so, Phoebe was not without the resources to gain attention.

It was warm beneath the lime trees, pleasantly so, for there was a light breeze, but enough so that no one expressed surprise when Phoebe murmured that she was uncomfortable. Fortunately she'd a simple remedy at hand. She wore a spencer to protect her skin from the sun, and having little need of the tiny garment now that she sat in the shade, she removed it.

The night Phoebe had come to dinner at Ridley, Susannah had wondered idly what O'Neill would think of the girl's décolletage. Now she knew at least that he would waste no time evaluating it.

Phoebe's afternoon dress did not sport a neckline as daring as her evening gown had, but it was not overly modest either. Cut square, her low dress revealed the beginning of a deep cleft. Connor sat across from the girl, and an impartial onlooker might have said Miss Limley as good as presented her bosom to him, for as soon as she removed her spencer, she leaned down to brush a crumb off the blanket.

Brazen cow. Susannah flicked her gaze from Phoebe to Connor, and was in time to see he had not missed the girl's display. Indeed, his eyes lingered upon it. And his thoughts? She could not tell.

She could not tell even when she found herself looking directly into his blue eyes. Connor lifted his gaze so swiftly, he caught Susannah, but his expression was so bland, she could not be certain he realized why she had watched him. And then, quite suddenly, he grinned.

Devil! He had known she was watching him admire Phoebe's charms. And that roguish grin seemed to say: what would you have me do, my lady? I am a man, after all.''

Susannah lifted her brow and glanced pointedly at James.

She did not think to question whether Connor had followed her thoughts, but she did wonder if he would heed her plea on James's behalf.

She was not to know. The unmistakable sound of a pony being ridden hard up the path from Ridley heralded a change in the afternoon. The rider was Dill Johns, the youngest son of Ridley's dairyman. Seeing the elegant company sprawled upon the grass, the boy went bashful. "E-excuse me, m'lady, m'lord," he piped in a high treble, bobbing his head at Susannah then at . . . It took Susannah a moment to realize Dill had addressed Connor O'Neill as a lord. She had only a second to concede the child had reason for his mistake before he addressed her.

"M-me mum sent me, my lady. 'Tis Nan! She's taken bad, sudden like, My mum thought you'd like to know."

"Nan?" Susannah rose at once. "She is at the cottage?" Dill nodded vigorously. "I shall go, of course. You stay and have a drink of lemonade, Dill. You must be hot. I . . ."

Susannah looked around uncertain how she would get away, but the question was answered almost as soon as she formed it.

"I shall take you in the gig, Lady Susannah." Connor rose as if the matter were settled. "Your guests needn't be disturbed that way."

"Thank you, Mr. O'Neill, that is very gracious of you." Susannah said it firmly, for even then Bunny was rising to offer his services too. The very thought of riding any length of time at all alone with the young man who annoyed her far more than he amused her steeled Susannah against Bunny's look of disappointment. She said without a hint of irony, "No, Bunny. It would make me feel quite wretched to drag you out in all this heat, when you could be here comfortable in the shade."

Susannah gave Connor directions to Nan's cottage, explaining as she did that the old woman had been her nurse and had been given a cottage at Ridley for her own after Susannah had grown too old to need her.

Connor's eyebrow lifted. "You must have held her in especial esteem to make such a gesture."

"Yes." Susannah paused a moment, then said, "My mother died shortly after I was born, you see, and to a great extent Nan took her place. Along with Gussie, of course."

Connor smiled slightly at the thought of Lady Augusta as a mother, but he referred to Nan when he spoke. "I understand now why you were so willing to leave the pleasures of your picnic. I was surprised that you would be summoned from your hostess's duties to attend a servant."

"She attended me often enough over the years. The least I can do in return is forgo the end of a picnic for her. Actually, I think you are the one who made the sacrifice, Mr. O'Neill." Susannah's tone changed for the drier. "As you've no connection at all with Nan, I consider it gallant in the extreme that you would tear yourself away from the particular pleasures the picnic offered you."

"Particular pleasures?" Connor pretended puzzlement, but Susannah could plainly see the laughter in his eyes. "Ah! You mean the view I was offered. Of course. And I cannot but agree. It was an exceptionally pleasing view."

"Hmm" or some such sound was Susannah's retort.

Connor chuckled at the thinness of it. "You did raise the subject, my lady," he reminded her.

"I did," Susannah conceded, honesty and his grin forcing her to it.

That she was trading quips with Connor over another woman's bosom, Susannah did not remark, or if she did, she ignored the thought. It was not particularly difficult. Recalling the shameless display Phoebe had made, she thought of James. "How can he be so blind?"

Connor heard the question that was more a sigh than anything and understood it. "Somerset is in love with the girl, then? Lady Augusta hinted at it, but I could not be certain she was not merely teasing him."

"Would that she had been. No, James is well and truly smitten. And Gussie does not object to Miss Limley. She has a heavy purse, you see, while James's is excessively light. His father, I'm afraid, was not the most frugal of men."

"And you agree that her guineas will compensate Somerset for the cuckold she will surely make of him?"

Though she had said much the same thing herself, Susannah winced a little at Connor's directness. "I can only say that Gussie maintains James will prove no more faithful than Phoebe. It is her belief, he'll be the same as most other husbands, going his own way after he has an heir.''

Susannah looked off but did not remark the wild rose vine clambering over the stone wall that bordered the lane. She was seeing a ball in London. Gussie had not exaggerated the general behavior. Most husbands and wives arrived separately at the entertainment of the evening, greeting each other with little more than politeness if their paths happened to cross. And there were worse marriages. Susannah knew of more than one in which the principals had not exchanged a word for years. Oh, she did not think her marriage to the Viscount Sunderly would become that distant. His devotion to her was too great, but would it not, in time, come to resemble most other marriages among members of their class?

"What do you think, Mr. O'Neill?" Susannah swung her gaze abruptly to Connor. "Do all marriages end in distance and infidelity?"

The question taking him by surprise, Connor glanced down before he answered. He appreciated what he saw. The sun shining through the straw of her chipper bonnet sprinkled Susannah's nose and cheeks with little squares of light and shadow, making her look unusually and appealingly young. Connor's initial impulse was to flick her nose and tell her no man married to her would look elsewhere.

The impulse died the moment he looked into her eyes, however. A woman's uncertainty, not a girl's, flickered shadowlike in their sable depths. She would marry soon. He'd known that from the first, of course, but the knowledge struck him more forcibly than before. Was it possible they would marry her to a fool or blind man?

"I can't make you any assurance about your own marriage, if that's what you really want."

Connor did not need to see Susannah's eyes widen to know he had spoken curtly, and for a half-second he felt almost helpless. He had not meant to make any reference at all to her own marriage, and certainly he had not meant to speak so sharply. The thought that her family might wed her to a faithless fool had disturbed him. Naturally enough. He disliked waste, and she would be wasted upon such a man. Perhaps he would address a letter to the Duke of Beaufort and tell him so. The thought seemed to steady his mind. Susannah Somerset's marriage could not be—was not—any concern of his.

"As to your general question, my lady, I would advise you to consider the source of the opinion that all marriages are mere matches of convenience." On firm ground, Connor was able to smile with just the amount of wryness correct for the moment. "You will forgive me, I hope, if I observe that Lady Augusta is a jade of the first order, albeit a delightful one."

Susannah was not so diverted by Connor's humor as he'd have liked. For a long moment she regarded him steadily, her dark eyes still questioning. But Connor had thought and said all he wished on the subject of marriage. Seeming unaware of her silent study, he looked away to the horse he guided.

He was right to resist her, Susannah decided after a moment. She wasn't really concerned about marriages in general, and he could not make her any assurance about her own.

What of his marriage? Susannah slanted her companion a gaze from the corner of her eye. He'd made no secret of enjoying the sight of Phoebe's charms. But if he were married to a woman he loved?

No. Susannah put an abrupt halt to the train of her thoughts. She would not speculate over the romantic life of a man she scarcely knew. She would keep to her determination to think as little as possible about marriage—her own or the Irishman's.

Just to be certain her thoughts did not take an errant turn, Susannah resumed conversation, this time on the quite neutral subject of Nan.

"Did I tell you Nan's mother came from Waterford, Mr. O'Neill?"

"You did not reveal that pertinent fact, no, my lady." Connor, quite as ready as Susannah to take up a new subject, gave her a real smile. "Is that why she was such a wise nurse?"

"She was wise, but whether it was her English half or her Irish . . ."

7

MRS. JOHNS had taken alarm unnecessarily. She had had difficulty rousing Nan only because the old woman had taken an herbal concoction to combat a persistent case of the sniffles. By the time Susannah and Connor arrived, the only fuzziness Nan exhibited was that she insisted upon addressing O'Neill as "my lord." Susannah did not exert the effort to correct her, but Connor did, reminding her that he was only Mr. O'Neill. Nan's reply was a seraphic smile and, "Oh, aye, to be sure. The O'Neill."

Susannah chuckled—Connor shrugged so helplessly—then shooed him out that she might attend to Nan without any distraction.

Concern for Susannah's old nurse uppermost in his mind on his way into the cottage, Connor had not taken much notice of her garden. Mrs. Johns, following him outside, smiled when he looked around in obvious pleasure at the small Eden he found waiting for him.

"I see y' admire her ladyship's garden, Mr. O'Neill. An' well ye might. 'Tis a green thumb our Lady Susannah has. Loves to potter about in the dirt, she does. Why, she was here only yesterday plantin' the alyssum yonder."

Connor could easily imagine Susannah Somerset sketching a design for a garden. Distinctly more difficult to conjure was an image of her kneeling on the ground, rooting about in the soil.

Curious, and perhaps a little skeptical as well, he mentioned Mrs. John's revelation to Susannah soon after they left Nan's. Her response succeeded in intriguing Connor the more, for she shrugged and said, glancing off into the distance, "It is Nan's."

Cool and composed, Susannah's profile advised Connor to try another subject. He did not. "I did not make myself clear, I see. I know the garden is located at Nan's cottage, but I meant to say that Mrs. Johns indicated you are responsible for the design and much of the planting."

Susannah could, as Connor learned, not only be but also look stubborn. "Mrs. Johns, as you have reason to know, Mr. O'Neill, exaggerates."

"I do not believe she has in this case."

"Why are you persisting with this?"

"Why would you deny that lovely place is your creation?"

Connor knew for a certainty then that it was indeed Susannah's garden. Before she could avert her gaze from his, he saw a spark of pleasure light her remarkable eyes. He did not give her time to deny the truth again. "And now you may thank me for my compliment."

"I do not think I need you, Mr. O'Neill, to teach me my manners." A rankling glance accompanied the remark, but Connor detected, beneath it, a suggestion at least of softness. He was not surprised when Susannah said, after a pause, simply, "Thank you."

"You are welcome," he returned, unable to keep from smiling at having wrung the truth from her. "But why the denials? Surely you are not ashamed of your gardening?"

"No. I am not ashamed at all, but it would seem that old habits of secrecy are hard to throw off." Susannah read the puzzled look Connor gave her and continued, almost reluctantly, "Nan encouraged me to garden when I was very young, but after she retired to Ridley, my . . . ah, governess disapproved heartily. I was to tell the gardeners what I wanted them to do, never work in the soil myself."

"And that did not suit you?"

"No." Though he admired her poise a great deal, Connor found that Susannah could be appealing indeed when she looked at least a little self-conscious. "I like feeling good loam crumble between my fingers; even smelling all that fertility appeals. Mad, I know." She shrugged. "Only Nan and Sebastian ever understood."

It touched him, that last. But only reluctantly did Connor admit it. First he told himself it was a small thing for a child, who must have had everything, to be denied one pleasure. But then he found himself imagining her as a little girl, full of life and enthusiasm, trotting out, pail in hand, to grub about in the dirt, only to have some hatchet-faced governess snatch her up, spank her, and forcibly thrust her elegant little girl's hands into a harsh cleansing concoction.

"I am glad you persisted, my lady. The result of your efforts proves you were right to sneak off to the nearest pile of dirt despite the strictures of your governess. As we would say in Ireland, I found your garden, a wee bit o' heaven."

Susannah had not exaggerated when she said only Sebastian and Nan had understood her love of watching the growing of what she—not a gardener—had planted. Her father had said flatly it was no occupation for a young lady, and even Gussie had chided her for enjoying so plebeian an occupation. Now here was O'Neill saying, again, that her garden had pleased him.

Tilting her head a little, the better to see from beneath her brim, she gave him the smile she gave so rarely. "Thank you again, Mr. O'Neill." Her chuckle was rich and playful. "You've my permission to visit it anytime you like."

Connor had had considerable experience with women, and yet he lost himself a little then in the pleasure her smile gave him. There was such warmth in her eyes, all her lovely face seemed aglow with it.

And she bestowed that look, that radiance, upon only a few. He knew that as well.

That night, in her room, Susannah thought back on her day, or the part of it she'd spent traveling to and from Nan's with, she admitted, pleasure. There had been a change in the atmosphere between the Irishman and her. She thought their conversation in the library marked the beginning of the change, but an exact chronology did not seem so important as the fact that there had been an improvement. There were fewer sparks, more smiles, and more banter. She was glad. Her summer at Ridley ought not to be marred by strife.

She was seated in the window seat in her room, looking out at the sky as she often did before she went to bed. With no moon, the stars made magic of the night.

But her eye wandered rather soon to earthier spheres. From her window she could make out the clearing where the head trainer's cottage lay.

She could not see a light. Was he alone in the dark? The unexpected question produced an unpleasant sensation that dimmed a little of the warm glow she'd enjoyed. Immediately Susannah was irritated with herself. That very afternoon she had resolved that the amorous side of O'Neill's life was no concern of hers. And what did she imagine, anyway? That he would live as a monk? Something between a smile and grimace lifted her mouth, but the expression faded in the next moment. Something moved in the lane leading to his cottage.

Her gaze sharpening, Susannah distinguished a large shadowy shape. It moved so fluidly, she knew it could only be a man mounted on a dark horse. When he reached the next lane, the rider did not turn to Ridley, but rode away toward the heath.

It was O'Neill she had watched ride off in the dark of night. The next day, Susannah learned from Lady Augusta that the Irishman had departed for Ipswich on business. To herself she wondered why he rode out at night. Aloud she questioned what sort of business would take him from Newmarket with the meet only three weeks distant, but O'Neill's employer did not know.

"Perhaps he heard of the sale of some horses, my dear." Lady Augusta looked supremely unconcerned. "I cannot say as I did not press him. I've complete confidence O'Neill will have my horses ready for the meet. And besides, I never think to question him, somehow."

Of course not, Susannah thought half-irritably. "The" O'Neill makes his own rules. But when she began to suspect she was disgruntled because he had not made known to her his intention to leave Ridley, though they had been in each other's exclusive company two or more hours the day of his departure, Susannah dismissed her grandmother's head trainer from her mind and resumed the pleasant pattern of her days: galloping with the grooms in the morning, visiting Lady Danu afterward, sitting with Nan in the afternoon, gardening a little, then going off for a swim.

Her evenings, however, were claimed by local society. A day after Connor's departure, Bunny Townshend brought an invitation to a small dinner party his parents were giving the next night at Bascom Lodge. Unhappily, Lady Augusta was compelled to cry off at the last moment. She'd come down with Nan's sniffles, complete with dripping nose and red eyes, but she insisted Susannah and James go without her.

Alone in the carriage of her cousin, Susannah found it natural to ask after his courtship with Phoebe, then regretted the impulse, his face fell so.

"I am mad about her, Susannah!" James declared as he had more than once before. "But I can't tell what she feels toward me."

"Oh?"

James nodded morosely. "She can be so charming. The way she smiled at me makes me quite wild about her, but she can make me furiously jealous too. After you left the picnic the other day, I thought I might kill Drew, the two of them carried on so. Bunny says it is because I wear my heart on my sleeve that she treats me so. I've half a mind not to pay her court tonight just to see if he has the right of it."

James was looking at her expectantly, awaiting some words of wisdom, but all Susannah could think of to say was that his murderous impulses ought more properly to have been directed at Phoebe. It was she who had, no doubt, thrust her décolletage at Drew, not the other way about.

"Well, I think holding yourself aloof is not such a bad

notion," Susannah brought herself to say finally. "It cannot hurt to show her you will not allow her to run roughshod over you."

Unfortunately, to Susannah's mind at least, James's new tack worked wonderfully. Phoebe seemed to realize she had pushed him a little too far, and afraid she might lose her chance at a connection to the Duke of Beaufort's family, she set about making amends.

When James only greeted her with studied casualness before sauntering off to join some young men gathered on the far side of the room, Phoebe followed him with narrowed eyes. When he ignored her altogether for over quarter of an hour, she went to him, bringing him a glass of punch and smiling a particularly inviting smile. For the rest of the evening she confined all her attention to James, and when dinner was announced, she accorded him the honor of leading her in to dinner.

The result of Phoebe's efforts was that James, flushed with success, drank a great deal more than he normally did. And when some of his friends announced after dinner that they were off to the Rutland Arms in Newmarket to hear what the locals had to say of the upcoming meet, he joined them, though his defection left Susannah to ride home alone.

It must be said Susannah made no objection. She was pleased to see James enjoying himself, and besides she was certainly not, in the year 1811, afraid of highwaymen.

Some few miles distant from Bascom Lodge, Susannah had cause to wonder if she had not been foolish. Above the quiet clicking of the carriage wheels she heard the sound of a horseman advancing quickly upon them.

Just as she was debating whether to look out and see who it was, she heard a male voice call, "Whoa, there!" And on an instant her faint alarm dissipated. The rider did not have to cry out the coachman's name for her to recognize his voice.

As the carriage slowed, she did lean her head out the window. On a black horse, a black cape covering his black coat and trousers, Connor O'Neill looked like a highwayman, until she saw a gleam of white and knew he was smiling at her.

"Lady Susannah! Well met. May I cadge a ride with you? I've ridden straight through from Ipswich and would dearly love to rest."

"By all means, do join me, Mr. O'Neill. I wouldn't want you to be uncomfortable."

He laughed, and she was aware that she, too, smiled into the night.

After Connor had tied his horse to the back of the carriage, he joined her, his gaze sweeping the interior as he climbed inside. "You are alone?"

"Yes, James went to the Rutland Arms in Newmarket with friends."

"And left you to make your way home alone at night?"

With some surprise, Susannah realized he was both incredulous and displeased. Half-amused, she replied lightly. "Well, I daresay Dibble knows the way."

"He is unconscionably self-absorbed!" Susannah was in no doubt who it was O'Neill thought self-absorbed. "What if something had happened, your wheel came off, say?"

"If you had but looked, you'd have seen Dibble's son on the box with him."

"You felt secure with a lad of no more than ten to protect you?"

"But Will would not protect me," Susannah protested, thoroughly engaged. "He would stay with his father, while I rode one of the carriage horses to Ridley for help." A muted growl informed her what O'Neill thought of her humor. For some reason, she smiled again. "At any rate you are here now to protect me. How was your business in Ipswich?"

"Inconclusive. How was your entertainment?"

As it was obvious Connor would not tell her anything of his business in Ipswich, she told him of the Townshends' dinner party and James's successful strategy.

Connor was not vastly impressed. "That should do well enough until someone new wanders within the range of her eye."

Susannah agreed to a point. She did not think it was novelty in itself that piqued Phoebe. The girl might see O'Neill, for example, a dozen times and still be moved to bat her thick lashes up at him. "At any rate he was pleased for a little."

"He was pleased by deuced little," Connor returned curtly. "And no matter if he was ecstatic, he ought not to have been so overcome that he forgot his duty to you." As he spoke, Connor stretched his long legs out, resting them on the opposite seat. "Do you mind?" he asked.

"No, of course not."

What Susannah did mind was the lack of light in the carriage. She wanted to know if it was fatigue made him so irritable over James's desertion. He sounded weary, and she wanted to ask after him, even to wonder aloud why he had been moved to travel to and from Ipswich at night. But most of all, Susannah realized, she simply wanted to look at him.

Susannah no sooner registered the thought than she thrust it away. It helped that she was, again, surprised to hear the sounds of riders overtaking the carriage.

"Whoa!" another male voice called out in the night. "In the name of his majesty, halt!"

As Dibble pulled up, several soldiers, the color of their red coats identifiable even in the night, surrounded them.

"What is the meaning of this?" Susannah once more leaned out the window to address a rider. The man to whom she spoke was a square, stout man. He held up a lantern another handed to him.

"Forgive the inconvenience, my lady . . . ?" His gruff voice trailed off on a questioning note.

"I am Lady Susannah Somerset. And I wish to know why I am being inconvenienced."

The soldier stiffened at the imperiousness in her voice. "We've orders to search all carriages and conveyances we came upon, my lady. The jail at Norwich has been raided."

"And you suspect I've an escaped prisoner hidden in my skirts?"

Her withering tone caused the poor man to grit his teeth, but orders being orders, he held up his lantern that he might peer into the carriage.

"This is the trainer of my grandmother's racehorses," Susannah snapped. "You may know of her. She is Lady Augusta Somerset. If you do not know her, however, you will know of my father. He is the Duke of Beaufort and will hear of this night's work, I assure you. What is your name, man?"

"Sergeant Wilkins, my lady," the fellow admitted in a strangled voice. Beaufort's daughter! Of all the luck. "We are only following orders, your ladyship."

"I understand, and having followed your orders and ascertained we are not dangerous, I am certain you will wish us a hearty Godspeed, Sergeant Wilkins."

"Oh, aye! Godspeed, my lady!"

The carriage rolled forward even before the words were entirely out of his mouth. In the next moment, Connor gave a low, appreciate laugh. "Remind me to have you on my side in a pinch, Lady Susannah Somerset. I am not certain I have ever witnessed anyone tying up a sergeant in the English militia quite so efficiently."

Susannah ignored the compliment. "I wonder why I think their search has something to do with you, Mr. O'Neill?"

There was again the flash of his white smile in the dark. "You are overly imaginative, perhaps?"

"I've never been accused of being fanciful before," she replied readily. "Traveling by night is odd in itself, and I've only your word that you came from Ipswich. You might as easily have come from Norwich. Indeed, given how tired you sound, I think that more likely, because Norwich is farther."

"Are these fancies the reason you did not give my name to the good Sergeant Wilkins?"

There was not the least bit of gratitude in his voice, only, and distinctly, amusement. Susannah ignored it. "I did not care to be delayed, should your distinctly Irish name be of interest to the sergeant. Did you plan to throw them off by joining me in the carriage?"

"As I had not the least notion you would be clattering along this road late at night without an escort of any kind, I could have planned nothing of the sort. But do I understand you correctly, my lady? You willingly risked the charge of acting as an accomplice for no reason but that you are eager to reach your bed?''

Without pause Susannah replied, "That and because I owe you a favor.''

"What?"

He sounded thrown off his stride, and she smiled to herself. How pleasant it was to confound "the" ever-assured O'Neill.

"Come, come, I am sure you recall the morning you were kind enough not to reveal my presence to James and Bunny, when I wished to avoid them.''

"Ah, yes. I do recall, now you mention it.''

"So now we are quite even.''

"But I beg to differ!" She could hear the laughter in his voice. "I did not ask you to send the militia off with a flea in its ear, much as I enjoyed your performance. You acted for your own benefit, as you yourself said. To discharge your debt to me, you must perform a service of benefit to none but me. Like this one.''

Susannah saw the flash of his smile again, then saw the shadow that was his hand reach up to cup her chin. His touch startled her so that she might have pulled away, but by then Connor had caught her lips with his.

It was the gentlest of kisses, feather-like, promising more than it gave. Susannah could have ended it. She considered doing so, after she absorbed the shock that he had, in fact, as he had hinted would delight him, presumed so utterly as to kiss her.

But it was dark in the carriage. Susannah did not have to open her eyes and face the man who was her grandmother's trainer. Under the cloak of darkness, he was . . . a man, only. And it came to Susannah that she had wondered a very long time how his kiss would be.

It was tantalizing, his lips warm, teasing on hers. She no longer thought to pull away, thought of nothing, in fact, but that she wanted more, and she opened her lips to taste his.

Instantly Connor's kiss intensified. Susannah swayed into him as his mouth firmed on hers, demanding more and receiving it, returning even more.

Quite some time later, it was Connor who broke off abruptly. "You are a heady wine, my lady," he whispered, his voice husky as his breath stirred the tendrils of hair that curled just by Susannah's ear. "We've come to my lane," he added as softly, when she tightened the hold she scarcely realized she had on his shoulders. Dazedly Susannah became aware the coach was, indeed, slowing.

"Sleep well, my lovely lady." It was the merest thread of sound in the darkness. Then he was gone, calling out a farewell to Dibble as he untied his horse.

Connor's form had not quite merged with the shadows when Susannah sank back into her seat and began to take in what she had done.

She lifted her hand to her mouth to stifle a sudden cry, only to jerk it back immediately. Her lips were sensitive to her touch. Appalled, she clamped them into a tight line. Were they swollen? Might anyone who looked at her know what she'd allowed?

He would know. No matter how tightly she held her lips, he would know, and know, as well, that she had done more than merely allow. Susannah groaned. Allow! She had returned his kiss and in full, full measure.

8

CONNOR ENTERED the cottage that was his home at Ridley by the kitchen door. It squeaked as he closed it, bringing Liam, nodding by the fireplace, awake with a start. "Och, now, there you are! Took you a mite longer than I expected."

"I see you lost sleep from worry."

Liam ignored the dry remark in favor of studying the lines fatigue had etched on his friend's face. "It was a bad business then?"

"A futile business, rather."

Having delivered the succinct reply, Connor unearthed a bottle of Irish whiskey and two glasses from the cupboard, then settled wearily into a chair.

Liam waited until Connor had tossed off a glass of the smoky whiskey. "Seamus was not there?"

"No, he was not," Connor replied in a voice made soft by weariness and anger too. "I imagine they hanged him on some excuse soon after they captured him."

Liam struck his thigh hard with a hand so large it could justly have been called a paw. "The bloody—"

"He knew what his fate would be," Connor cut in harshly now, "if he or any other in his band of Greenboys were caught attacking a paywagon, Liam. He knew and still threw himself away. Damn, but he'll not take Rory down with him!"

"How will you find the lad without Seamus to tell you who aids the Greenboys in England? And if you can't be findin' Rory, how'll you warn him there's naught at Norwich Castle but a bloody Sassenach trap?"

Connor tossed down another glass of the whiskey as if he would wash the question away. He'd no good answer for them.

"I can only hope Rory will hear of the breakout and will work out that Seamus Fitzgerald was never incarcerated at Norwich, when Seamus fails to appear at whatever door shelters the remains of the Greenboys."

"A breakout!" Liam's expression changed completely and he gave a great shout of laughter. "You did not free them all, lad!"

"Every one," Connor affirmed, but though Liam hooted again, he did not smile, only gazed into the flames of the fire, seeming lost in thought. Most of the men he'd released had been harmless drunks or poor farmers in arrears on their rents. One or two, though, had been cut of a different cloth. Violence and cruelty had gleamed in their crafty eyes, and it had been of them he thought when he found Susannah traveling through the dark night alone.

Which only showed he was . . . tired beyond rational thought, for the escapees would have had to ride like banshees to come upon the Somerset coach before him. None had had horses waiting, saddled and ready.

"But how did you manage it and still get away?"

For the first time Connor's expression lightened a little. "Through your good advice, Liam. The vicar's disguise you suggested worked brilliantly. They never questioned that I was a harmless soul come to console a sinning parishioner, and I was able not only to have free run of the records of all the men incarcerated, but to visit the cells as well. I had gotten to my first one when a fortuitous explosion ripped an old building apart on the far side of Norwich and half the garrison rushed off to investigate. It was child's play then to open the cell doors and release the petty criminals within."

"And there was no pursuit of you?"

"There was, actually. They fanned out in all directions

to recover as many prisoners as they could. In the end it was
Lady Susannah who delivered me from the Sassenach redcoats.''

"Nay!"

Connor regarded Liam's thunderstruck expression wryly.
"Perhaps in the interest of accuracy I ought to say she did
not deliver me to the Sassenach. I came upon her as she
returned from a dinner near Bury Saint Edmunds. Truth to
tell, I didn't know how hard the militia was upon my heels.
I only thought to rest my legs, but I hadn't been in the coach
long before it was stopped. Had they looked closely, they'd
have seen my horse was winded, but she sent them packing
before they could do more than draw breath.''

"Her ladyship surely did not know it was you they
sought?''

"She only suspected I might be of interest to them." The
corner of Connor's mouth lifted. "She's no fool, nor is she
inconsequential. The hapless sergeant in charge of that troop
will be scratching the flea she put in his ear for a fortnight
at least.''

Liam shifted uneasily in his chair. '' 'Tis all well, I'm sure,
but do you think she'll be keepin' her suspicions to herself?''

"Yes.''

"Ah! She's fallen for you, then?''

But Connor did not respond with the assuring grin Liam
expected. "She's not fallen into my bed, if that's your
question. She'd not see me hang, that's all. You needn't
worry though,'' he added when Liam began to frown. "I've
a stout alibi in Ipswich, should she—or anyone—decide to
shout their suspicions to the winds. I took care to be seen
in Ipswich yesterday and to cultivate a certain widow there
who will say I was with her until midnight.'' Liam exclaimed
with an approval not unmixed with pride, but Connor cut
him off. "Enough, Liam. We must think now what to do
next. I want to extend our search. Perhaps we've not found
Rory because we've only looked for him in and around
Norwich. I want you to go to London. Play the part of a
Yorkshireman, looking for an Irishman who is to sell him
a horse. You'll have some disguise that way, but you'll also

have an excuse to visit alehouses frequented by the Irish. It won't do any harm, either, if you quietly spread news of the outbreak in Norwich. I can't travel so far afield, but I think Cambridge is worth a try. I'll do the same there. 'Tis all we can do but pray to God that Rory learns we are in Newmarket before whoever it is who betrayed the Greenboys the first time does so again.''

Later, in his room, Connor fell into his bed with a weary sigh. He was growing too old for so much activity. First he'd ridden through the night to Ipswich to visit the lush widow he'd cultivated for just such a purpose. He made no apology for using her. She was lusty and understood he made no promises, but his dalliance with her had not increased his energies for the ride to Norwich. And playing a country vicar come to inform a parishioner of the death of his mother had not been an easy part for him. He'd had to stretch to look both pious and inoffensive. Excitement had carried him out of Norwich, but the ride had been long, and then at the end . . .

He began to smile finally there in the dark. Whatever her feelings for him, she had responded to his kiss. And he? He would remember that kiss long after he forgot the evening he'd spent with the widow in Ipswich.

She'd lived up to the promise of her eyes. And more. When she'd yielded, opened her mouth to him, he'd felt a desire fiercer than he'd been prepared for. And now that he'd had a taste, he wanted more of her.

The thought brought Connor a slight unease. Until he thought of Susannah; then a smile chased away the faint alarm. He would not find it easy to satisfy his desire to taste her again. With the daylight, he suspected Lady Susannah Somerset would not be well pleased to recall the liberty he'd taken, or the response he'd aroused in her. She would take care to be armed against him when they met next.

His eyes drifted closed, though a smile still curved his mouth. She was formidable. Poor Sergeant Wilkins. And a beauty. All golden and tasting of honey . . .

When Connor did not appear for the early morning gallops,

Emma Lange

Susannah knew herself to be the most foolish of cowards. As she must eventually face him, must endure the light that would be dancing in his eyes, she ought to want to get the horrid meeting over and done with. She told herself she would breathe more easily then. That was what she told herself, but what she felt was the most intense relief that the devil had not, predictably, proved accommodating.

Susannah did encounter James, however. He was returning from his riotous night as she returned Barley Boy to the stableyard, and at the sight of him, Susannah bit back a smile. If James had slept at all, he'd slept in his clothes. Everything he wore was creased and rumpled, and his hair stuck out at odd, unexpected angles, but when he saw her, he managed a crooked suggestion of a smile.

"Susannah." James swayed, momentarily battling with eyelids that looked heavy as stones, then rallied briefly. "Glad to see you got home safely. Heard there was a dust-up somewhere or other, and worried for you."

His head sagged, then seemed to pull him around in the direction of the house. Susannah forgotten, he lurched off toward his bed. His cousin watched him go with an affectionate smile. James was not so self-absorbed. Even three sheets, perhaps four, to the wind, he had remembered to be worried for her.

The encounter with James served to remind Susannah of her carriage ride. She had told Dibble not to speak to anyone of their being stopped the night before, either by O'Neill or by the militia. She had given the coachman the excuse that she did not wish to worry Lady Augusta. Dibble, ever loyal, had not questioned her, though it was the thinnest reason ever given. Gussie would have relished the story. And she'd have come to the same conclusion Susannah had, that O'Neill's appearance in the dead of night just ahead of the militia was no coincidence. Others might come to the same conclusion, if Dibble were to talk and the gossip spread. Susannah might be thoroughly put out with the man, but she was not so vindictive she wished there to be dangerous speculation about him. Gussie would simply have to wait to hear the story.

Curiously, it never occurred to Susannah she was being

disloyal not to confide her suspicions about the Irishman to the authorities. Had she been asked, however, she'd have said she imagined O'Neill and whatever confederate he had freed, or tried to, from the Norwich county jail were only struggling to secure freedoms even the humblest Englishman already enjoyed. After reading her history, she'd no defense for her country's actions in Ireland, many of which seemed to have been based on the reasoning that the Irish deserved the worst treatment possible because they insisted upon loyalty to a different church. She thought it a paltry justification indeed for snatching an Irishman's lands from him, for denying him the vote, and even for forbidding him to make his own goods.

Though the question of Susannah's loyalties was settled easily enough, her nerves proved less tractable. She had too much pride to hide, but as she went her way about Ridley that day, Susannah kept an eye on the lane to the trainer's cottage.

In the late afternoon, as she returned from her pool in the woods, her steps were distinctly lighter. Whatever she might tell herself about the advantages of getting a difficult moment over, the longer the moment was postponed, the more Susannah could toy with the notion it might never come. No, she would see him, of course she would, but surely with the passage of time the memory of how she had responded to him would fade—from his mind as well as hers.

At the house, Soames did not have the best news to impart. Bunny Townshend and Phoebe had ridden over, and as James was still "indisposed," Lady Augusta, alone, presided over tea with them. Susannah understood from Soames's lifted brow that Gussie was not pleased to have been caught so, and wished her presence forthwith in the Green Saloon.

She'd have gone straight in, but that she had mud on the hem of her dress and did not care to explain where she'd gotten it. Mary, her maid, was aghast at the very idea, for Mary had the notion that Susannah must at all times be turned out to better advantage than whatever other young lady happened to be on hand. Rushing about, she had Susannah dressed in a trice in a lemon-colored dress of a fine jaconet muslin that did, Susannah allowed, flow nicely about her slender figure and long legs.

Susannah was to be grateful for Mary's competitive nature. Lacking James, Lady Augusta had sent for another to balance the number of gentlemen against ladies. Susannah saw him the moment she crossed the threshold of the saloon where her grandmother liked to take tea. Seated upon a settee with Phoebe Limley, the Irishman was smiling down at the girl, whose head was tilted at a coy angle while she made the most of having a striking man all to herself.

"Susannah!" Bunny leapt to his fashionably shod feet. O'Neill, she saw from the corner of her eye, rose less impulsively. "Susannah! I say, you are looking well!"

"Why, thank you, Bunny." Susannah allowed him to bow over her hand before she greeted her grandmother with a commiserating smile. James's darling received a "Miss Limley" then finally Susannah glanced at O'Neill.

She had steeled herself for it all day, but at the sight of the devilish gleam dancing in the rogue's too-attractive eyes, Susannah flushed. She did not turn tail, however. As she felt the infuriating heat rise in her cheeks, she lifted her chin higher and willed an admirably cool, composed "Mr. O'Neill" to emerge from her mouth.

But she could have kissed Bunny for providing a distraction. "What a relief it is to see you appear so unruffled, Susannah!" he cried even before she'd quite finished inclining her head in the Irishman's direction.

"Whatever do you mean, Bunny?" She regarded him in genuine surprise as she took a seat.

"Do you not know? There was a mass escape from the Norwich county jail last night. I was so alarmed when I heard of it, I came right along to assure myself you came to no harm all alone."

Susannah commanded her eyes to stay upon Bunny, though it took the greatest effort of will. She wanted so much to see if O'Neill was worried that she might announce he'd been only a step ahead of the militia.

It was not in her to take such irrevocable revenge, but it

was quite in Susannah to hesitate a moment and allow, she hoped, the rogue to languish just a little in suspense.

She spent the moment arranging the sleeve of her dress to her liking, then gave Bunny a smile. "I thank you for your concern, Bunny, but as you can see the events of last evening . . . affected me not at all."

Phoebe leaned forward, blocking Susannah's line of vision before she could slide an assessing look the Irishman's way. "When Bunny told me of the breakout, Lady Susannah, I shuddered to imagine what might have occurred had you encountered any of the villains!"

"Fancy we've that in common, Miss Limley!" Lady Augusta plunged into the discussion with an arch look. "Villains tend to spark my imagination as well!" Phoebe blinked, trying to make sense of the remark, as the dowager turned from her to address Susannah. "I am wise enough to know, my dear that while imaginary villains are exciting, villains in the flesh would not be at all. I am very glad that you did not suffer from James's desertion."

"I ought to have accompanied you in his stead!" Bunny cried in self-reproach.

Susannah made only a little effort to keep her exasperation from her voice. "Don't be absurd, Bunny. In the first place, James never deserted me. I urged him to go off to the Rutland Arms. I did not think I needed an escort, nor did I."

"Any journey at night, even over the most familiar ground, can be dangerous for a woman alone, Lady Susannah."

The assertion, made in flat, authoritative tones by the very man who had taken advantage of her position, alone and unattended in the dark of night, brought Susannah's gaze snapping to Connor. "As you have cause to know, Mr. O'Neill?" she challenged ever so innocently. It was a purely rhetorical question. Almost at once Susannah went on, "Now, I do appreciate everyone's concern, but enough has been said on this subject. Truly. My journey last night was quite unmemorable. Yet, had I encountered an unscrupulous rogue upon the road, I am certain I would have survived the unfortunate encounter quite unscathed."

She smiled superbly, including everyone in her confident look. To the others it seemed the purest chance that of them all, Susannah's gaze came to settle, as she said that last, upon O'Neill.

Connor had to bite his lip to keep from smiling when her eyes fairly stabbed him, though he was tempted, with one or two grim stories, to disabuse her of her foolish sense of safety. Perhaps later he would. Just then the light of battle sparkling so brightly in her dark eyes was far too appealing to douse.

She was behaving exactly as he'd predicted, except that she looked even lovelier than he'd expected as she set him in his place. It was, in part, her dress. The soft yellow of it brought out the honey-gold of her hair. She looked so very good, in fact, all Connor wanted to do was lift her onto his lap and resume where they had left off the night before.

Something of his thoughts must have gleamed in his eyes, because Susannah colored and turned abruptly from him to address a remark to Bunny. Connor watched her, wondering now why she had not revealed to her grandmother at least, the truth of her not-so-solitary carriage ride. He had almost given away his part in her evening, until he realized from Lady Augusta's reply to the Limley chit's tedious chatter that the dowager duchess knew nothing. All day he had been considering how he would quell the speculation he felt certain would arise when it became generally known he and the militia had been out together on the roads. Now, thanks to the unlooked-for discretion of the elegant, enchanting English witch across from him, he had a great deal less to worry him.

9

CONNOR PAUSED a moment at the door to the Rosy Maid's public room. Though the hour was late, the room was crowded with men determined to make the most of the time they had before the closing hour. A group of young men seated in the far corner drew Connor's seemingly idle glance. In interesting contrast to the other patrons, they wore earnest expressions on their faces and leaned close together so that their low voices might be heard above the room's din.

He made his way to an empty table near them and was just settling himself when a barmaid appeared out of the smoke lying heavy upon the room's hot air. "What can I get ye, then, luv? An ale?"

As she appraised her latest customer, the barmaid's smile broadened. She had thought him negligible when he'd entered the room. He wore a long dusty jacket frayed at the cuffs and stood with a stoop. She'd not been able to see his face, for he'd pulled a battered slouch hat low on his brow, but now, up close, she saw that his legs beneath his rough trousers were well-muscled, and glancing swiftly upward, she found herself lost in the glimmer of extremely blue eyes.

"An ale'll do fine," Connor told her in a voice tinged with a Yorkshire accent. She gave him a grin before sauntering off.

Anyone watching would have thought Connor interested in the blowsy barmaid, for he seemed to follow her progress through the crowd, turning away from the young men at the nearby table as he did so.

It was Connor's fifth watering hole that night. He'd made his way to Cambridge soon after his tea with Lady Augusta . . . and her granddaughter. The faintest of smiles quirked the corner of his mouth. Lady Susannah. Had she been abashed or flustered upon meeting him after she'd returned him that kiss? No, thoroughbred that she was, she had nipped at him whenever she got the chance.

The barmaid returned with Connor's ale. "There, now, luv, call fer Annie if ye've a need." The smile she gave him promised more than ale, but would she give him what he really wanted—word that she'd seen a young man of Rory's description in the place recently? Rory had not been seen elsewhere in Cambridge.

Connor scowled as he sipped the dark, bitter brew he'd ordered. Damn, but he would give a great, great deal for a swallow of Irish whiskey. Clear and pure it might look in the bottle, but it turned to fire on the tongue.

Like . . . Connor winced. Lord have mercy upon him, he was comparing her to Irish whiskey. The Lady Susannah Somerset, daughter of the Duke of Beaufort, lately of London, now of Ridley, long of shapely leg, golden of beauty, fiery going down, and English to her core.

No, English to her marrow. Her core was her feminine own. Sipping the ale, Connor allowed himself the pleasure of recalling the scene they'd had just after tea.

Lady Susannah had accompanied Bunny Townshend and the Limley chit to Ridley's steps, intending, Connor did not doubt, to evade further contact with him by slipping up to her rooms after she had closed the door on her guests.

He forestalled her, padding up behind her quietly so that when she turned, she turned into him. She'd recovered her poise, inquiring as coolly as if he were only an unexpected servant, "Mr. O'Neill?"—but she had, first, taken an inadvertent hop backward.

He'd not been able to control his grin at that undignified little jump. She was not so cool and collected as she'd have liked him to believe. When her eyes had flashed with resentment for his humor at her expense, however, Connor had schooled his features as best he could.

"I've something to show you . . . give you, actually, my lady. Will you come with me?" He put out his arm, not at all certain Susannah would accept his invitation. Indeed, he'd been so uncertain, he had thought it prudent to add, "It is in the gardens."

With some amusement he watched a spark of interest light her eyes. "The gardens, Mr. O'Neill? Now you do intrigue me—as you no doubt planned."

He laughed, because she guessed his strategy, because he knew then she would come, and because there was deep in her eyes the faintest suggestion of a smile.

In a silence that was oddly companionable, they made their way around the house to the gardens. It was late in the afternoon, the day balmy, and the roses that were the pride and joy of Ridley's gardeners sweetened the air around them.

Connor felt Susannah take a deep breath, savoring the pleasure of that scent, but when she spoke, it was not of the roses. "You are not thinking to put me in your debt again, are you, Mr. O'Neill?"

"Could I?"

"No," she replied, her expression studiously unaffected by the teasing look he slanted her. "You could not, for I've no intention of paying you another forfeit."

"No? But I did not think you minded paying the last one so very much, my lady."

A direct hit, and cloaked in the most innocent of tones. Connor heard Susannah's breath catch and watched her gaze fly off. But she was up to his attack, after a half-second.

"You are no gentleman to say so, Mr. O'Neill." She swung her gaze back to him, her dark eyes remarkably steady, in all. "However, I cannot chide you overmuch, for you say no more than the truth." If the admission caused her discomfort, the only sign was an additional bit of color on her high, sculpted cheeks. Her golden skin tinged with rose, she looked the more beautiful for that flush. "I did enjoy the . . . forfeit, in fact. Stolen kisses in the dark from a highwayman are the stuff of every girl's dreams. However, I would not care to render the experience trite by repeating it. In short, Mr. O'Neill, I am not at your disposal.''

Her father was the fifth duke of his line, the eighth marquess, and the twelfth earl. He had not had to train Susannah to a regal air. She'd been born to it. It flashed through Connor's mind that he ought to go down on one knee and beg her pardon for any dishonor he had done her.

The thought that she would take the homage neatly in stride made him smile. ''I never made the mistake of thinking you were at my disposal, Lady Susannah.'' Smoothly, before she could protest that he had told her little and assured her even less, Connor made a sweeping gesture. ''Here we are, my lady.''

They had arrived at an unremarkable section of the high evergreen hedge that separated the flower gardens from the lawns. Susannah looked around, then at Connor, surprise giving way to suspicion. ''And exactly where is that, Mr. O'Neill?''

He could not resist grinning. ''Why, in your grandmother's gardens.'' When she arched a displeased brow at him, he laughed. ''And where I've hidden your gift. I'd not the time to give it into Budget's care, you see, and so I hid it from his minions lest one stumble upon it and dispose of it.''

As he spoke, Connor knelt down to feel beneath the hedge, and after a little pulled out a bucket. ''Devil it!'' he exclaimed then, his tone carrying enough genuine displeasure that Susannah peered over his shoulder.

The bucket seemed to contain a great deal of dirt and a limp wad of green she took to be a plant. ''What is it?''

She leaned so close beside him, Connor could smell the lemony scent of the soap she used. ''It was a plant for you. I found it a little time ago, but I'm afraid I didn't care for it properly.''

''What sort of plant?'' Susannah knelt down by him and took the bucket from his unresisting grasp. ''Oh, look, the bloom is lovely," she exclaimed, lifting the leaves. "And though the plant is a little wilted, it's not dead. Where did you get it?"

"It really hasn't died?" Connor asked, skeptically eyeing the prone stem she held in her hand.

"It is in distress, not in extremis, Mr. O'Neill." Susannah glanced up with a twinkle in her eye. "I suppose you don't know the name of it?"

"You suppose correctly. I dug it up because I liked the flower, not because I was enchanted with the name."

Susannah ignored his teasing as she examined the long stalk bearing some ten satiny golden flowers. "The flower itself reminds me of mullein, but I didn't know mullein ever grew on such a long, delicate stalk. Where did you find it?"

"Just outside of Newmarket, in the garden of a house that has been empty a month now."

"You stole it from someone's garden?"

Connor's expression remained very bland. "Because the house is empty, it is no one's garden. And anyway, there was too much of this plant. I only tidied up the place a bit by removing it."

Susannah laughed, and Connor felt a particular satisfaction. He had feared it would take much longer to make her face light up again. "You are a rogue, Mr. O'Neill, but," she chuckled, "I cannot regret your impulse—in this case. It's a lovely flower, and one I don't have."

It was not precisely the color of her hair. Her hair was not so bright a yellow, but it would have looked lovely braided into a coronet on her head. The fanciful thought had been the reason he had picked it from among several choices. Sometime, perhaps, he would tell her.

"You will be able to revive it?" he asked instead.

"Yes, you needn't worry there." She stood, lifting the pail. Her eyes looked very dark and velvety with a smile warming them. "It only needs some water. I'll plant it tomorrow. Thank you, Mr. O'Neill."

"You are welcome, particularly if I've been able to creep back into your good graces with this token."

"Creep?" Susannah, for once, took Connor completely by surprise, laughing outright. "I doubt you've ever crept anywhere in your life, Mr. O'Neill. Nor were you out of my good graces, as I explained earlier, but . . . you are certainly more firmly in them now. I am very pleased to have a new specimen for my garden."

"I am glad, and hope you'll be predisposed to forgive me if I tell you you've a smudge of dirt on your left cheek. Just there, above the hollow. No, no." When she wiped ineffectually, Connor took the task upon himself. At his touch, Susannah stiffened, but he kept his face expressionless and said casually, "Stand still. You don't want to look silly, I'm sure."

She did hold still, but only because, Connor suspected, he had taken hold of her chin by then. Reminded doubtless that he had held her just so when he had kissed her the night before, she studiously avoided his eyes, which was just as well, perhaps because Connor found it impossible to drag his gaze from her mouth. It was a very soft, perfectly molded, inviting mouth.

Susannah grew restive, though, and flicking her eyes up to his, saw where Connor looked, and likely something of his opinion of her mouth. Connor let her go when she pulled against him, though he didn't much want to, and he gave her a lazy bow. "You look lovely as ever now, my lady. Lovely enough to rival the roses behind you, in fact."

In the smoky, boisterous public room in Cambridge, Connor smiled to himself. She had arched her brow at that last, as if she'd not believed him. She'd been right to suspect there had been no smudge on her cheek; that he'd fabricated the story as an excuse to touch her. But she'd been wrong to question the sincerity of his flattery. If anything, her silky hair shining a warm gold in the late-afternoon sun, she put the roses to shame.

A rather more overblown rose swayed up before him then, and Connor gave the barmaid, Annie, a smile. "Drink with me, sweetheart?" he invited.

"Can't on his hours." She jerked her head to the bar where

the publican kept a proprietary eye on the proceedings. "But later, my hours are my own."

"I'll keep that in mind," he promised. "In the meantime, though, perhaps ye can help me." Eager to please a man with eyes like his, Annie nodded readily. "I've come lookin' for an Irishman, a friend of mine. I was to meet him in Cambridge at an inn, but devil take it, I can't find him anywhere. Mayhap ye've seen him. Lad's name is Rory. He's tall, a bit thin, with brown eyes and hair as black as coal. On occasion he swaggers a bit, but he's a good boy for all that."

The barmaid wanted to please, but in the end she shook her head. "Nay. Can't say I've seen such a one, sir."

"No matter, but if ye should see him, tell him 'the goose' is in Newmarket. It's a fancy of his to call me that name, you see. You'll not forget?"

"Oh, nay. But mayhap you ought to come back and see fer yerself, if he's been around?"

"I will, indeed." He gave her a wink that made her giggle. "Be sure and tell him I will, if ye see him."

After the maid departed, Connor drank his ale, seeming wrapped in his own thoughts. In no way did he reveal he was aware the group of young men nearby had ceased all conversation the moment he'd said he sought an Irishman. It might be coincidence. Or it might not.

They could be young Anglo-Irish Protestants. It was possible, and if they were, they might be disaffected from English rule in Ireland, and if they were disaffected, it was also possible they might be acquainted with Rory, for the Greenboys, the group Seamus Fitzgerald had founded to harass the English in Ireland, had made an effort to recruit Protestants as well as Catholics into their ranks.

Hearing all his ifs and mights, Connor downed the last of his ale. The worst frustration was he could not drag the answers out of the pups whispering nearby. He couldn't expose himself so. There was a traitor about somewhere. There had to be. The Greenboys, when they had tried to ambush the paywagon on its way to English soldiers stationed in Munster, had been ambushed themselves. Anyone in the group could have betrayed them, but Rory had thought it was one of the Anglo-Irish in the group, or one of the few Englishmen who supported the cause.

10

CONNOR REMAINED in Cambridge the next morning, making the rounds of the more established inns. He told the host at each he was seeking a younger brother, the truth being as useful as a falsehood at times, but still he met with no one who had served a young man of Rory's description.

While Connor was going freely, if unrewardingly, about his way, Susannah was trapped. She'd thought to go to her garden at Nan's after a pleasant luncheon with Lady Augusta, but James rushed into Ridley's smaller dining room, catching her.

"Bunny and Phoebe have come!" he exclaimed with lamentable, if appealing enthusiasm. "They are off to visit a camp of Gypsies on Warren Hill. Phoebe hopes to have her fortune read, and they wish us to accompany them."

James looked too hopeful to deny. It was the first time Phoebe had sought his company.

Phoebe had not come to Ridley entirely on James's account, however. While she and Susannah waited for the young men to work out the travel arrangements, Phoebe asked, with an attempt at casualness, if O'Neill were about. Susannah said no, nothing more. Phoebe waited a moment, obviously hoping more information would be forthcoming, but Susannah only regarded her with an expression that caused Phoebe to shrug her shoulders disinterestedly.

"Oh, well, I only thought of him because of the Gypsies.

He is as dark as they, but for his eyes, of course. It was my maid saw the Gypsies,'' she rattled on, too conscious of Susannah's cool look to allow a silence. ''She said they are ever so exciting. Especially the men! Ah, here are our young men now.''

Bunny and James drove up to the front steps, where the girls awaited them, in separate gigs. The Gypsy camp was between Bascom Lodge and Ridley, and they reasoned that if the hour grew late, Bunny and Phoebe might wish to drive directly home.

Susannah was not well pleased to be traveling alone with Bunny, but there was the compensation that she would be without Phoebe. And James gave her another appealing look.

The Gypsy camp consisted of eight brightly painted wagons pulled into a circle under the shade of several large oak trees. When the two gigs arrived, a half-dozen barefoot children raced up to inspect the visitors and hold their horses.

Behind the informal greeters came a tall, fine-looking older man. He had black eyes and a proud face and wore his hair caught back beneath a kerchief. Introducing himself as Antonio Romero, he welcomed them, and when James explained the reason for their visit, sent a child off for the woman who told fortunes.

She was an old crone, bent with age, but possessed of a pair of bright, shrewd black eyes Susannah didn't doubt could see a great deal of a person's character, if little of the future.

Susannah went first with her into one of the wagons, and took a seat on a bench built into the wall. The old woman settled herself more slowly, then took her customer's hand and studied it.

''You've generosity and spirit, good miss. I see those qualities in these two lines. And you possess courage. Hold to all three. You will need them in your life.''

Susannah smiled to herself. Her ''fortune'' could have been anyone's, but the old woman was not done. She lifted her wise old eyes to probe Susannah's. ''Choose the man who matches your spirit, young miss. You will find little pleasure in your life if you do not. But if you do win through to him, if you do not take the easy path, you will be fulfilled indeed.''

Susannah stared into black eyes that seemed to gleam just a little, though whether with amusement or wisdom it was impossible to say. Most likely it was amusement that animated them, Susannah told herself as she resisted an urge to demand that the old crone name the man who matched her spirit. Fortune-telling was merely a game, a way to amuse the English and earn the Gypsies a few coins. The crone had spoken of marriage only because she'd have known romantic matters would be uppermost in the mind of a young woman Susannah's age.

"Thank you, madam. I shall keep your advice in mind. And if I find a man of my spirit, I'll cut a path to him if need be."

The old woman cackled, seeming as delighted by the rejoinder as by the bright coins Susannah left upon the table.

When Phoebe descended after her time with the fortune teller, she looked very pink. "I cannot conceive how that woman could know so much about me!" the younger girl exclaimed when James asked if she were satisfied with her fortune. "She knew all about Papa being wealthy, and about my Season, and even about . . . Well, she knew so much!"

Susannah bit her lip to keep from smiling. How astute of the old Gypsy woman to guess Phoebe had committed an indiscretion with one of her flirts.

As if she had been waiting nearby for the correct moment, a young woman appeared with a tray and four tiny steaming cups. Bunny looked dubious about tasting a Gypsy beverage, and after the smallest of sips, he regarded his cup with alarm. "Great heaven, I have never tasted anything like it! Is it coffee?"

The young woman seemed to smile, but it was not possible to say for certain, as she ducked her head. "It is coffee, yes, good sir."

Romero strolled up to them, smiling broadly. "You like?" He gestured to the cups. "It has taste, no?"

Susannah chuckled. "It has taste, yes. Good taste."

He swept her a bow that was courtly in its grace. "You prove, my lady, that beauty and grace go hand in hand."

Susannah took the flowery praise in the spirit it was given, and inclined her head with a smile of thanks.

"Will you and your people still be about when the meet gets underway in Newmarket, Mr. Romero?" James inquired.

The Gypsy smiled. "Yes, good sir. We come to see the fine horses race. And perhaps to win a little."

James laughed at that. "Put your money on the horses from Ridley and you will win, you may be sure of it."

"Ah! That is the stud of the Lady Augusta, no? I have known her well in the past. A very find lady. You will give her the regards of Angelo Romero?"

When Susannah found herself speculating how well Mr. Romero had known Gussie, she winced. To form such a question about one's grandmother was a clear indication that living with said grandmother was not without its deleterious effects.

James promised they would convey Mr. Romero's regards. "Gussie will be delighted you remembered her. And may I thank you again, sir? You have been most hospitable."

"But, James!" Phoebe pouted when James rose. "I don't wish to leave yet! The camp is so interesting."

Phoebe gave a seemingly idle glance around, but Susannah, following the direction of that gaze, saw a newcomer had strolled into the circle of wagons. He was a young man, surely no more than twenty, but he had a hard, taut body he carried with bold grace. In his ear he wore a bright gold ring.

Catching sight of the camp's visitors, he swept them with a direct assessing gaze and turned abruptly to stroll in their direction. Susannah glanced at Phoebe. There was a smile just curving the girl's mouth.

While James stood, obviously waiting to go, Phoebe turned her bright glance to Mr. Romero. "I have never seen a man wear jewelry before, sir. Is it the Gypsy custom?"

Mr. Romero glanced from Phoebe to the young man approaching, a guarded expression replacing his broad smile. "It is our custom, yes, miss."

"Well, it is a very dashing one!" Phoebe proclaimed, openly eyeing the Gypsy, who returned her look.

"This is my son, good sirs." Mr. Romero stiffly indicated the young Gypsy who was a half-foot taller than he. "Dario."

Dario was truly a fine specimen of manhood, in tight black pants that fit him like a glove and an open white shirt. When he flicked a raking glance from Phoebe to her and back again, Susannah did not have to look at James to know he would be bristling at the young man's boldness.

But Phoebe seemed unaware of the tension in the air and addressed the younger Romero directly. "I saw some horses as we approached the camp, Mr. Romero. Do you ride?"

"Like the wind, pretty lady."

His voice was young, but his smile was not. Dario looked as if he wished to sample Phoebe on the spot. She did not look as if she would object.

James could not see the look his darling gave the Gypsy, he stood behind her, but he could follow the direction of Dario's gaze. "Come along, Miss Limley. You did say you promised Mrs. Townshend that you would return in time for tea."

"We've hours until tea!" Phoebe lifted her chin at James. "And I wish to stay. I've never seen a Gypsy camp before." She tipped her head slightly. "Do not be in such a hurry, James! You wouldn't wish to spoil my fun, surely."

It was a shameless effort to wrap James around her finger, and might have succeeded, Susannah judged, but that Dario grinned.

James saw that smile at his expense and stiffened. "I don't mean to spoil your fun at all, Miss Limley, but it is time we went." He held out his hand. "Come along."

"No!" Phoebe had never been denied much, and certainly not by a young man. Miffed, she forgot she had decided to marry into the Somerset family, had decided James would make the perfect compliant husband, she even forgot the young Gypsy who was so intriguing. She saw only James's hand, and she tossed her fat, sausage curls at it. "If you must go, then do so, Mr. Somerset. We brought two gigs. Bunny can drive me home.''

"I say—" Bunny began, but James was already speaking.

"Very well, if that is what you want, Miss Limley. Susannah?" James scarcely waited for his cousin to rise before he whirled about and stalked off to their gig.

Susannah bid the elder Mr. Romero, Bunny, and Phoebe, too, a hasty farewell, then hurried after her cousin. A smile was on her lips, for Phoebe was looking after James in almost comical astonishment. Susannah thought to congratulate him for his firmness, but after a look at James, she decided against speaking at all.

An angry flush on his cheeks, James flicked his reins sharply when the young Gypsy holding the horses let them go.

"Careful, James, there is a hill to be got down," Susannah broke her self-imposed silence to warn, for she was alarmed by the pace he set. The Gypsy camp was already disappearing into the trees behind them.

James was not in a mood to behave temperately, however. "I think I know how to manage a hill, Susannah! Kindly leave me to concentrate upon my driving."

She was glad to comply with that instruction. He would need to concentrate. Had it been someone else driving, she would not have been quite so concerned. James, however, was not famous for his ability with the reins.

It seemed almost as if James thought to console himself for Phoebe's behavior by playing the daredevil. When they came to the hill, he flicked the reins again.

"James!" A cry escaped Susannah when they hit a rock and the gig bounced so sharply she had to clutch the seat to keep from flying off. "Slow down!"

But James did not slow their pace. To Susannah it seemed, in fact, as if the gig suddenly gathered speed. "James!" she called out again, looking to see what on earth he was about. To her genuine alarm, she saw he had gone pale. Then she saw why. He had dropped one of the reins. It slapped the ground, frightening their horse.

As they gained speed, Susannah clung to her seat for dear

life. The trees along the road flashed by with nightmarish rapidity, and everywhere she looked, there were fearsome rocks. Built to be dashing, not stable, the gig seemed certain to overturn, and when it did tilt crazily, Susannah's mouth went dry. She squeezed her eyes shut as they teetered on the edge of disaster, then they came down with a hard jolt and careened madly on.

Susannah's bonnet slipped onto her shoulders, and her hair, coming loose from its pins, whipped at her face. She couldn't release her hold upon the gig to brush it away, and half-blinded, praying for a miracle, had no idea help had arrived until James cried hoarsely, "Oh, God, yes!"

It was O'Neill. Susannah recognized him immediately, though he had his dark head down close to his mount's neck as he urged the animal alongside the gig.

Her heart leapt into her throat. He had chosen to overtake them on the outside of the road, on the side that was bordered by a few feet of grass before it fell away in a dangerous drop.

Fear for him made Susannah shut her eyes tightly, but she had scarcely closed them before they flew wide again. She couldn't bear not knowing how he did. The gig bounced wildly again, and she cried out. O'Neill seemed not to hear her. He had gotten his horse alongside the bay by then, and Susannah watched, almost unable to believe her eyes as suddenly, with his horse running full out, Connor leapt from his mount onto the back of the bay.

It seemed too unbelievable a feat to be true, but already they were slowing. Susannah became aware that she could taste blood in her mouth, that she gasped for breath, that her hands were cramped, she held the seat so tightly.

The moment they rolled to a halt, Connor leapt from the winded bay and found Susannah with his eyes. White-faced, heart still thumping painfully, she could scarcely believe they were safe. Connor had only to hold out his arms for her to half-fall, half-launch herself into them. Had he been a magnet and she a piece of metal, Susannah could not have gone into his arms with more force, nor experienced such a feeling as she did, when he pressed her hard to him.

"Dear heaven!" was all she could get out on a half-sob

before she buried her face in his shoulder. He held her the tighter.

Connor's heart beat hard and loud beneath her ear, filling her awareness, and only gradually did Susannah realize he spoke to her too, murmuring soft, soothing nonsense.

"Ssh, sweetheart, ssh. It's all right now. It's all right." She let the words flow over her, less intensely aware of his heartbeat, but needing it all the same. "There, now. Ssh. You are safe. All safe. Thank the Lord."

That pricked Susannah's awareness a little, and she pulled back just far enough to look up at Connor. "Thank you, sir," she whispered with an unsteady emphasis. " 'Twas all your doing. I think the Lord was busy elsewhere."

The expression on Connor's face was not a smile so much as a look of profound relief. "Those who know of such things say He works in mysterious ways. I am so glad I managed. You are not hurt?"

Undoubtedly Connor had appeared to greater advantage at other times, but to Susannah he had never looked so good as he did then, hot, dusty, grim almost, but with his eyes softened by concern for her.

"No, I am not hurt," Susannah answered, thinking a sore bottom little enough after what she had feared. Assessing the damage to her person, however, brought Susannah to the awareness both that she stood in Connor's arms and that she wanted to stay in them. Shy suddenly, she straightened. Connor let her go to the extent that he allowed her to take a step back, but he kept his hands upon her arms.

"You are not feeling faint?" he asked, frowning. "Or about to lose the contents of your stomach, as your cousin is doing?"

"James?"

Connor smiled a little crookedly, as if he were having to learn all over again how to smile. "Did you have another cousin in the gig?"

She returned him much the same ragged smile. "Only James. Poor thing, he has lost a great deal this afternoon. First Phoebe to the Gypsies, then control of his horse, and now his dignity. But you needn't look so concerned for me," she told Connor softly. "I feel neither faint nor ill, only very, very relieved. Thank you again for that bit of bravery you displayed."

Connor did not appear to register either her thanks or her praise. His expression had turned grim again at the reminder of the danger in which she'd been, and his reply was a harsh, indistinct grunt.

Susannah had only to think what would likely have happened had Connor O'Neill not come along, not been brave, and not been a superb rider to feel more than a little grim herself. As if it had a will of its own, her head sank forward to rest upon his chest, and once more he gathered her against him, pushing her tilted bonnet aside completely that he might stroke the hair tumbling loosely down her back.

"I have wanted for the longest time to see your hair down," Connor murmured so softly, Susannah almost did not hear. "It feels like silk, you must know, and looks like a waterfall of sunshine tumbling down your back."

Knowing he was saying the merest nonsense to soothe her, Susannah gave a dry chuckle into his chest. "Perhaps this is another example of the Lord working in mysterious ways."

Connor's laugh rumbled so beneath her ear, it felt as good as it sounded and Susannah looked up to smile, albeit a little shakily, at him. It was odd how natural it felt to be in his arms, to hear him whisper her hair pleased him, to exchange a smile with him. Perhaps it was natural to feel so, as he had just saved her life. Susannah didn't know, nor did she brood on the question. For that moment she simply gave thanks to be where she was.

She was smiling up at Connor when James called out her name. He sounded ill and looked worse, as Susannah saw when he rounded the back of the gig.

"Are you hurt, Susannah?"

"No, no. Only shaken, James." With a sigh she was not even aware of, Susannah moved out of Connor's arms and went to her cousin. "And you?"

James only shook his head before he looked over her head to their rescuer. "I owe you the deepest thanks, O'Neill. If not for you . . ." His voice faltered, and he took

Susannah's hand. "Dear heaven, if not for you! Susannah, will you ever forgive me? I am so sorry."

He looked dreadfully rumpled, painfully shaken, and entirely penitent. Susannah smoothed back a lock of hair that had fallen into his eyes. "I do forgive you, love. And now we've that settled, let us think about getting home. I hear a gig in the distance, and I would prefer to avoid Bunny and Miss Limley, if possible."

Her words had the effect of a tonic. James straightened at once and color surged into his cheeks. "Yes! I think I hear them too. Up then, and we'll make it to the lane to Ridley before they see us."

"Well, I don't think—"

"Surely you cannot expect your cousin to ride with you, Somerset!' Connor broke into whatever far gentler phrasing Susannah had had framed to convey the same message. "I'll drive her. You may ride my horse."

James blinked uncertainly, but Connor simply led his sorrel up to the young man and handed him the reins. "Hurry, now!" He moved James along. "You must, if you want to avoid them."

Keenly aware what a shabby picture he would make as disheveled as he was, James allowed himself to be convinced he was not a coward to avoid the gig, the mere sight of which made him faintly ill.

The bay, though exceedingly winded, responded to Connor's command, and soon they were on their way, remaining just out of sight of Bunny and Phoebe. Susannah rather wanted to lay her head on her escort's broad shoulder. But she knew that would be going too far, and so she contented herself with sitting close enough that she could feel him strong and reassuring beside her.

11

THE NEXT morning, when Susannah returned from the gallops, a footman awaited her at the stables with a letter. "It's from Sebastian!" Susannah reported to Murdoch with a great smile. "I think I shall go and read my prize to Lady Danu."

At the mention of the mare, Murdoch flicked his cap against his thigh. "As to Lady Danu, she passed a fretful night, m'lady. Mayhap she'll be soothed by you as usual, but have a care with her."

"Do you think her time has come, Murdoch?"

The head groom nodded. " 'Tis close now."

Lady Danu was, indeed, more fretful than usual. Though she came to the fence to nuzzle Susannah in greeting, when her mistress offered her a carrot, the mare tossed her head at it.

Concerned, Susannah almost forgot her letter, until the mare came to sniff the unfamiliar vellum.

"You wish to know Sebastian's news?" Susannah inquired then with a chuckle. "Well"—she began to skim her brother's letter—"he says he has been training Portuguese soldiers much of this time and recently had the honor of seeing his men fight 'admirably.' " Susannah made a face at the mare. "Sebastian can be so very spare at times. I am certain they fought with the greatest courage, but Sebastian would never think to describe their feats. Ah! But look here, he does go on at some length about his hosts, the Portuguese. They are 'proud, courageous, and warm and possess an extraordinarily high sense of honor. Though I have been befriended by many, I am particularly fond of the d'Estalba family. Their son, the Comte d' Estalba, fights with me. He has a sister, Maria, who is near your age.' '' At that Susannah regarded Lady Danu wisely. *"Cherchez la femme,* Lady Danu. I would wager my next quarter's allowance that Maria d'Estalba is a beauty.''

Lady Danu snorted loudly, but even so, Susannah distinguished the sound of a male chuckle behind her. Taken unawares, she had no defense against a thrill of pleasure. She had not seen O'Neill since he had lifted her down from James's gig the day before.

''Is this a new strategy you've developed for soothing the mare, Lady Susannah?'' He nodded to her letter, a twinkle in his eyes. ''Reading your mail to her?''

It helped that Connor addressed Susannah as he might any friend, for she was finding it difficult to actually look at him. He seemed so very handsome for one thing, with his white shirt open at the throat and his black hair still damp from his toilette. She could almost imagine him in his bath, the water sluicing over him. Oh! She must not think of such a thing, nor that he had held her in his arms the day before.

Connor had offered her reason to look away from him to her letter and Susannah took it. ''Actually, she has taken more interest in this bit of vellum than in the carrot I brought her.''

Connor swung up onto the fence, taking a seat by Susannah without invitation, as if they were old friends who did not stand on ceremony. His action agitated her, though not because Susannah thought it presumptuous. He seemed very close to her. From the corner of her eye she could see his hand upon the fence. It was a man's hand, squarer than a woman's, and strong. Without any effort Susannah recalled how gently that capable hand had touched her.

Lady Danu. Susannah forced herself to focus upon the mare across the paddock. It was of Lady Danu she must think, instead of allowing her thoughts to run off into unacceptable channels. Resolutely ignoring Connor's hand and jerking her gaze from the lean, sinewy thigh upon which her eye had just fastened, she took a steadying breath.

"Murdoch believes Lady Danu's time is near." To Susannah's relief her voice sounded natural. Hearing its evenness, she steadied, and her concern for Lady Danu overcame to a degree her acute awareness of her companion. "I am concerned for her, Mr. O'Neill. She is so restless, I fear she will waste all her strength before the foal comes."

Connor studied the mare a long moment before he said slowly, "I've seen other mares do much the same but still come through nicely." Seeming to know they spoke of her, Lady Danu trotted up so close to Susannah, Connor's expression softened. "If she lays her head in your lap, though, my lady, I shall be amazed. That I have never seen."

"We are old friends," Susannah said fondly. "You will send for me, when she begins to foal, Mr. O'Neill? I would like to be there."

"I should be glad of your presence," Connor replied.

Susannah looked at him sharply. "You do fear she may have difficulty then?"

"Any mare in foal is a cause for concern," Connor said carefully. "I would wish you present, my lady, because you calm her."

Susannah studied him a moment, then gave a brisk nod that, unbeknownst to her, endeared her to Connor. He'd been afraid she meant to press him further, and he could not in honesty assure her without condition that all would be well. He shared some of her worries. Lady Danu was exceedingly restless.

When Susannah leaned forward to flick an offending bit of straw off Lady Danu's back, Connor found some distraction from his concerns. The movement had pulled Susannah's jacket tight across her body, revealing the soft, inviting curves of her breasts and slender waist.

"Are you very sore today?"

Susannah glanced up from Lady Danu. "Only a little. In all, I am remarkably well thanks to you." She chuckled low.

"Gussie said she made you endure quite a lecture on your merits."

Connor nodded, a wry smile lifting his mouth. "My ears are still burning, in fact."

But Susannah did not laugh at the jest. "You deserved all the praise she gave you." There was a moment's pause, then she heard herself say softly, "I owe you another debt, Mr. O'Neill."

Her eyes fast upon his, Susannah did not miss seeing Connor's eyes glint very blue. She intended to say something about repaying him handsomely, if differently than she'd repaid her first so much more minor debt, but seemed unable to form the words as she gazed up at him.

Oddly, it was Connor who broke the spell of the moment. Almost abruptly he looked off, tension in his jaw. "Your safety is payment enough, my lady. I feared . . ." He shrugged. There was no point telling her he'd had a particular horror that if she were thrown into his path, he would not rescue her, but trample her beneath the hooves of his mount. "Whatever I feared it did not come to pass, and that is recompense aplenty."

A moment's silence ensued, as they both contemplated the injuries Susannah had escaped. Then, as unexpectedly as he'd looked away, Connor looked back at Susannah. Her breath caught in her throat. He'd thrown off his gravity. A wicked, rogue's look danced in his eyes now.

"Will you not commend me for gallantry, my lady? I have sacrificed a great deal saying you owe me naught, with this being a far greater service than the first one I did you."

Susannah blushed, unable to master the reaction, as she imagined what payment might be commensurate to the greater service. Seeing the color rise in her cheeks, Connor laughed softly. "Nay, my lady, to be sure the repayment would not be so much as that," he teased.

"Oh!" Susannah's cheeks heated so, she put up her hands to cool them. "You've put me to an even worse blush! Fie on you, Mr. O'Neill!"

It was no reprimand. Susannah's tone lacked any bite, and all because Connor was grinning lazily at her, his eyes very warm and very blue as he distracted her from thoughts of how near she'd been to serious injury.

Then she was not even trying to look stern. She was laughing herself. If Susannah had, for one reason or another, forgotten breakfast, her stomach had not, and with a loud, clearly audible growl, it reminded her.

It was well, in the end, that Susannah fortified herself. Just before luncheon one of the grooms came to the house to fetch her to Lady Danu.

When she arrived, Murdoch and O'Neill were keeping watch outside the mare's stall, looking over the half-door. " 'Tis good ye've come, my lady," Murdoch greeted her, pushing his cap back upon his head. "She'll not have much of us."

Susannah hurried forward, her eyes going from Murdoch to the Irishman. "She is fretful?"

"Most fretful," Connor concurred wryly. "She took a portion out of Kevin Smith he can ill afford to lose."

Susannah smiled despite her anxiety for the mare. Kevin Smith was renowned for being the thinnest groom in any English stableyard.

Lady Danu lay on her side, but when Susannah slipped into the stall, the mare jerked her head up and bared her teeth.

"Easy, now. Stay by the door until she's accustomed to you," Connor called out quietly. Hearing concern for her in his voice, Susannah did not remind him she knew better than he how to insinuate herself into the mare's good graces.

The skin stretched taut over the mare's belly rippled suddenly, and Lady Danu flung her head distractedly as if she strained against an invisible weight. "Is Dr. Williams coming?" Susannah asked of the men behind her.

"Aye, we sent for 'im as soon as we knew," Murdoch replied.

When the mare's contraction eased, Susannah moved slowly forward. Speaking quietly, she persuaded the mare to accept her presence, and after a little, began to stroke Lady Danu's head, at which the mare seemed to calm.

An hour, perhaps longer, went by. As Lady Danu's

contractions became stronger, she fought them harder so that her coat was soon streaked with sweat.

Susannah thought Dr. Williams had arrived when she heard a stableboy come pounding into the stables. Her relief was short-lived, however, for the boy announced breathlessly, "Dr. Williams's wife has sent word he can't come, Mr. O'Neill! He was kicked by a horse only an hour ago and has been taken into Newmarket."

"Damn!" The voice was Connor's. "Is there anyone else?" He had turned, Susannah could tell, to address Murdoch.

"There's Jenkins, but he's over on the other side of Newmarket. Ah, well, we'll have to try to get him here. Do you know where to go, lad?"

Evidently the stableboy did, for Susannah heard him run out again. "Have you ever attended a mare foaling your-self, O'Neill?" Murdoch asked the question in Susannah's mind.

"Aye, more than once . . . " He glanced over the stall door at Lady Danu with a frown, then shrugged as if he did not know how to finish his thought, or did not care to with Susannah there.

Murdoch, however, nodded wisely. "She's fightin' it harder than any I've ever seen."

"Yes," Connor agreed almost reluctantly. "She will tire herself, I fear."

"Is there nothing we can do?" Mindful of the mare beside her, Susannah spoke low, but the anguish in her voice was evident nonetheless.

"Yes, there is," Connor said, as if he had made up his mind to some course of action he had been contemplating. "But it will be neither easy nor pretty. I would understand if you decided to go."

"And leave her?" Susannah thought it would be the most disloyal act in all the world if she were to abandon the mare just when there might be real difficulty. Then it occurred to her that Connor might be trying to tell her tactfully she would be in his way. "Is it that you fear my presence may cause more harm than good?"

Connor gave her a smile in which, had she not been distracted, Susannah might have read a great many things, admiration not least among them. "No, my lady, not at all. You are the only thing helping to soothe her. I only meant to warn you of what's to come."

Another contraction distracted Susannah so she did not even think to answer. Dimly she was aware of O'Neill issuing instructions to Murdoch, of the head groom striding off, of his rougher voice calling out orders to the other grooms waiting outside the stable, but for the most part all Susannah could think of was how violently the mare seemed to strain.

In time, Lady Danu became so fatigued that in the shorter and shorter intervals between contractions, she went utterly limp. When Connor entered the stall, she reacted not at all and scarcely lifted her head as he knelt down to examine her.

Susannah marked with relief Connor's assurance. He seemed to know just where and how to touch the mare. He did not look well pleased when he was done.

"The foal's turned about the wrong way," he said, looking up at Susannah.

"Can you turn it, perhaps?"

"I shall try."

Susannah thought the reply characteristic of O'Neill. He promised no more than he could do, and thereby, managed to reassure her far more than he could have done with any far grander promise.

While Connor went off to assemble what he would need, it seemed to Susannah that Lady Danu weakened markedly. Her coat had no luster left, and her eyes were dull.

Deeply anxious, Susannah turned pleading eyes on Connor and Murdoch when they returned. "Can we not do something? I am so worried for her."

Susannah looked a mess. There were bits of straw in her hair, her nose truly was smudged, and her skin glistened with sweat. But Connor thought she had never been more appealing than she was then, weary and disheveled on behalf of a friend.

"Yes, I think it must be close to time." He assumed a deliberately brisk manner. "Murdoch will be by you, my lady, but be mindful of Lady Danu's teeth. She may object to what I shall do.''

Susannah nodded her understanding, caring little for any danger to herself. Absently she rubbed a piece of straw from her nose before she settled into place.

Murdoch knelt by her, prepared to hold the mare's head if she became vicious, or push on her belly if that was needed. Susannah turned away from Connor, not caring to watch what he would do. Nonetheless, she was aware when he first touched Lady Danu, for the mare jerked convulsively. At once Susannah spoke in a low, calm voice and began stroking the horse slowly.

''Ah, yes, she's ready!'' Connor said after what seemed an interminable time but was in reality only a few moments. ''Push upon her, Murdoch, when the next contraction starts.''

Murdoch nodded curtly, and putting his hands in position, ignored Lady Danu as she jerked her head and eyed him wildly. When the contraction began, however, the mare forgot Murdoch, though he pushed so hard Susannah could see the strain in his arms. A quick peek down at Connor, and she saw that he too was working hard, the sweat beading on his brow. When the contraction ended, both men sagged back.

Susannah looked to Connor. When he smiled at her, it seemed as if the dread shadowing her lessened perceptibly. ''Keep a good heart, my lady. We are close.''

She had no time to react, for the contractions were coming very hard and very fast. For some time there was no sound in the stable but the hard breathing of the two men and the mare, and Susannah's low crooning.

It began to seem to Susannah that she had spent all her life sitting on a hard floor, hot and anxious, bits of straw clinging to her skin. If something did not happen, she feared they might all wilt of heat and fatigue. Then, just as she became convinced none of them could go on, Connor cried out, ''It's coming! By Saint Patrick, it's coming!''

And it did. Headfirst, the foal seemed to spurt out, all wet and spindly and perfect, to blink dazedly at the new world in which it found itself.

The afterbirth followed almost at once, and a collective sigh went up in the stable as all three sank back to gaze upon the fruit of their considerable labors.

The colt's first instinct was to stand. Susannah laughed raggedly as the little thing began pushing this way and that with its spindly, unfamiliar legs. They all three cheered aloud when somehow it managed to heave itself up; then they watched like anxious hens as it wobbled woefully. The colt struggled forward a step, another, then one more, before it sank down by its mother with something very like a sigh of relief.

Despite her fatigue, Lady Danu lifted her head to examine her newborn. She seemed to approve of what she saw, for she nuzzled him a little before she licked him thoroughly.

Susannah was crying. She realized it only when she smiled and tasted a salty tear. Brushing her cheeks with her palm, she looked at Connor.

He smiled, his eyes not exactly dry either. "I think even Lady Danu would agree it was all worthwhile."

Susannah gave something between a sob and a laugh. "He is beautiful, isn't he?"

"Oh, aye," Murdoch agreed, his voice suspiciously gruff. "Look at those legs. When it comes his time, he'll win the Two Thousand Guineas, and that's a fact."

12

LADY AUGUSTA presided over a small but exceedingly festive celebration that night. As was her custom upon the birth of a new colt, she invited all the stablehands to the house for champagne. Scores of toasts were made to the newborn and his dam, but Lady Augusta did not forget her trainer. Lifting her glass high, the dowager duchess proclaimed him "a noble man to his fingertips." Because the old woman had enjoyed a considerable amount of champagne and slurred her words slightly, it sounded as if she had called O'Neill a nobleman, but everyone understood and cheered.

In honor of his success, Lady Augusta gave Connor the honor of naming the colt. He accepted, but insisted before he got to the task that he must recognize the services rendered by Lady Susannah, for, as he said, "her brave presence lent Lady Danu a calm without which my efforts and Murdoch's would have gone for naught." Quite the greatest cheer of the evening went up at that, with every groom lustily crying "Hear! Hear!" and smiling as proudly as fathers.

Susannah could not have been in a happier mood. She gaily drank to herself, to Connor, to Murdoch, and certainly joined the others when they raised their glasses to the new colt, after Connor declared that, in keeping with tradition and his own interests, Ridley's newest hope would henceforth be known as Whiskey.

Delightfully tipsy, Susannah kissed Murdoch's weathered cheek when he told her he thought her "the bravest, finest lady in all England," and raised such a blush there, a toast had to be made to the bloom. She was not done, though, for upon the second time that James remarked wonderingly, "I say, Susannah, you were not really on hand for the entire, er, ordeal, surely?", she giggled delightedly and thought he merited a kiss as well.

As did Connor, in the end, when he cocked an amused brow at her as she accepted her fourth or perhaps fifth glass of the marvelous bubbling drink she was enjoying so. In answer to his looks, Susannah smiled brilliantly before she went up on tiptoe to whisper in his ear that she thought him "quite, quite wonderful." And then, on tiptoe still, she saluted his cheek, too, with the softest of kisses.

The next day Susannah paid for her elated spirits, of course. She woke very late. Her mouth felt dry and thick, and her head ached so that she wondered if the training gallops were not being conducted inside it.

Mercifully James was not at breakfast when she crept down, and so she was quite alone, forcing toast and weak tea down her throat, when Soames brought her her second letter in two days.

She knew at once who had authored the letter. The neat, precise writing was that of her father's secretary, Hemmings. Her queasiness seeming to double, Susannah laid the letter aside for a little. A small act of defiance, perhaps, but all she could manage just then.

When she did read the letter prone upon a settee in the library, she found its contents as little to her liking as she had feared. Hemmings succinctly informed her that his grace had arranged a "small gathering" at Deerbourne Park; that his grace desired her to be present for said gathering; and that the duke's carriage would arrive the next day to transport her.

Susannah reread the letter twice. How like her father not to reveal what had inspired him to arrange a gathering, nor to mention whom he had invited, but only to instruct

Hemmings to, in essence, command her presence. He was Beaufort. Matters were arranged to suit him, with an elegant minimum of effort.

Balling up the letter, Susannah threw it across the room. Perhaps she wouldn't go. He would come for her. No, he would not come to Ridley. It seldom suited Beaufort to enjoy his mother's company. Their estrangement was no mystery. Susannah knew her grandfather and Gussie had had nothing more than a marriage of convenience. Both of them had gone their own ways early on, Gussie to town and frivolity, the old duke to affairs of state. They had two boys, whom they remembered on occasion, but children had had little place in either of their lives. That Beaufort grew up resembling his father in character was more by chance than design, but nonetheless it followed he did not abide well with his mother. A true Somerset, he was too cool and aloof to be amused by either Gussie's outspokenness or her eccentricities.

Susannah had never thought to change the situation. She'd the wisdom to realize Gussie likely made a far better grand-mother than she had a mother, and Susannah guessed that in Beaufort's place she might have viewed Lady Augusta with as little affection as he did.

Susannah made a face. Beaufort would not come to Ridley and bodily remove her, mayhap, but he would make his dis-pleasure known somehow if she ignored his summons. A weak sigh broke the stillness of the room. She had matched wills with his grace enough to know she could survive his displeasure, but also enough to know she cared to endure it only in a very good cause.

And he was not taking back her summer from her. Though the specific amount of time her presence would be required at Deerbourne had not been given, Beaufort knew how much she looked forward to attending the meet now only a fortnight distant, and whatever else could be said of him, the duke was not heedlessly cruel.

But he was exacting, particularly when it came to the family name and honor. Did he know? Susannah leapt up from her settee and half-flung herself out the French windows. The warmth of the day came almost as a surprise, as did the beauty of it. Her thoughts seemed to steady a little.

Her father was not, as she had imagined in her youth, omniscient. And if he were? She had kissed the Irishman only once—and once again upon the cheek. Her father would not approve, but the sudden stab of panic that had sent her flying out-of-doors could not be justified. There was nothing between her and O'Neill. They were friends—no, acquaintances with a shared interest in horses. No more.

Then why the summons? Who was being gathered? Sunderly?

A groan escaped her. Tallish, attractive, attentive, exceptionally well-mannered, unexceptional Philip Mountjoy, the Viscount Sunderly and the future Earl of Grafton. He had been a friend of Sebastian's at school and had come once to Deerbourne to visit.

When they had met again in town, Susannah remembered him only vaguely. Sebastian had towed home dozens of friends, but Sunderly had remembered her, and come after her as if he had been waiting for her.

Susannah gave a pained laugh. He *had* been waiting for her. But she had not guessed because he had been too much the gentleman to press her right away, and, too, he'd seen how impatient she could be with the men who thronged about her.

Susannah believed most of them were interested in her for her wealth and position, which was a part of the truth, of course—she was Beaufort's daughter—but Susannah had never truly appreciated the effect the contrast between her golden beauty and her dark slanted eyes had on men. While they vied with one another to show her their interest, she came to resent tripping over yet another suitor every time she turned about, particularly as not one seemed to have anything even moderately interesting to say for himself.

Of them all, only Sunderly made her laugh. He hid the depth of his interest, kept his attentions moderate, and told her stories of his schooldays with Sebastian. It had been a particularly clever stroke, for Sebastian had just departed for the Peninsula, and Susannah missed him greatly.

To Susannah's great chagrin, Sunderly had assumed a great

deal more from her pleasure in his stories and her laughter than she had intended to convey. He'd come to believe she returned his feelings, and so he had revealed at last that he had fallen in love upon his first sight of her. In his words, not only had she been beautiful then, but she had possessed, though she was only sixteen at the time, "the poise and elegance of a young queen."

Poor Sunderly! He had misjudged her all around. The poise and grace of movement he had so admired had been entirely forced. For daring to ride bareback at night, and dressed in breeches yet, her governess of the moment had given Susannah the punishment of ascending and descending the grand staircase at Deerbourne thirty times in succession. Sebastian and Philip had entered the house as Susannah made her final descent, but she had curbed her desire to launch herself into her brother's arms. Miss McElwaine stood sternly at the bottom of the stairs, fully prepared to make her charge repeat the punishment another thirty times if she transgressed so horribly as to lift her skirts and run.

Susannah heaved a sigh. Poor Sunderly. He had been a sort of replacement brother, and she'd enjoyed his company well enough until his fervent declaration of love. Now she only felt guilty and uncertain and a little vexed when she thought of him. Had she led him on? Perhaps she had. She had wanted to laugh with someone, and his stories of the pranks Sebastian had led him to commit had been like a breath of fresh air in the hothouse of London society, where every eye had been upon her, not least Beaufort's piercing ones.

The memory of how strongly her father had favored Philip Mountjoy's suit brought Susannah's head up, and she found her feet had brought her to the stableyard. Billy Whitlow, one of the grooms, whistling as he went about his errands, called out a greeting. Susannah returned it, but not so cheerfully.

She had just drifted to Lady Danu's stall when she heard O'Neill's voice. He called out to Billy, sending the young man upon some errand. Susannah didn't attend to his exact words. She was fighting an impulse to run away.

He was there, strong and tall and impossible to dart around before she could act on the impulse, and certainly before she could determine why she wanted to fly from him.

"Good morning, my lady." Smiling teasingly, Connor made a play of looking up at the sun. "It is morning, is it not? Yes, I see it is, and that you have defied all my expectations by arising before noon."

Susannah could not quite meet his eyes. Her gaze glanced off his face as she murmured softly, not matching his light tone at all, "Now you know the stern stuff of which we Somersets are made, Mr. O'Neill."

Connor gave her a searching look Susannah felt more than saw. She was looking at her hands. They had almost lifted from the door to Lady Danu's stall and reached for him. The knowledge that she wanted to touch him did very nearly send her fleeing.

It was not just that he looked so very good, though he did. She had thought him dangerously handsome from the first. Now, however, she knew exactly how it felt to be in his arms. And she wanted that feeling again just then.

Abruptly Susannah asked, "How is Lady Danu?" Even to her own ears her voice sounded strained.

There was an infinitesimal pause, but she avoided Connor's eyes. And finally he told her Dr. Williams had come. "He says Lady Danu and Whiskey are both doing very well. But you can look for yourself to see as much."

Susannah flushed a little, aware how strangely she was behaving. At the prompting, she did look into the stall before which she had been standing for several minutes, and saw that Lady Danu lay resting comfortably, while Whiskey explored the stall upon legs that already did not seem so thin or unreliable as they had the day before.

She gazed at the mother and colt, a tight feeling in her chest. They were alive because of the man beside her. He had taken charge, decided what needed to be done, and done it. And that was not to mention what he had done for her and James. They might not have died had the gig overturned, but they'd have been badly mangled.

"Dr. Williams himself is recovered?" Susannah asked.

She saw Connor's shoulders lift briefly. "He suffered a deep, ugly gash on the leg, but I suspect he suffered most from his failure to be on hand when he was needed."

Susannah nodded. "He has always been most conscientious." She glanced at Connor from the corner of her eye and found he was watching her. Caught, she had to face him and his intelligent, perceptive eyes.

Connor made no secret he studied Susannah. At first he had thought her subdued spirits the result of the champagne she'd so thoroughly enjoyed the evening before. He was revising his opinion. She was too changed. He'd not have been surprised had he seen tears in her eyes.

"Do you feel ill, my lady?"

Susannah made a swift negative motion with her head. "The champagne . . ." She bit her lip, afraid for an awful moment she might, in fact, cry. It was only her beastly headache followed by the unexpected jolt of her father's summons making her emotions so unsteady, but all the same, she could not simply bury her head in his shoulder as she inexplicably wanted to do. "I must go, Mr. O'Neill. I only came to see Lady Danu." She turned, then stopped to glance back over her shoulder directly into his eyes. "You were wonderful yesterday, Mr. O'Neill. I want you to know it was not champagne prompted me to say that."

Lady Augusta was as taken aback as Susannah that Beaufort had issued his sudden summons. "Something's afoot, my dear! Mark my words. He has a reason for his sudden gathering. I've never known Beaufort to do anything without a reason, nor anything suddenly when it comes to it. Do you suppose he means to force the issue over Grafton's whelp?"

Susannah did not know, but that her grandmother should voice her worst fears caused her spirits to sink further. She drifted off to Nan's, gave the old woman a full accounting of Lady Danu's foaling, then with a sense of relief, closed Nan's garden gate behind her and directed her steps to her secret swimming hole, the one place she knew she would be quite alone.

* * *

Connor saw Susannah disappear into the woods. He was returning from an errand in Newmarket, and assumed, because she carried a basket, she was off to pick berries. He never considered that she might be going for a swim. Had the thought occurred to him, though, he'd have dismissed the possibility out of hand. Young ladies of her class did not swim. Actually, few women or men of any class cared to submerge themselves in water. It was generally considered an unhealthy practice.

Uncharacteristically, Connor fudged a little as he found the path Susannah had taken. He did not admit to being concerned over her low spirits. He had two sisters, not one, and knew girls could be moody. He only acknowledged a desire to catch her alone for a little, and he'd the perfect reason to give for pursuing her. He wished to hold several simulated races to give Saracen the feel of running with other horses and wanted her to take part in the exercise.

As he expected to find Susannah easily, Connor gave more thought to his strategy with Saracen than his whereabouts as he walked along, and he was, as a result, taken aback when he came out of the woods on the far side, having seen no sign of her. Nor could he see her in the wheat field before him or further off in the distance. Faintly alarmed, he turned about. It seemed unlikely anyone had been lurking in Ridley's woods and done her harm, but he couldn't dismiss the possibility out of hand.

His brow drawing down, Connor recalled, too, her odd mood of the morning. His concern had been vague enough that he could deny it earlier, but now it nagged him more sharply, causing him to scan the path carefully as he retraced his steps.

As a result Connor did not overlook the single thread of periwinkle blue that dangled from a bush some midway through the woods. Worrying the thread between his fingers, he studied the ground below the bush.

It seemed oddly worn, and on merest impulse Connor pushed the bush aside. He found it had obscured the entrance to another path.

This one was a great deal narrower and more overgrown than the main path through the woods. Connor was obliged to dodge bushes and duck branches frequently. He found another thread a little further on and, encouraged, quickened his step. Absently he noted the gurgle of a stream, but of more interest was a particularly low branch he was obliged to lift out of his way. When he stepped under it, he found himself, without warning, standing in a small open meadow.

After the green, filtered cool of the woods, the dell seemed awash in warmth and light. Tiny white and blue wild-flowers intermixed with grass formed a carpet that spread to the stream he'd heard. One tree dominated the place, a giant, kingly oak that seemed fully capable of holding the other trees of the forest at bay. Several of its roots were exposed by the stream. They looked as thick and massive as its limbs, and he saw they had grown across the stream, creating a pool. Drawn by it, he was taking a step forward when, without warning, the water broke and Susannah, water cascading over her, lifted her face to the sun.

She was gone again in the next moment, only to surface immediately. Her head was tilted back, and Connor stared, disbelieving his eyes almost, to see she was smiling.

Then she stood.

The pool was deep. The water came just above her waist.

Venus rising from her bath. No. Transfixed, Connor rejected the comparison. It brought to mind pale, demure Botticelli goddesses. The living English maid before him did not shyly cover her body with her long tresses. Her hair flowed sleekly down her back as she paused again to lift her head to the sun above. Nor was her skin pale. Anywhere. Touched by that sun, it glistened warm and golden all over.

She was gloriously beautiful. Proud and lithe and slender, and so very generously curved. Her breasts were full and firm above her slender waist.

Whether he made an inadvertent movement or whether some sixth sense warned her she was observed, Connor could not have said. But Susannah stiffened suddenly and her eyes flew wide as they locked with his.

Surprise held Susannah absolutely still. She had just been

thinking of Connor O'Neill. At first she had fought the urge to do so, but to so little avail she finally had let herself wonder inconsequential things about him: did he swim, had he brothers as well as a sister, had he a sweetheart?

For the space of a heartbeat, staring wide-eyed, she thought she must have conjured him, that he could not be real. No one knew of the secret path or her secret place.

The look in his eyes, when she finally took it in, was all too real, however. Perhaps because the expression on his face was set, his eyes seemed to leap out at her, to jolt her with the awareness of herself she saw in them.

Instantly crying out, she splashed inelegantly down beneath the concealing water again, and stayed submerged for as long as she could. Even so, though she was certain he would be gone, her cheeks were burning when she came up.

"Oh!" Anger replaced mortification. He had not taken himself and that tense look away. He stood there yet, so still, she'd have taken him for a statue, but for the intensity of his gaze. "Damn it!" The oath burst from her. She did not want to be exposed. She did not want to be looked at in such a way. She did not want to feel her heart hammer so hard in her chest she thought she might faint. "Go away! Go away!"

"I don't know if I can." Connor said it slowly, as if giving voice to a thought that surprised him.

Susannah slapped the water, causing a splash. Unfortunately the indignant gesture only made the water recede. His eyes followed the water line down. At once she sank lower. "Go." Her voice surprised her. It had lost sharpness and sounded almost husky. Immediately Susannah cleared her throat and repeated, more adamantly, "Go!"

Absurdly the thought that occurred to Connor then, of all the thoughts that might have, was that Lady Susannah Somerset would be beautiful if she lived to be ninety. Without any artifice, without even the crowning glory of her honey-gold hair, she was one of the most beautiful women he had ever seen. She had enviable, elegant, spare bones. And those sable, seemingly fathomless eyes.

"Please."

The single low throaty word roused Connor as her command had not. He gave a start almost, and visibly collected himself. "Forgive me, my lady." He made her a graceful bow, then said simply, "You are very beautiful."

13

SUSANNAH PAUSED a moment before the door to her father's library to smooth the skirt of her striped afternoon dress, then, lifting her chin, entered without knocking.

Beaufort stood by the windows looking out over Deerbourne's formal garden, his figure elegant and severe even from the back, and she'd a moment of something close to panic. But even before the duke turned and Susannah saw his expression, she had herself in hand. Only a sorcerer could know what had happened her last afternoon at Ridley, or guess how she had reacted to it, and even Beaufort could not lay a claim to witchcraft.

Still, it was not until she saw the cordial expression her father wore that her tension lifted entirely.

"My dear." Beaufort kissed her cheek lightly. "You are a pleasure to look upon. Traveling agrees with you, perhaps. I hope you left everyone at Ridley well?"

"Yes, very well." Susannah seated herself in the formal Adam chair Beaufort indicated. "Gussie is eagerly looking forward to the meet. As am I, actually, for at least two of Ridley's horses stand excellent chances."

Though Susannah had said the last casually, her father gave her an ironic look. "The meet is ten days away, I think?"

"Yes. Not long at all." She returned his gaze steadily.

"Do I detect a concern, Susannah, that you will not be let free of Deerbourne in time to cheer your favorite on?"

"I'd not have put it quite that way, Father, but I would be sorely disappointed to miss the meet. It is a high point of the summer."

Beaufort did not keep her in suspense, but inclined his head as if conceding she'd the right to her interest in racing. "You needn't worry yourself, my dear. I think you ought to be returned in time for your high point, if all goes well."

"If all goes well, Father?"

"The weather, Susannah," Beaufort said more patiently than was his wont. "If it rains heavily, the roads may be turned to mud, but otherwise, you will be free to return in five days or so."

Having settled the question of her departure to her satisfaction, Susannah was free to wonder again why she'd been summoned. Somewhat to her surprise, her father made no mention of the gathering he'd arranged.

He asked after Mrs. Mimpress, Susannah's faithful traveling companion, who had been deposited with a sister in nearby Guildford, and they discussed James a little. Somehow Beaufort knew of his nephew's interest in Phoebe Limley, and he expressed his disapproval.

More time slipped away as they exchanged the news they each had received from Sebastian, talked of some improvements Beaufort thought to make to Deerbourne Park, and observed how fine the weather had been that summer. When Haselford, Beaufort's butler, entered with the tea tray, Susannah poured, and as she handed her father his cup, she decided to prod him a little. "When do your guests come, Father?"

"Tomorrow."

Beaufort missed the curious look his spare reply earned him. He was occupied with smoothing a quite invisible wrinkle from his impeccable trousers.

To a great extent, Susannah thought her father appeared as always. His keen gray eyes seemed to see more than they revealed, quite as usual. And his ability, though he was not a large man and was at all times meticulously polite, to dominate any encounter was entirely in evidence.

And yet there was something amiss, or if not amiss, then

different about her father that afternoon. He seemed distracted. Susannah might have said unsettled even, but that it was impossible for her to think of Beaufort being unsettled.

As ever, though, Beaufort was aware of himself. When he looked up from the study he had been making of the depths of the fragile teacup he held, a rueful smile lifted his mouth.

"I find myself in quite an unusual position, my dear, and it is not one I can say I relish." The duke's smile deepened, and Susannah realized, rather belatedly in life, that the many women who had pursued her father over the years might not have been motivated entirely by his title and fortune. "I've a favor to ask of you, Susannah."

There was no need for Susannah to hide her surprise. They were both equally aware that his grace, the Duke of Beaufort, was not given to asking for anything.

"Yes, unprecedented, I grant," he addressed her lifted brow. "But I've a desire for you to be on your very best behavior for the next several days."

Now Beaufort had rendered Susannah not only surprised but also intrigued. "I do not think I am accustomed to behaving badly," Susannah observed as mildly as she could, given her curiosity over why he should ask of her something he had heretofore simply expected.

"Far from it," Beaufort agreed. "You are, in fact, very like me in company, Susannah, for you invariably display a perfectly polished, polite, yet distinctly aloof manner that you know, as I do, nicely serves to keep the world at bay."

"And you would have me become a gay nodcock at your gathering?"

Amusement lit his gray eyes. "Mercifully, being a nodcock is beyond you, my dear. However, warmth is not. I know how you are with Sebastian, your friend Lady Anne Demaurice, and even with me upon occasion. When you choose, my dear Susannah, you display a side of yourself that has a rare and compelling power."

Susannah inclined her head, as any more articulate response was beyond her. Her father had remarked favorably on one thing or another before, but never had he been so extravagant. "Rare and compelling" was high praise from anyone, but from Beaufort!

And why had he chosen to inform her of his opinion now? Why did he wish her to display the warmer side of her nature? Had he—she stiffened at the thought—invited the Mountjoys? Did he wish her to impress them with her warmth?

"I know your warmth is a gift you give, Susannah," her father continued. "I do, I assure you, understand that it is not an attitude that can be compelled, but nonetheless I ask now, as a favor to me, that you make an effort to exhibit at least a little of it. You see, I've invited someone very special to me to come to Deerbourne to meet you."

Someone. One. Not a family of Mountjoys, but one person. Whom could he have invited? Another suitor? At the thought, Susannah's thoughts went wildly astray. As had happened at odd, random, unnervingly frequent moments, she found herself reliving in vivid detail that moment when she'd risen, refreshed, from the pleasant waters of her pool and looked, all unexpectedly, directly into Connor O'Neill's fixed blue eyes.

Mercifully, Susannah's half-second of distraction went unnoticed. Her father was equally distracted. He was loooking off into the distance, gathering his thoughts.

His gaze remaining upon a charming arrangement of roses his housekeeper had done, Beaufort said quietly, "You will not know her," and quite missed the startled look Susannah gave him.

Her. Her! No Mountjoys, no mysterious suitor, but a woman! Susannah very nearly laughed aloud. How off the mark and self-absorbed she'd been, fearing this gathering had been arranged on her account.

Her curiosity was quite as piqued as her humor, however, for her father had never made a special to-do over any of the women with whom he had had affairs over the years. He'd never even spoken of any of them to her. She'd known the identity of most, of course, but only because others were eager to tell her.

Now he had gone to pains to drag her down from Newmarket that she might actually meet a woman who was—what had he said?—"very special" to him. The implications were obvious. Susannah gave her father her undivided attention.

"Her husband was in the diplomatic service, and as a result they lived abroad a good deal," Beaufort went on, still studying the roses. "He died a year or so ago in Russia, and though she is out of mourning now, she came up to town only after you had left for Ridley. It was in town I met her again. You see"—he shifted his gaze to Susannah, and she was astonished to find he regarded her a little defensively— "we, ah, knew each other when we were younger. And when we met again, we seemed to take up almost where we left off. She is a very worthy person, Susannah. I think you will like her exceedingly."

"Father!" A brilliant smile sparkled in Susannah's eyes. He was in love. Beaufort! She could swear it. "I am certain I shall like your 'special' friend very much. I shall even go to the extent of greeting her by her name, you know, if you will give it to me."

"Hmm." Her father, unaccustomed to inspiring amusement in any breast, eyed her narrowly, but to negligible result. Susannah was far too delighted to see her father just a little uncertain and so very human. She'd have told him the look became him enormously, but he'd have been certain to poker up if she did, and so she contented herself with regarding him as warmly and fondly as she knew how.

She won the battle of looks. A rueful smile lifted his rather stern mouth. "As you seem to have guessed, I have fallen head over heels in love. It is a lowering thing to admit, though I hasten to say Lady Esther Kerr quite deserves my interest. She is a delightful lady, Susannah, and I hope very earnestly you will admire her as I do."

Susannah admired the woman, Lady Esther Kerr, sight unseen. She'd seldom seen her father so engaged, and she quite made up her mind to be very warm indeed toward the woman who had put that smile in his eyes.

"You may rest easy, Father. I am quite certain Lady Esther and I shall get along famously."

* * *

"Faith, an' how private can we be in this place, Connor?"

Liam stared around the public room of the Rosy Maid. As usual, men stood three deep about the bar, and every table, or nearly every one, was filled.

"As private as our voices are low, Liam. Come on."

Connor spoke so brusquely, Liam stared a moment, brow lifted, before, suppressing a sigh, he followed his companion to an empty table in the farthest corner of the room. Connor had been foul-tempered for days, and showed no signs of improving. When Liam joined him, Connor did not speak at all, but gazed without expression into the smoky room.

Liam followed his gaze, and relaxed a little upon the discovery that Connor watched a serving wench. She was young, comely, and possessed a bright gold head of hair. The last attribute gave Liam pause.

"Is she the one?" he asked cautiously.

"No."

Connor did not spare Liam a glance. Playing with a match left lying upon the table, he continued to stare almost broodingly at the blond.

"Blast it all, Connor! If she's not the one, what do you mean starin' a hole through her? Nay, you've no need to say. I can tell well enough by the hair o' hers why it is you can't take your bloody eyes off her, when you ought to be lookin' for the wench that has some word of Rory."

Still Connor did not shift his gaze from the new serving wench, only said in a low, flat voice, "You fash yourself for naught, as usual, Liam. Annie's coming even now."

A buxom brunette Liam had indeed missed bustled up to their table, smiling brightly at Connor. "Hello, luv! Jem's gone for the young man who asked after ye, just like ye wanted. He should be along shortly now. Can I get ye an ale in the meantime?"

"Aye, Annie. Dickon"—Connor indicated Liam with his head—"and I'll both have one."

The smile he'd summoned for Annie faded the moment she left. The match once more playing in his hand, Connor found the other girl, the blond.

"Nay! You're not lookin' after her again, man!" Liam

half-groaned. "You'll have this Annie up in arms if you're not careful."

"That ceaseless tongue of yours grows wearying, Liam. I'll thank you to give it a rest."

"Aye, no doubt you would," the older man grumbled. "But then, you've not had to live with yourself. 'Tis I who have had to put up with looks so sour they'd curdle milk. You were never so grim even in ninety-six, when you only just escaped the hangman's noose. And I know in my soul it's Lady Susannah has you starin' off after light-haired wenches, then bitin' off the nose of anyone comes near you. Why—"

"Enough!"

The word was snapped, low and short. But it was the look in Connor's eyes that made Liam shift uneasily. "No harm meant, man. 'Tis only—"

"I know full well what it is, Liam," Connor cut in, but not quite so harshly. Indeed, he sounded almost weary of a sudden. "And there's no need for discussion. Leave it."

Liam knew when Connor had reached his limit. Settling back with the ale Annie brought them, he left Connor to his thoughts.

They were not pleasant. Connor, studying the blond again, found her no more appealing. The gold of her hair was too brassy, the pores of her skin too large. Yet she'd have pleased him well enough once. New to the Rosy Maid, she was fresh, slender, and not uncomely.

His tastes had changed, it seemed. The match flew straight up in the air. Damn. He couldn't hold on to a bloody match for thinking of her! He couldn't look at a blasted serving wench with interest. He couldn't speak a civil word to an old friend.

A grim smile curled Connor's mouth. How lightly he'd assured Liam that Susannah would be only a diversion. A diversion. He, who had never been faithful to any one woman—he was not married!—found himself unwillingly faithful to her, to a diversion. He could not force an interest in any other woman.

Connor scowled, the match again in his hand. From

experience he knew he had only to let his concentration waver the least bit, and an image of her rising from the pool would form in his mind.

How much more instructive to force himself to recall how he'd responded when Murdoch told him she would not be riding out to the gallops, as she had been called away to her father's home. The announcement had come the morning after he'd seen her in her pool. He had gotten to the stables early, making the feeble excuse to himself that he must check on Lady Danu and Whiskey. In reality, he'd been as eager as a boy to see her, to tease her, to see her blush, to confirm for himself that she was as beautiful as she had looked in that pool.

For a half-second he'd stood staring blankly at Murdoch, stunned to have her snatched from him without warning.

And then, merciful heaven, when Murdoch had helpfully given it as his opinion that her ladyship's departure had to do with the young man her father wished her to marry! Connor tossed off a long swallow of his ale. He'd wanted to wring Murdoch's scrawny neck. And that did not speak to his impulse in relation to the Viscount Sunderly.

The best that could be said of that moment was that it had shocked him into awareness. He ought to be grateful to the Duke of Beaufort. He had needed awakening. There was no saying how far things might have gone had he not been forced to acknowledge the truth. When she had become so much more than a challenge to spice the summer, he had no idea. He had not allowed himself to mark the moment.

She was English! The word tasted like ashes on his tongue. Her people regarded his as barbarians. His people returned the feeling with interest. And he? He had said the truth when he told her he did not hate every man and woman born in England, but to marry one? To take the daughter of an English duke home?

It was mischief worthy of the Tuatha De Danann to put a lovely, nearly perfect woman before him, then give her one insurmountable flaw. She was English. He could not expect his people to forget the enmity of centuries and welcome an Englishwoman, a daughter of the ruling class that had made rubble of Ireland, as their mistress.

Connor took a very long drink of his ale. She would be so very difficult to forgo. Little wonder he'd been bad-tempered. But he had forgone other pleasures on account of who he was. He would put Lady Susannah Somerset behind him as well.

There would be no more teasing with her; no more traipsing after her into the woods; no more snatching excuses from the air to touch her. He would concentrate on the upcoming meet, for he'd given his word to Mulcahey he would do his best there, and he would concentrate on Rory.

"Look now! Can he be the fellow?"

Connor's gaze snapped forward. He understood the doubt in Liam's voice when he saw the boy with Annie. The stripling could not have been above eighteen.

But Connor recognized him as one of the young men who'd been at the inn before, and he murmured confidently, "Aye, Liam. He's the one."

The boy was nervous as a cat, glancing repeatedly over his shoulder as Annie led him forward and announced, "Here's Roger, then, the lad what knows your friends with the horse. Take you a seat, then, Roger," she instructed when the boy hung back. "They're good gentlemen."

"An ale, Roger?" Connor asked when the boy still hesitated. He nodded once, curtly, before finally dropping into the chair when Annie left to fill the order.

There was a moment's silence as the two older men studied the newcomer openly, and Roger assessed them in darting, hurried glances. It was Connor who spoke first. "This is a friend, Roger. You may call him Dick and be assured that he too is a friend of Rory's. You did tell Annie to send for you if we came again?"

"Aye." His eyes were large and intense in his pale face. Wetting his lips, he said abruptly, "I've word of the man you seek. I'm to tell you he's well and going about his business."

A faint lilt colored the boy's voice, but nonetheless Connor spoke as obliquely as he. "Tell Rory, if you can get word to him, that there is no business for him in Norwich, only the hangman's noose. It is a trap."

The boy blinked. "H-how would you know that?"

"I looked for myself," Connor replied with quiet authority. "Get word to Rory that I've been in the place he wishes to enter and know for a certainty that no one of interest to him is there."

The boy looked staggered. "Not there? But we all thought . . . How do I know to trust you?"

Liam broke in impatiently, though he took care, as Connor had, to mimic a Yorkshire accent. "Tell Rory it is the one goose that did not fly over the water that sends him the message."

The reference was obscure; only those acquainted with Irish history sufficiently to know of an episode that had occurred two centuries before, termed "the flight of the earls," would have understood it. The boy responded by turning a wide, intent look upon Connor, who, in turn, met the searching gaze steadily, though he knew he was exposing himself. At last the boy let out his breath. "I'll try to get the word to him. And 'tis an honor to meet you, my—"

Connor cut him off with a swift hand motion. "Enough of that, lad. There is one more thing I would have Rory know. If he needs help, he is to come to Newmarket to Ridley Stud."

The boy repeated the information softly, then, being young, brightened as the address sank in. "Will you be racing horses at the meet, m . . . sir?"

Connor was moved to chuckle. "You could say that, and if it's a tip you're wanting, Roger, lad, I recommend Barley Boy. He's as close to a certainty as one can come in a race."

When Annie returned with the boy's ale, she asked if Roger had been of help. Connor smiled the smile of a good-natured fellow who had no more on his mind than a horse trade. "He's been a great help, as you have, lass. Come here and let this Yorkshire man give you a reward!"

Giggling happily, Annie hurried to his side, only to gape down at her hand as Connor slipped two coins into it. "But there's two guineas here!" she gasped.

"You're worth every penny, Annie," he told her, meaning it. He'd have paid a great deal more to have Rory safe.

14

"LADY ESTHER KERR! Well, well, well."

"You know Lady Esther, then, Gussie?" Head tipped,
Susannah studied the smile with which her grandmother had
responded to her news of Beaufort. In all it was a very pleased
smile.

"Yes, dear heart, I remember everyone who has lived in
the past half-century. Everyone who is anyone, that is," Lady
Augusta amended regally. "Therefore, it follows that I recall
Esther Winston."

"Winston? I did not know that was her maiden name. The
vicar nearest to Deerbourne was named Winston. Is there
a connection?"

"How sharp you are, my lovely dear!" Lady Augusta
regarded her granddaughter approvingly. "That vicar was
Esther's father, and she was your father's closest friend when
they were young. As a vicar's daughter would never do for
the future Duke of Beaufort, however, Alistair married your
mother, who had both wealth and position, while Esther
managed through the offices of a wealthy aunt to aspire to
a diplomat, Lord Kerr. But now . . . well, it is rather nice,
isn't it, to have them end up together again?"

Lady Augusta was rather dreamily contemplating her son's
good fortune when Susannah asked quietly, "Did Beaufort
ever love my mother, Gussie?"

"No, dearest, he did not," Lady Augusta replied with

characteristic forthrightness. "It was a good match, but one of convenience. Marianna was much younger than Alistair and never really up to him. He was always meticulously courteous and respectful. I do not mean to say he was not. She was very easy to be kind to, for she was exceedingly pleasant and pretty. Though you look nothing like Marianna, my dear, you do remind me of your mother when you walk. You've her grace of movement, Susannah, and may thank God for it. Otherwise you might move like a martinet of a Somerset. But as to Alistair, do you mind that he may have had an affection all these years for someone other than your mother?"

The question had been posed abruptly, but Susannah was not unprepared for it. "If you are asking whether I am offended on behalf of my mother, the answer is no. I cannot even remember her, Gussie."

"And yet something does not sit well with you, *ma chère*. What is it?"

A faint smile lit Susannah's eyes. "You see a great deal, Gussie. Yes, I suppose something does not sit well. Lady Esther's advent has changed Father for the better. He's not undergone a radical change of character, of course, but he is warmer, less aloof, more engaged, somehow." She gave her grandmother a wry look. "What a serpent's tooth I am, to speak so of my father, but it is true. And I cannot help but wonder if it would not have been better for him had he married Lady Esther in the first place, despite her lack of wealth and position."

"It would have been far better for Alistair to marry someone closer to his level in intellect and strength of character," Lady Augusta agreed easily. "But he could never have done it. Alistair learned from his father the attitude that marriage is more a mating of properties and families than a union of individuals. Your father felt his duty to his title so keenly, he never seriously considered marriage to Esther Winston. And I do allow that, by his marriage to Marianna he did succeed nicely at increasing his lands and wealth, not to mention producing two inestimable children." She paused to blow a fond kiss at her granddaughter, then resumed her

dispassionate appraisal of her son's life. "If Alistair did grow
increasingly detached and aloof over the years, it was the
price he willingly paid for acting the Duke of Beaufort to
the inch. However, I must say, reprobate that I am, I am
pleased he has a chance now to enjoy a little of what he gave
up. And I think we ought to celebrate."

With a sly smile Lady Augusta poured two fingers of
sherry from the decanter beside her into a glass and handed
it to Susannah. "Take it, my dear! How can we celebrate
if you do not? Now . . ." She lifted the rather fuller glass
she already had at her disposal. "To Beaufort and love,
however late it may come!"

The sherry was good, rich and full-flavored. Susannah
looked at her grandmother, a twinkle in her eye. "I see why
your nerves require this particular potion, Gussie. It is
delightful."

Unruffled, Lady Augusta returned, referring to her late
husband, "Alfred prided himself on putting down the best,
my dear. The least I can do in honor of his memory is to
enjoy the fruits of his labors. But, Susannah, you've only
discussed a part of your news. You must tell me how it is
you came to bring Philip Mountjoy back to Newmarket with
you."

Susannah kept her face free of expression with an effort
of will and the assistance of her sherry. She took a sip of
it before she answered her grandmother.

"I had intended, as you know, to drive straight through
from Deerbourne Park to Newmarket, but when Lady Esther
was obliged to return to town to attend to some business
concerning her husband's estate, I accompanied her."

"You do approve of Esther, then?" Lady Augusta interrupted to ask.

Susannah's smile appeared again. "I do, very much. She
is not only all that is gracious, but she takes little nonsense
from Father. I overheard her telling him once that she would
not be cowed by his grim look, it was too tedious by half,
but that she would be open to reason, should he care to try
that upon her."

"Bravo for her!" Lady Augusta set her glass aside to

applaud. "Oh, yes, I am delighted Kerr had the good grace to die off early! Now, back to young Sunderly, before you scold me for outrageousness."

Susannah chuckled. "You *are* outrageous, but I shall not scold you for it. As for Lord Sunderly, I met him in the park by merest chance. He was in town gathering a few things together for a fishing trip to Scotland with Richard Markham."

"Ah! So it is the Markhams he visits here in Newmarket. And when you learned he meant to join Richard here, you invited Sunderly to ride with you."

In fact the viscount had invited himself to ride with Susannah. He had begged, almost, when he learned she was leaving for Newmarket the next day. "I don't want to intrude, my dear, you know that, but think how pleasant it would be to ride up together. You can tell me all about Newmarket, the horses and the traditions. I shall feel an old hand when I get there."

His smile had been so very eager. What could she say? That she would prefer to ride alone than have him accompany and amuse her? That his unexpected decision to attend the meet, when she had thought they had agreed to spend their summer apart, made her want to cry out in frustration? That he seemed even blander than she remembered, now that she saw him again after . . . ?

"It seemed the thing to do," Susannah abruptly broke the train of her thoughts. "We were both traveling to the same place on the same day. He will be staying the week with the Markhams before going on to Scotland. But how have things been here, Gussie? The horses are all well I hope?" Susannah glanced down at her skirt, and found reason to rearrange its graceful folds. "And O'Neill? He has matters in hand?"

"Do you doubt it?" Lady Augusta's brow lifted superbly. "My O'Neill has worked himself and all the rest in the stables ceaselessly. He's even refused my invitation to dinner tonight to meet my 'race regulars'—says he's too much to do."

Lady Augusta's "race regulars" were a group of confederates who had been coming to Ridley to enjoy the summer meet at Newmarket for close to three decades. Susannah

knew and enjoyed them all, from Lady Amelia Dennys, with
her trio of Chinese dogs, to Sir Alden Windrop and his
unflagging determination to devise a mathematical system
that would infallibly predict a winning horse.

Dinner that night, the first gathering of the group, as the
meet was to begin the next day, was as festive as ever.
Susannah could not object to being told repeatedly that she
was lovelier than anyone had a right to be, and she enjoyed
immensely all the talk of the horses, for Gussie's "regulars"
were mad about the races.

There was, of course, discussion of Ridley's "temporary"
trainer. Lord John Farthington called out skeptically that he'd
never heard of such an arrangement. "Hear the man's a
temporary replacement, Gussie! A temporary replacement?
Is he up to Mulcahey? Tell the truth, now!"

Lady Augusta, got up in a fantastic creation of bold scarlet,
laughed richly. "Is a falcon up to a robin? Is a blooded
stallion up to a workhorse? I should say O'Neill is up to
Mulcahey. What say you, Susannah?"

"What?" Susannah glanced around slowly, taking her time
to allow the sudden fierce leap of her pulses that had occurred
at the mention of O'Neill's name to slow before she spoke.

"Is O'Neill comparable to Mulcahey as a trainer, my dear?
Jack, here, would know."

"Ah, O'Neill. I think he is a fine trainer, Lord Jack."

"There, you see, Jack! You know Susannah possesses the
best instincts when it comes to horses. Ridley will dominate
the meet. Put your money on it."

Susannah turned back to Sir Alden, who was trying to
explain the intricacies of his latest mathematical system. She
could not keep straight what was to be divided by what, and
smiled so vaguely she wondered Sir Alden could not tell how
distracted she was.

But no one, not her father, not Lady Esther, nor Sunderly
had seemed to notice how often she left them, suddenly, midsentence. Perhaps, at last, she'd something for which to thank
the legion of strict governesses she'd gone through. They
had instructed her often enough on how to smile politely.

Now she seemed able to wear that smile no matter where her thoughts were, and as to the blush that invariably arose on her cheeks when she was distracted, her companions had mistaken it as a sign of interest in their remarks.

Susannah clasped her hands tightly in her lap and tried heroically to concentrate on Sir Alden's theory that magical results could be had from dividing the horse's weight by the jockey's, while adding the age of the horse, multiplied by a factor of seven.

Her effort went for naught. As Sir Alden waved his pen in the air, Susannah's thoughts slipped away.

She would see him soon.

Her hand clenched tightly about the glass of claret she held, but Susannah did not hear Sir Alden explain how he had arrived at the number seven. Her treacherous thoughts were fixed upon O'Neill, who had seen her bare and wet to her waist.

Heat seared her cheeks again, and she gazed unseeing at the paper upon which her companion made rapid notations. What would she do when they were face-to-face? Susannah asked herself as she had done repeatedly for the past ten days. She had an awful fear she would turn red as a beet. And that he would laugh.

The thought of his laughter made her warm again, but in a different way. She had only to let her thoughts drift a little, and she could see him laughing, his eyes lit with that lazy, teasing light.

Or she might, if she let her thoughts drift further, see O'Neill staring at her in her pool. Would he look at her like that when they met—as if he would never get enough of the sight of her?

Would he say, "You are very beautiful," in that way that had made her naked beauty seem a gift she'd bestowed upon him?

The nearer Susannah had come to Ridley, the more their meeting had occupied her thoughts. How would it be? What would he say? The wheels of the carriage seemed to repeat the question over and over as they rolled along. She had not heard half of whatever Sunderly had said, but had listened, instead, to the wheels.

Impatient to know, impatient to see him again, Susannah had wanted to fly out to the stableyard the moment she arrived at Ridley. Only with the greatest effort of will had she gone first to her grandmother, to tell Gussie Beaufort's momentous news.

Soon, though, she would be free to go to the stables. And she was, finally. After dinner Susannah excused herself. Gussie's guests had been looking after themselves since before she was born, and waved her off fondly when she said she wished to walk out to the stableyard before she retired.

He was not there. Susannah absorbed the disappointment only slowly. Before a meet, John Mulcahey had stayed in the stableyard sometimes until midnight.

Two young grooms, Billy Whitlow and Kevin Smith, were there instead, playing cards by the light of a lantern. Billy greeted her with the broadest of grins. "I'm that glad to see you, my lady! I wagered Meeks you'd be back tonight. He thought you'd not return from Surrey before midweek, but I told him you'd never missed the first day of a meet before and wouldn't start now."

The stables smelled pungent as always. The familiar scent lifted Susannah's spirits, as did Billy, who was only a year older than she. When Susannah asked if she had made him a wealthy man, the young groom shook his head disgustedly. " 'Tis only a mite richer I am, my lady. Meeks couldn't make me wealthy if he lost everything he had. Why, he'd not enough blunt even to wager me on Ruin's race tomorrow."

"No?" Susannah gave him a measuring look. "You wouldn't by merest chance be interested in a wager with me, would you?"

Billy grinned delightedly. "I was that afraid you'd not ask, my lady!"

Kevin Smith had no intention of being left out. He took a colt named Prince Martin because the colt was a roan and she had a partiality for roans; Susannah took Hermano, a horse she had seen run at Ascot the year before; while Billy, stoutly maintaining loyalty to Ridley, chose Majestic Ruin, the only horse they had running the first day of the meet.

When she left an hour later, Susannah knew from the two grooms that Barley Boy had continued to run strongly in the gallops and that O'Neill's Saracen had experienced several simulated races, complete with a pistol and crowd noise. The boys thought it an excellent idea and commended the Irishman.

"He's the best trainer I ever saw," Billy confided, while Kevin nodded sagely. "None of us thought he'd manage to train the black, but he has."

"He's even trained you to work, Billy," Kevin threw out laconically.

Billy only grinned. "I'll admit I'd rather face one of Boney's armies than have O'Neill take me to task. He doesn't shout and curse like Mulcahey, only looks at you." When Billy attempted a dire frown, he sent Kevin into gales of laughter. "Laugh at me if you will, Kev, but I didn't see you laughing when the Irishman pointed out you were slow with the feed today."

Kevin sobered. "Nay. I'd not make the mistake of laughin' at O'Neill. He'd have no difficulty takin' me apart with one hand, but I'll say, as well, that when he's pleased, there's no better man."

Casually, after she had strolled back from a peek at Lady Danu and her colt, Susannah managed to learn that O'Neill had left the stables no more than a quarter of an hour before her arrival, and that he did not intend to return that night.

It was not until then that Susannah learned precisely how much she had looked forward to seeing the Irishman. She had never suspected that when she left the stableyard without having seen him, she would look off down the lane to his cottage and entertain, if only fleetingly, the thought that she could surprise him, could go to see him at night at his cottage.

The next morning, retracing her way to the stableyard, anticipating the coming gallops, Susannah did not find it quite so difficult as she had expected to command her feet to patience. And she shushed the flock of geese that always surged out to greet her with loud, piercing honks. Prepared with stale bread, she suggested strongly that they moderate their enthusiasm on account of Gussie's guests, none of whom appreciated the dawn's light.

But she knew she lied, and to geese at that. The truth was, she did not want them to announce her arrival in the stable-yard. Now that the moment truly had come when she would face O'Neill again, Susannah felt absurdly shy.

Already she could feel a telling warmth creep into her cheeks. Perhaps if she hurried her pace just a little, it would seem she was flushed from exertion.

"Lady Susannah!" Murdoch looked around as she entered the stables, his face splitting into a wide grin. "Billy said you was back, but I was afraid your trip had tired you so, you'd miss the gallops."

"Miss the gallops?"

Susannah gave the leathery groom such a surprised look, he chuckled. "Aye, ye're right to look so. I was off the mark to forget you've ever been a game 'un, my lady."

Smiling a little, Susannah turned slowly to look about. Several grooms were leading horses out of their stalls. She greeted them, but even as she did, her eyes continued on, sweeping the area, then caught on a tall figure at the far end of the stables. Susannah's heart leapt so suddenly, she bit her lip. And immediately looked back to Murdoch. "Shall I ride Barley Boy, Murdoch? Or ought he to be spared, as his race is tomorrow?"

" 'Tis O'Neill who'll have some notion about that, my lady, not I. He knows his horse—as good as or better than Jack Mulcahey, though I'd not say so to Jack's face. Ah, here he comes now."

Conscious of her heartbeat, Susannah turned in the direction Murdoch nodded. At first, in the dark of the stables, she'd only an impression of him, the wide shoulders, long limbs, and easy, fluid movements.

When he came into the light spilling through the open door behind her, she took in all at once, with a jolt almost, that her memory had not exaggerated his looks. His hair was as black as she thought; his features as chiseled and strong.

Then she was looking into Connor's eyes. They were so very blue, blue as the sky, startlingly blue against his dark lashes. Lost in them for the space of a heartbeat, Susannah became aware only slowly that they were animated by no spark at all, either friendly or unfriendly. She might have been a post for all the interest he displayed in her.

"Lady Susannah," he greeted her briskly, tonelessly. "I trust your journey was enjoyable?"

His mouth, at the corner of which there had so often been the faintest lift, was a straight, implacable line.

"Yes," Susannah said slowly. "It was most enjoyable, thank you, Mr. O'Neill. I trust your time at Ridley was productive?"

"We shall see this week whether it was productive." He spoke flatly, as he would to a groom. "Jack is saddling Barley Boy. Ride him light. I want him exercised, but not tired."

Susannah just restrained an impulse to salute. "Which horse needs a hard riding?"

She had thrown him off. For a half-second their gazes locked. Susannah had no idea what might have been in her eyes, only saw something hard and unyielding in his; then even that was gone. He veiled his gaze again. "Demon doesn't run until later in the week."

She stared at him, but got nothing more in return. "Then I'll take him."

Demon was named for "demon rum," not his temperament. Still, he was a strong horse and afforded Susannah some challenge. She needed it. She could not remember ever being so disappointed. She had thought him . . . She did not know. A friend? Perhaps. A kindred soul? Perhaps that too, perhaps more.

He had approved her garden; he saved her when James lost control of the bay; had wanted her assistance to save Lady Danu and Whiskey. He had seen her in her pool and had made no secret of liking what he saw. Yet now had acted as if she were a stranger.

Susannah's eyes narrowed as she set Demon to a pounding

pace. She would know how deep the change in him was, and she vowed, as well, to know its cause.

He was an Irishman, a horse trainer, no more. She knew it. She'd reminded herself often enough over the previous ten days or so that he was no worthy object for her thoughts. Still, his indifference affected her. Damn the man, but it affected her deeply.

15

LADY AUGUSTA liked to say she had attended the races at Newmarket for so long, she had wagered upon the first one. Of course, she had not been alive in the time of Charles the First, but she was treated by all and sundry with the awe and reverence a founding member might have been accorded.

Everyone who was anyone at Newmarket knew Lady Augusta's box. When Richard Markham took the Viscount Sunderly to it, they found the box densely crowded with such a variety of people that Sunderly stared, caught off-guard, though Richard had warned him that social distinctions became somewhat blurred at the track.

Specifically, Richard had said, "You will find all manner of people speaking to the dowager Duchess of Beaufort," and he had not, as the viscount saw, exaggerated. Of the two men speaking with the dowager duchess just then, in fact, he did not believe either was a true gentleman.

Responding to a signal from Richard Markham, the viscount moved forward, inching through the crowd toward his hostess.

Her voice rang out loud and distinctive in the next moment, and to Sunderly's sincere amazement, she poked the bluff, hearty, overly got-up man beside her in the ribs with her fan.

"So, Dick Macaffee! You want to know if the black has the manners to run? Ha! What I will tell you is this: he has the speed to leave your Bugle's Air in the dust!"

''But that's not what Macaffee would know, Lady Gussie,'' objected a man whose smooth tones proclaimed him born slightly closer to the manor than the other. ''Your black may have the strength to win, but he must have the disclipline as well.''

''Sir Ralph! Surely you do not mean to imply that I might run an undisciplined animal?''

''Ha!'' Dick Macaffee's booming laugh echoed off the walls of the box. ''You'd run a hare, Lady Gussie, if 'twould win.''

All three laughed with such abandon, Sunderly winced ever so slightly. It was much the same reaction he accorded the bright, bold hue of green Lady Augusta wore. Only when his hostess turned, sensing newcomers, and he saw her face, did the viscount accept that the old harridan was truly Susannah Somerset's grandmother. She had her granddaughter's eyes, and even, if one looked beyond the paint and powder, something of Susannah's fine, elegant bones.

''Richard Markham!'' Lady Augusta called out imperiously when she saw the two fashionably clad young men. ''Come down and pay your respects! I cannot receive your homage properly if you stay a league distant. And bring your companion. I would meet Grafton's boy.''

Standing at the front of the box between Sir Alden Windrop and James, Susannah studied the crowd upon the track below, and seeing her distraction, her cousin leaned over to announce, ''Sunderly has come, Susannah.'' Her first impulse was to say merely, ''Oh?'', but she disciplined herself and gave up her perusal of the throng. Beside her, James murmured, ''He'll be glad if you hurry along. He doesn't look too cozy with her.''

Susannah saw at once what James meant. Sunderly looked very stiff. He'd only the smallest smile for his hostess, and even that little held more wariness than warmth.

''Perhaps it is Gussie's hat has him looking so pokered up,'' Susannah mused aloud, causing James to cough into his fist. Lady Augusta's bonnet was a bizarre creation, covered in the same bright green silk of her dress and adorned with a spray of white plumes and, amazingly, a half-dozen small white birds.

Given more easily to pity than Susannah, James took her elbow and hurried her forward. As they approached, they heard Lady Augusta remark ambiguously, "Well, you've the look of Grafton about you, boy."

Philip did resemble his father, who was of a good height, if rather slender. Both were attractive in an unexceptional way, with even features, adequate hair, and pleasant, unremarkable eyes. Why the viscount should stiffen at Gussie's remark, Susannah was not certain. Perhaps it was the "boy." At twenty-eight, he would not be accustomed to the appellation, but Gussie addressed every man below fifty similarly.

Whatever it was that had put him on his guard with her grandmother dropped away entirely when the viscount saw Susannah. The smile he gave her was both pleased and approving, and ought not, by any lights, to have made her heart sink as it did.

"Lord Sunderly." Susannah let him take her hand, but reclaimed it as soon as she turned to greet Richard Markham. "Have you shown Lord Sunderly all about Newmarket, Mr. Markham?"

"I have shown him around a little, but I am certain to leave something to you, my dear."

"We visited the Birdcage." Sunderly referred to the paddock at Newmarket, where the trainers and grooms saddled the horses for the next race. "There were so many people crowding about, however, it was impossible to see much."

"Opening day is generally crowded," Susannah replied lightly. "Did you pat the Red Post for luck?"

Richard Markham shook his head. "No. I thought you might want to introduce Philip to that tradition, Lady Susannah."

"Do you truly believe touching a post brings luck?" Lord Sunderly asked, smiling indulgently at Susannah.

Perhaps fearing that Susannah would not object sufficiently to either the superior smile or the condescending sentiment,

Lady Augusta chose to interject herself into the conversation. " 'Course she does! It's the way of the track to believe in tokens and talismans. I've got mine here."

Poking about in the depths of her reticule, Lady Augusta unearthed a rabbit's foot. It was almost as ancient as she, and had seen far less respectful use. Ragged, moth-eaten, none too clean, it was not at all pretty.

"Saints preserve us, Gussie!" James exclaimed, laughing. "If you expect that to bring us luck, we are in trouble."

Susannah and Richard Markham both chuckled their agreement, but Lady Augusta was unchastened. "We shall apply to Hughes, here. What do you think, sir? Is a dirty rabbit's foot as good as an old one?"

Hughes, one of the foremost touts at Newmarket, beamed at being singled out. "The older, the better, Lady Guss. The more a lucky token is used, the more luck it acquires."

Susannah gave the dapper gap-toothed man a fond smile. "I, for one, stand convinced. At Newmarket you are the uncontested expert on luck and the odds, Hughes."

"While you, m'lady, are the last word on beauty. I'd wager anyone any odds that you are the loveliest lady present today—but, of course, for Lady Gus."

Susannah grinned. "Now I know why you are called the 'silver-tongued tout,' Hughes. And as ever, it was a pleasure to hear your tongue at work. But we shan't stay and keep you from your business with Gussie. I know the two of you have a great deal to discuss," she added, for Gussie and Hughes made numerous side bets throughout the meet.

The tout tipped his hat in farewell, and Susannah allowed the viscount to take her arm as she strolled with him and James and Mr. Markham to the front of the box. They were only just out of earshot of Hughes and Gussie when Sunderly asked, "Who is that man, Lady Susannah? I mean, can he be a friend of your grandmother's?"

"Hughes?" she asked, though she knew very well to whom the viscount referred. "Ah, he is a tout. He sets odds and takes wagers, my lord. At race time he and Gussie are very close, actually."

"But they are not friends, precisely," James spoke up to clarify the point. "They only meet at race time to wager with each other."

"They meet frequently three times a year," Susannah observed, acting on an entirely unworthy impulse to appall the viscount as much as possible. "I am sure I do not see many people I call friends so often." James looked at her oddly, but Susannah ignored her cousin as she disengaged her arm from Sunderly's and called to Sir Alden.

At the sound of his name, Sir Alden looked up vaguely from the sheet he studied. "Oh, hello, there, Markham, Sunderly. Like the races, do you? I'm afraid it will be Hermano, Susannah. His numbers are simply too good!"

Amused for several reasons, not least of all by the lack of interest Sir Alden displayed in Sunderly, Susannah laughed, then took some pity and stooped to explain Sir Alden's tangent. "Hermano runs in the next race against Gussie's Majestic Ruin, and Sir Alden has developed a numerical system for determining the winner."

"Numbers never lie," Sir Alden observed stoutly.

Richard Markham was intrigued enough to pursue the matter, and, with James, begged an explanation. As a result, for a few moments Susannah and Sunderly were left to themselves.

She had been curious how the viscount would do at the track. As it was a world she loved, she did not apologize for making his reaction to it something of a test.

And he ought not to have done too badly. There had been odd characters in the stories he'd told of his adventures with Sebastian, but glancing at the viscount, Susannah could not find any pleasure or even amusement in his eyes as he surveyed the less august crowd far below them in the area of general admittance. Indeed, judging by the downward curve of his mouth, she thought him far more disdainful than intrigued.

Rather at random, Susannah began their conversation where Sir Alden had left it. "I am afraid, though I cannot say I understand his system, that Sir Alden is quite right."

Sunderly had not followed her thoughts, and frowned. "I beg your pardon?"

"About Majestic Ruin. I think he will come in second to Hermano, who belongs to Sir Ralph Badgett."

"Oh." His frown cleared a little. "It's an odd name that, Majestic Ruin. Where did it come from?"

Susannah smiled. "Even Gussie would not name him Blue Ruin, but she came as close as she could. She also has Barley Boy, Demon, for Demon Rum, Amontillado, Madeira, and now Whiskey."

Sunderly did not respond directly. Instead, looking out over the track, he said slowly, "Your grandmother is . . . unusual."

"Yes, she is," Susannah agreed. "And I am exceedingly fond of her."

At once the viscount looked chastened. "Yes, yes! You have always spoken of her most fondly. But, that is, she does not seem much like you, Lady Susannah."

"No?" Susannah glanced back at her grandmother. Lady Augusta was speaking with Hughes still, gesturing so emphatically that her plumes waved wildly. "I regret to hear you say so, my lord. I should like to have half her spirit when I am her age. She is seventy-odd, you know."

Let him think that over! Susannah knew his grandmother. The old thing had almost to be dusted, she was so immobile. And she was not yet seventy.

Almost at once Susannah repented of her uncharitable thoughts. She ought not to have taken Sunderly's reaction to Gussie in bad part, when only a very few took her grandmother in easy stride.

The Irishman had. No! The comparison was unfair. O'Neill was common. Susannah bit her lip. Of course, Connor O'Neill was not common at all. She was only vexed with him because she had not seen him at all that day, and had even been denied the opportunity to wish him luck.

Whether Connor had avoided her by chance or design, Susannah could not know, but a little later that afternoon, there was no question.

In a group swelled with the addition of Mary and Drew Wardley as well as Bunny Townshend and Phoebe, Susannah and James took the viscount to the Red Post, a tall pillar situated on the Beacon course that generations of wagerers had patted for luck.

It was Phoebe Limley who peered over the throng to spy the Irishman. "Why, look!" she cried, standing on tiptoe. "There is Mr. O'Neill. Fetch him, will you, Mr. Wardley? I wish to ask him how Ruin does."

As O'Neill was ahead of them, making his way more easily than they through the crowd, Drew was obliged to hurry to catch him. Susannah saw the Irishman smile when he turned in response to Drew's call, and even at a distance she felt the power of his smile.

But when he glanced back, prompted by something Drew said, and his eyes met hers, there was no smile to warm his handsome face. There was only that one stabbing look; then he said a few abrupt words to Drew and strode off at the same determined pace as before.

"He'd not the time to chat," Drew explained when he returned to the group. "He's Ruin to see to just now."

"But I thought there was an hour or so before that race!" Phoebe might have stamped her foot, Susannah thought, but there wasn't sufficient room in the crowd. "Surely he could have spared us a moment."

To Susannah's surprise and satisfaction, it was James who replied to Phoebe, pointing out, in so many words, that the world did not revolve around spoiled heiresses. "O'Neill is a busy man, Miss Limley, particularly just now, and his first obligation is not to us, but to the horses."

"Whatever his obligations, he did not seem a very amiable fellow," Sunderly observed. "That was a deuced unfathomable look he gave us, or rather, gave you, Lady Susannah."

Susannah had not realized anyone noticed who it was that had received O'Neill's unfriendly look. But she had more pride than to reveal the blow that look had been to her.

"Did O'Neill look unfathomably at me, my lord?" She shrugged as if she had neither realized it nor cared. "Perhaps he has some superstitions about speaking to ladies before a race.''

"I've heard of such a superstition," Drew remarked, and Connor O'Neill was forgotten, at least by all but Susannah, in the ensuing discussion of unusual superstitions.

As Susannah had expected the colt to do, Majestic Ruin lost to Hermano, but only by a length. Lady Augusta was vastly pleased with her colt's showing. Very privately she and Mulcahey had reckoned Ruin's chances of finishing even in the money as close to nil, and she had decided to race him only because she wanted a horse running on opening day.

As a result, her party of "regulars" returned well pleased if fatigued to Ridley. Opening day was always exhausting. Mindful of that fact, Lady Augusta had invited only Major Hornbeck to join her and her guests for dinner, but still Susannah dressed with great care.

No weariness at all dimming her eyes, she slipped out of the house a little before it was time to join the others and made her way to the stables. If she experienced a disappointment at finding only Billy Whitlock and a few other grooms about, she did not show it.

Indeed, she smiled, for Billy's eyes widened at the sight of her and an awed "Cor!" escaped him.

It ws a compliment of the highest order, but Susannah did not allow her old crony to become entirely lost in his appreciation of her. Remorseless, she held out her hand, whereupon Billy's bemused look became a sheepish grin.

"Cor!" he exclaimed again in a far different tone. "I should have known you'd not be wrong, my lady, but I never thought a Spanish-soundin' horse could beat our Ruin."

"Alas!" Susannah closed her hand about the coin he dropped ever so reluctantly into it. "Hermano's bloodlines are purely English, however foreign his name."

Billy watched her toss his coin, and his grin broadened. "Double it for tomorrow, my lady? Another of Badgett's horses is runnin' in the second. Can't remember the name, but it's foreign too."

Susannah thought a moment. "The second? Who runs against him? Not one of ours."

"No, no. That Macaffee's runnin' one o' his then. Clarion."

"Billy! Jim!"

The grooms leapt to attention, turning alertly to the door and the man striding through it. "Murdoch—" Connor broke off when his gaze fell upon Susannah. He did not seem pleased to find her there, but Susannah had steeled herself to expect a cool welcome and simply waited as composedly as she could, with her heart racing, while he sent the two boys after Murdoch. When they had departed, Connor slowly, almost reluctantly it seemed, transferred his attention back to her.

A black eyebrow lifted sardonically. "You've come a little overdressed to the stables, haven't you, my lady?"

It was not the comment Susannah had hoped for upon the contrast between her fashionable silk and the straw bales behind her. But at least he had noted her appearance.

"Yes, I suppose I have, but I hadn't time to get out here earlier, and I'd a debt to collect." When his brow lifted, Susannah explained as if there were no strain between them, "Billy did not think a Spanish name could master Majestic Ruin."

There was the faintest altering of O'Neill's expression. Susannah only realized she waited, almost holding her breath, for him to smile, when he did not. Instead Connor shrugged his shoulders. "Ruin did well to come in second."

"I did try to warn Billy last night, but he would not listen. He seldom does, when he's made up his mind."

"You have wagered with him before?"

He did not seem to approve, which surprised Susannah. She'd not have thought O'Neill would fault her for wagering with a stablehand. "We started long ago with candy, actually, but now we are older, we've graduated to half-crowns. You don't look as if you approve, Mr. O'Neill."

"It's not for me to approve or disapprove what you do, Lady Susannah."

He sounded very curt, but Susannah noted that he did not take his gaze from her, grim though the gaze was.

"Are you dining with Gussie's regulars tonight, Mr. O'Neill?"

His mouth did turn up then, at the corner, mockingly. "It is the July meet, my lady. I've not the leisure to socialize into the morning hours. Good night."

"Good night. Oh, Mr. O'Neill?" Susannah put out her hand, catching his arm.

She made note that his muscles tensed abruptly at her touch. "What?"

She rather thought the snapped question was not a bad sign. Surely if he had been unmoved by her, he'd have asked more mildly why she detained him. "I wanted to congratulate you on Ruin's showing. As you said, he did better than expected."

Connor had the oddest impression her eyes had deepened in color since the last time he had looked into them. Perhaps it was the apricot color of her dress, but they were so rich a sable brown, they seemed to have taken on the texture of velvet.

"I think you rode him a time or two in June, my lady. You may as easily congratulate yourself. Good night, again."

He did leave then, turning on his heel, no parting smile or even nod for her. Susannah drifted off to Lady Danu's stall. The mare greeted her with a nicker, but had nothing to say when Susannah observed softly that some men could be contrary as the devil. "Or perhaps it is I am contrary," she amended, nuzzling Lady Danu's neck. "With a respectable, eminently suitable suitor who pursues me devotedly, I am all impatience, but with O'Neill, a perfectly unsuitable, eminently disreputable servant"—she stressed the word—"who shuns me, I am . . . Oh, Lady Danu! I dare not think what I am with him."

16

"LORD SUNDERLY." Susannah reined in, taken by surprise when the viscount appeared suddenly around a bend in the woods through which she was riding. "This is unexpected."

The viscount seemed not to take her reserved greeting amiss. He smiled at Susannah with more enthusiasm than he had all day, though he had been with her for most of it, including the moment Barley Boy charged ahead just at the last to win his race.

"We've Richard to thank for our meeting. He's the one set me upon this path, saying it would bring me eventually to Ridley. I see you shared my desire to ride after standing about at the track the day long."

Susannah would not have characterized attending the races as "standing about," and she seemed to recall she had said something aloud about wanting to ride out when she got back to Ridley. Hadn't she also remarked she wished a moment alone? No, likely she'd only thought that. Now here he was, no apology for intruding on her lips, no request to join her forthcoming. He assumed a great deal, did the Viscount Sunderly.

"I did wish to ride, yes. Shall we make for Ridley, then?"

Before he could agree, Susannah turned her mount about. She could not fault the viscount for his destination. Lady

Augusta had invited several people for dinner, among them
the Markhams and their guest.

"You have been riding ever since you arrived home?"
he asked amiably as they started off.

"No." Susannah toyed with saying nothing more. She'd
been enjoying the soft sounds of the evening, but then she
felt churlish and added, "I went to visit my old nurse, Nan."

The viscount turned a look of approval upon her. "How
good you are to take the time to visit an old retainer, Lady
Susannah, particularly as you must have been tired when you
reached home."

"Actually Nan is a restorative, my lord. She knows a great
deal of the real things of this world. It is I am the more
invigorated by our meetings."

"I see."

Of course he did not understand. Susannah did not imagine
Sunderly had ever had a conversation with anyone below him
in class. Lesser mortals served him, and he accepted their
services graciously enough, for he knew what behavior
became his station, but he had nothing to say to them.

Sunderly was no different from most of his class. Susannah
could not really fault him. That she was different, she
ascribed to her mother's early death. Nan had been a mother
to her, and a loving one. Too, there was Gussie. The dowager
duchess observed the distinctions of class, but the classes
were her own. She'd one class for amusing people and
another for those who could produce winning colts. If a
person could do neither, she'd little use for him.

And if he could do both?

Susannah's mouth quirked very slightly. O'Neill had come
to the box that day, finally, the fourth day of the meet, to
accept Lady Augusta's commendation on Barley Boy's win.
Susannah had known he was there, though she had not been
looking at the entryway to the box, but out over the track.
The nape of her neck, the little portion exposed because her
hair had been pinned up beneath her French bonnet, had
grown warm, and she had turned abruptly.

Her eyes, accustomed to the bright sun on the track, had

not adjusted quickly enough. He had been a shadow filling
the doorway. She only knew it was he who stood there
because of his height. Then Gussie called out to him and
O'Neill stepped forward, looking to the dowager.

Congratulations had come from all sides. Connor accepted
the general praise with easy confidence. Susannah was not
surprised. She could not imagine him being either overly
humble or absurdly puffed up, but she was perhaps a little
surprised to see that he appeared to advantage in the company
of her peers.

Besides the gentlemen with their wealth and their titles,
all of them turned out in exquisitely cut coats of superfine,
gleaming high-crowned beaver hats, and elaborately starched
cravats, O'Neill was unmistakably at ease. John Mulcahey
had always turned a little red when he had been obliged to
come to the box. He'd spoken more sparingly than was his
wont, and had stood so stiffly Susannah had felt almost sorry
for him. Not so O'Neill. There was that almost mysterious
assurance about him that allowed him to return the greeting
of, say, the Earl of Braighton, as equal speaking to equal.

He had made a gallant to-do over Lady Augusta, executing
a faultless bow over the dowager's gloved hand after she
commended him for being "a dashed peerless trainer."

"I worked with what you provided me, my lady," he had
observed with a smile. "It was you who chose Barley Boy's
dam and sire, long before I came to Ridley. Allow me to
congratulate you for being a superb judge of horseflesh."

"You are generous to share your commendations with me,
my boy! But it is true, I will admit it, that judging physical
attributes has ever been my forte. My success, I imagine,
is owing to my enthusiasm for the task."

Lady Augusta had slanted O'Neill such an arch look then,
Susannah wanted to groan, but the Irishman rose with
devilish ease to the occasion. He grinned. "I've no doubt
of your enthusiasm for judging physical attributes, Lady
Gussie. It is too prodigious to miss, and too unerring not
to please."

The shameless return—Connor did not even blush, though

he knew very well Lady Augusta had been referring to an enthusiasm for men in general and him in particular—earned him a great delighted laugh and a kiss on the hand.

"My boy, I don't know what I shall do without you! I think I shall put my mind to finding some way or other to keep you on at Ridley."

"You must, Gussie! Two wins in as many days, and an excellent prospect of a third in the Two Thousand Guineas!" Major Hornbeck beamed enthusiastically, rocking on his heels. "You will make me a rich man if you stay on, O'Neill."

"But what will you do with Mulcahey, Lady Gus? You cannot have two trainers. I think the perfect solution would be for Mr. O'Neill to come and speak with me at Langley Stud."

The speaker, Sir Alfred Knightly, had an excellent stud not far from Ridley. It was his horse that had come in second to Barley Boy. An older man, in his sixties perhaps, he had a very much younger wife. In the forefront of the group surrounding O'Neill and Lady Augusta, Lady Marissa Knightly laid her elegantly gloved hand upon the Irishman's arm and agreed, with a meaningful smile, that she too would welcome him at Langley Stud.

Susannah observed that O'Neill did not immediately disengage himself from Lady Marissa Knightly, but smiled down at her in such a way that the woman's languid gaze sharpened momentarily.

In the next moment O'Neill had two women hanging upon him, for Phoebe Limley had no thought of conceding anything to a woman in her thirties, however alluring the more experienced Lady Marissa might be. She took O'Neill's other arm.

Susannah could not say whether Connor noticed that she alone of the women remained apart by the railing, looking on. He never glanced her way again, after that one time when he had first entered the box. In truth, Susannah could not have said with conviction he had looked her way then. She had not actually seen his gaze upon her. She might well have only fancied it had been, or that now it took an effort of will to keep his eyes firmly upon the circle about him and Lady Augusta.

She could say he left rather abruptly and after only a little time. James had called out unexpectedly that Susannah ought to come forward and receive her portion of the congratulations along with the breeder and trainer of the winning colt. "She's the one exercised Barley Boy these last weeks," her cousin had announced. "And that's no small thing."

"Indeed it is not," Connor O'Neill agreed, seemingly sincerely. "And I shall cede Lady Susannah my place, for I must be off to see to the horses. It is why I am here, after all."

"And I thought you were here to amuse me!" Lady Augusta chided, but to no avail. The Irishman merely smiled before he shed the ladies surrounding him and went off about his business.

With Connor's departure, Susannah's mood deteriorated. She ought to have been prepared for his avoidance of her, but she found she was not. Barley Boy had won! She'd exercised the horse for over a month, yet O'Neill had not spared her one pleased victory glance.

The cut was deliberate. There was no question of that. And it only made matters worse that she did not understand at all why he should be so cold suddenly.

"Lady Susannah, I think you are woolgathering."

Susannah roused with a start to recall she was on Delilah, her favorite of Gussie's riding horses, Sunderly beside her. She did not apologize for her distraction. She had not, she reminded herself, asked for his company. "Yes, my lord? What did you wish?"

Sunderly glanced at her. Her tone had not been sweet. "I, ah, bethought myself of James's remark that you regularly exercise your grandmother's racehorses. It seems a dangerous thing for you to do. I suppose Lady Augusta approves?"

"She does not object," Susannah returned scrupulously.

"And her trainer, O'Neill?" Sunderly persisted. "He approves?"

"I convinced him I could manage Barley Boy."

"He rides out with you, then?"

Susannah glared at her companion. Something in his tone
suggested the last question was of more concern to him than
her habit of exercising a racehorse. "Yes, most days O'Neill
rides out to the gallops too."

It cost Susannah to keep her voice even. She'd a desire
to snap, "Not that it is any of your business what mount or
with whom I ride."

Of course, as Sunderly thought himself in love with her,
it was not surprising he was suspicious of a man like O'Neill.
True, an Irish horse trainer was so beneath him as to be no
rival at all, but as a man . . .

But O'Neill had given Sunderly no cause for concern. He
had avoided her so completely, she could not think why the
viscount had even noticed him, unless it was that she had
given her suitor cause to take note.

No! Susannah did not define what she denied so
emphatically. Her thoughts seemed to freeze upon that "no,"
and before there was any danger she could clarify what in
her attitude toward O'Neill might give Sunderly pause, she
sought serious diversion.

"Come, Lord Sunderly!" She tossed her companion a
challenging look. "I shall show you, too, I can ride. I'll race
you to the lane beyond the stone wall there on the far hill."

"And take the wall?" It was not a particularly high wall,
only four feet or so, but the approach to it would be difficult,
for they would have to take it climbing a hill. Susannah
merely nodded in reply, but something in her expression
caused the viscount to nod. "Very well!"

Susannah was off almost before he got the words out, glad
to be gone, glad to have the air rushing at her face. The day
had been warm, and the box, inevitably, close. Nor did any
difficult thoughts plague her as she bent low over Delilah's
neck and urged the sturdy mare to a hard pace.

Delilah took a stream they came upon easily. Susannah
laughed as they soared high in the air and came down gracefully. They were well ahead of Sunderly. She could not hear

the viscount behind her as she and her mare started up the hill to the wall.

It looked higher than it was from their angle, but Susannah had taken it before. A subtle signal with her knees, another with the reins, and the mare gathered herself, leaping higher, higher.

It was in midair that Susannah saw O'Neill. He drove a gig down the lane directly in her line of vision. There was someone with him. A woman.

It was the last coherent thought Susannah had. Distracted, she was not prepared to adjust when Delilah stumbled ever so slightly as she came down on the far side of the wall.

It was the most minor of stumbles. Normally Susannah would have managed easily, but then, scarcely aware she was even upon a horse, her hold slack, she went flying over the mare's head to land with a thud hard upon the ground.

"Susannah! Susannah!"

The voice seemed to come from far away. Her eyes were closed, a fact Susannah found odd, and so she opened them. Ah. Connor swam into view. His blue eyes were dark. "Can you hear me, Susannah?"

She wanted to say, "Of course, now you are speaking to me, I can hear you," but became aware that she hurt all over. If she closed her eyes, perhaps she would not ache so.

"Susannah! Can you hear me?"

His voice sounded so urgent. And loud. She winced. "Yes, yes. Softly, please. Ugh." She put her hand to her head. "Am I all right?"

He made a harsh guttural sound. "You are the one would know best. All I can say is that you're not bleeding. Can you move your legs?"

She thought she could, tested the idea, then nodded, only to grimace when her head protested being moved.

Connor cursed when she put her hands to her aching head. "Damn! How could you be so cow-handed? Why did you even put Delilah to that wall? She's no hunter. Have your wits gone begging?"

Susannah scarcely marked his raging, for as he took her

to task, Connor set about examining her, and his hands moved over her with surprising gentleness, given his mood. Carefully he felt her neck, then the length of her spine. When he ran his hands over her arm, he hit a bruise, and Susannah shivered. Instantly he stopped. "Does that hurt?" he demanded, scowling blackly down at her.

Oddly, Susannah found she'd a desire to smile. At the sight of her wobbly attempt, Connor reacted harshly. "Why the deuce are you smiling? Was your reason knocked out of you? This is not a game, Susannah! You could have done permanent damage to yourself!"

"But I did not," she said rather softly, eyes on him. "Help me to stand, will you?"

Susannah could not but lean into Connor. He half-lifted her in his arms. She had not forgotten how hard and firm his chest was, nor how strong his arms, and she felt quite as at home in his embrace as she had the first time he'd held her to him.

On her feet, Susannah did not need to feign instability. Her legs might have been made of rubber, they felt so unsteady. Connor was holding her tightly about the waist when they heard a horse pound up to the wall behind them. Susannah had forgotten the Viscount Sunderly.

"Hello!" he called out. "Lady Susannah!"

His voice came to them from a little distance. Susannah heard O'Neill mutter, "Romeo at chase. No wonder you were riding hell for leather."

"I was not riding hell for leather," Susannah lied, though she could not think why she did. "I only—"

"Rode like an idiot and nearly broke your neck," Connor snapped rudely. He had not taken his arm away from her waist, but somehow his body was not so yielding as it had been.

He turned her to face the viscount. Sunderly was regarding her with utmost concern, Susannah saw, though even in her dazed state she noted as well that he first flicked his glance to the strong arm encircling her waist. "My dear, are you hurt?"

"Only my pride is severely bruised, really." She gave him a wan smile. "Otherwise I am well enough."

"It's fortunate you were on hand, O'Neill. I shall make use of your gig to drive Lady Susannah home."

It was an order, not a suggestion. Susannah scarcely noticed. She was only aware of Connor stiffening before he set her apart from him.

"Lady Susannah must remount the filly," he contradicted the viscount without expression. "It would not do for either her or the horse if she did not. And besides, Lady Marissa, who is in the gig, is not wearing riding dress. You can manage Delilah now, I imagine, my lady?"

Susannah's head ached. Her left shoulder felt stiff as a board. She wanted to ride in the gig. She wanted to scratch out Lady Marissa Knightly's eyes. The revelation was unwelcome. She closed her eyes to blot out the Irishman. She feared his blue eyes might see more than she wanted to see herself.

"She cannot ride a horse, man!" Sunderly was not accustomed to having his orders waved aside as if they were no more than annoying flies. "She is weaving on her feet."

"I am all right, really." Susannah made the effort to open her eyes. And she turned away from O'Neill. "He's right, Sunderly. I've never fallen off a horse and not remounted at once. Fetch her for me, O'Neill. I should like to get on with it."

He obeyed her order readily, but of course she only acted upon his suggestion. Meantime, the viscount found a gate and reached her as Connor returned with Delilah. Susannah expected the Irishman to give her a leg up. He did not. Perhaps out of a desire to test Sunderly's patience further, he clasped Susannah by the waist and lifted her onto Delilah. To steady herself, she had, perforce, to put her hands upon his shoulders. They felt very strong and warm even through his coat.

Their eyes met. She could not read his, could only see they were very, very blue, and then she was sitting on Delilah.

He arranged her skirts for her, a courtesy she appreciated, as she'd have forgotten.

"You can manage?"

His voice was low, as if only the two of them were present. As if the viscount were not glowering at them; as if Susannah could not see, from the corner of her eye, Lady Marissa sitting in the gig, holding the reins she'd been tossed before her escort had leapt out to run to Susannah, lying still as death upon the ground.

Susannah smiled slightly and perhaps not pleasantly. The sight of Lady Marissa, even at a distance, had made her aware of her looks. She had not been wearing a hat, but her hair had been confined in a neat chignon at the back of her head. Some of it still was confined, some of it straggled down her back, and some of it waved messily about her face. Susannah did not doubt there were leaves and twigs and bits of grass in it. "Oh, I shall manage nicely, Mr. O'Neill. Never doubt it. Thank you for your timely assistance. And enjoy the remainder of your ride. You are so kind to entertain Gussie's guests."

She made to pull the reins from his grasp, only to meet with unexpected resistance. Susannah thought Connor's behavior motivated by sheer perverseness. And he might have agreed it was.

At any rate he smiled almost as thinly as Susannah. "I do endeavor to please, my lady," he retorted, an edge to his voice. "And in that spirit, I'll presume to make a suggestion. Taking a spill can make one very sore. You would be wise to soak yourself. I've no doubt at all you know of a pool close by in which you might immerse yourself. If not, I may be able to break away later to take you to one I stumbled upon only a little time ago."

It was unfair to take advantage of her when she was hurt, but the knowledge that he acted unfairly did not diminish Connor's almost savage pleasure at the sight of the hot blush that rose to belie Susannah's cool expression.

His gratification was short-lived, however. By the time he reached Lady Marissa in the gig, Connor felt as grim as he looked, and his expression never warmed, though his companion used every wile she knew to win a smile from him.

In fact, Connor was scarcely aware of the sultry beauty beside him. Damn her, he could think only of Susannah. In that moment he almost hated her for the depth of emotion she'd made him feel. When he had seen her fly over Delilah's head, he'd experienced an agony the like of which he had never known.

A bitter laugh rose in him. The entire week had been an agony of sorts. He had had to fight merely to keep his eyes from her, and when he thought he was not observed, he had failed even at that.

And that was to say nothing of his murderous sentiments toward that insufferable bland English milksop who stuck to her like a leech. God, it was all he could do not to call the man out when he touched her.

He needed her desperately to be cool and remote. He could almost resist her then. But what had he done when, finally, he had snuffed that dangerously soft light from her eyes by refusing to inconvenience Lady Marissa on her account? What had he done when she wrapped about herself that cool, prideful mantle that was his only hope?

He had reminded her of the pool. He had made her blush, and surprised such a suddenly unguarded, vulnerable look in her eyes it had been all he could do not to drag her from that horse and fold her in his arms again.

17

ON THE LAST day of the meet, the day Saracen was to race, excitement ran high at the track. It seemed everyone in Newmarket had heard of the half-wild colt and of the unorthodox arrangement whereby he would run under Ridley's colors, though he was owned by Ridley's trainer. There had been questions, not surprisingly, but Lady Augusta had prevailed by pointing out she did have a financial stake in the colt. "First, I've paid a prodigious amount to feed him," she proclaimed grandly, "and second, I'm to have half the purse when he wins. Now, let's get on with it!"

Get on with it they did, but not before everyone in Newmarket had had ample opportunity to ruminate at length about the five horses that were to run in the Two Thousand Guineas and about their trainers.

Connor attracted the most attention, in part because he was the newcomer and something of a mystery, but there was, too, the fact that Ridley had done better at the meet than any other stable. Three horses, Barley Boy, Demon, and Madeira, a filly, had won their races, while two, Majestic Ruin and Amontillado, had placed second in theirs.

The night before the big race, Major Hornbeck reported at dinner that he'd seen a man who often did business for Prinny talking to the Irishman. "Colonel Hallett, Gussie, you know him."

Susannah was rather surprised by her grandmother's

reaction. Gussie looked half-amused. "I wonder what O'Neill said to him?" she mused, sounding more intrigued than concerned.

"He said he'd know the salary Prinny intended to pay him, that's what he said, Gussie!" Lord Farthington regarded Lady Augusta as if she had somehow, before his eyes, become a simpleton. "The man's no fool, even if he is an Irishman."

"No fool!" Sir Alden seemed to come awake at the last. "Why, he's made you and me a tidy fortune this week, Jack! I'd say he's no fool."

"And he'll have an array of offers to choose from, particularly if this colt of his wins." Major Hornbeck shook his head direly. "Badgett was talking to him overlong the other day, and Sir Alfred sought him out twice."

"You take on so, Becky!" Lady Augusta remarked dryly. "I imagine Sir Alfred, at least, only wished to see his wife."

The subsequent round of knowing laughter did not amuse Susannah. It left her, indeed, a little ill. Had she allowed herself to think on why, she'd have arrived at the answer, but for that precise reason she concentrated intently upon James, who was deep in conversation with, splendidly enough, Mary Wardley. They were discussing Barley Boy's run, and Susannah returned her attention to the general conversation much later, when Gussie and her regulars spoke of matters quite removed from the Irishman, his colt, or Lady Marissa Knightly.

Susannah had had only one conversation with Connor since her spill. The morning after it, when she had gone to the stableyard, he had been there, and seeing her, had looked unpleasantly surprised.

"What the devil are you doing here?" he had demanded, his brow lowering abruptly.

She had not been in a mood to take his curt greeting in stride. For one thing, her head still ached. "I have come, as I have every morning I have been at Ridley, to gallop a horse. Do you have any objections, Mr. O'Neill?"

"Only last evening you did not even feel up to dinner."

"No, I did not."

But I am certain my absence did not dampen your pleasure. The unspoken remark was full of hidden resonance, for Susannah knew from her maid that all the staff had been agog to see, at last, a woman wearing dampened undergarments. They had heard of the practice, but until Lady Marissa came for her first dinner at Ridley, they had not been able to judge the effect for themselves. "Scandalous it was, my lady!" Mary had reported, her eyes bright. "Why, she might have been wearing no dress at all, the way hers clung to her. Played up to Mr. O'Neill, she did, and he wasn't put off! No, indeed, but why should he be? There's not many a man would object to seein' beforehand the goods he's offered."

Susannah's eyes fell from Connor's. "I feel better now, after my night's rest. Which horse shall I take?"

"Agua."

Susannah jerked her gaze up again, her brow lifting. Agua was the slowest, smallest horse in the stables. She had not ridden a horse so plodding since she was thirteen. "I beg your pardon?"

"You heard me well enough, Lady Susannah. Agua is your only choice. Though you don't seem aware of it, you will be sore. And don't," Connor warned, eyes narrowing, "think to countermand my orders. You'll only earn the groom loyal to you hours of extra work."

Hateful man, Susannah had fumed, and continued to fume, though in fact, because her shoulder was sore and her leg had stiffened, she found Agua entirely sufficient exercise. O'Neill might have phrased his concern differently, however. He might have been at least courteous.

Though she had not spoken to him since, she had seen him, for he'd come to Lady Augusta's box twice more, when Ridley's horses won. One of those times, when O'Neill's low, amused laugh carried to them at the rail, Susannah heard Sunderly call him a "forward fellow." As she had little desire to champion Connor, Susannah had played deaf, but in truth she thought Sunderly wrong. It was not O'Neill who pushed himself upon Lady Marissa, or Phoebe, or Lady Augusta, or any of the other ladies eyeing him discreetly or not so discreetly, depending upon their characters. To the contrary, it was they who appeared forward to Susannah. She'd only have agreed that Connor did little to fend them off.

Perhaps it was for that reason that Susannah half-begrudged the nervousness that overtook her as the start of the Two Thousand Guineas approached. She told herself she did not really care if Saracen won; that it would serve the Irishman right, somehow or other, if his own horse failed to win.

But she did care. The flutters in her stomach told her that.

And if they were not enough, there was the feeling she experienced when she learned Sunderly had wagered against O'Neill and Ridley, putting his money upon Archer, a bay owned by the Earl of Bolton.

Susannah suspected the viscount would have cheered on any horse opposed to O'Neill's, but she had to admit he had chosen well. If one of Saracen's opponents could best him, it would be Bolton's Archer. Sir Alden's mathematical calculations made the bay the favorite by a length, and from Major Hornbeck Susannah knew that the large strong horse had the advantage of track experience as well. He had won twice at Epsom.

Accordingly, when Archer was led out to the track, he showed good spirit, with a toss of his fine head, but he did not waste his energies. He went right along to his place in the starting line.

Saracen was not so well-behaved. As with all the horses, a roar went up from the crowd when he came onto the track, but unlike the others, he danced sideways, flinging his head about and eyeing the mass of humanity in the stands with a wild look. James, beside Susannah, swore beneath his breath when Murdoch had to resort to his whip merely to force the colt to the starting line.

"He'll waste himself, blast him!" James muttered.

"I do believe you are right, Somerset." It was Sunderly, on Susannah's other side, agreeing, a smug smile in his voice.

Susannah's hands curled around the rail.

Dick Macaffee's horse, Bugle Boy, got off best when the pistol sounded, and shot into the lead. Close behind him thundered Sir Ralph Badgett's Curazon, then Archer, then the Langtry entry, Menace, and finally, well back of the others, Saracen.

The horses threw up clods of turf as they ran by, their riders leaning low over their necks.

Archer was stronger than Susannah had feared. When he began to move midway through the race, he challenged the others relentlessly. "That's it, boy! For England!" she heard Sunderly cry as the bay passed Curazon to take second place.

Menace was the first to drop out of contention. Susannah was aware she experienced a certain pleasure when the rather small but well-formed colt dropped back of Saracen.

As will happen in a long race, the early leader could not hold the pace he himself had set. At three-quarters of a mile, Bugle Boy ceded first place to Archer, and a roar went up from the stands. Saracen had moved up a little, but he still remained at least ten lengths back of the leaders.

"Jove, they are going at it!"

The exclamation was Sir Alden's. Looking at his watch, he gave the precise time when Archer passed the pole marking a mile. Susannah's heart sank. She had never heard of such a blistering time. It drained Bugle Boy entirely. At a mile and one-quarter there were only three horses left in contention, and Archer, in front of Curazon by four lengths, looked to be running easily. It seemed impossible that Saracen, who had not made any move at all, could overtake the bay.

But he could, and did, overtake Curazon. Susannah thought it likely that Curazon fell into third place because he had tired, but it was impossible to be sure. The certainty was that as the contestants neared the final turn, there were only two horses running seriously, and Archer was the leader by a good eight lengths.

The crowd cheered when Archer's jockey used his whip, for the racehorse spurted forward, seeming to know his rider wished him to pull away.

"Come on, boy, come on!"

Susannah was not even aware she called out until James took up her cry. "Yes! Yes! Listen to Susannah, boy! Come on!"

Of course neither Saracen nor Murdoch heard them. There were too many shouts on all sides, but if Saracen hoped to win, he must make his move. It was the last turn.

Murdoch gave Saracen the whip once on his flank. Just one stroke, no more, but it was as if the tap had been a secret signal. Suddenly Connor's black began to move, really move, against his opponent. The jockey up on Archer glanced back and deemed it necessary to apply his whip with more determination. Archer strained to answer the call, seeming to dig in. His effort was to no avail. Saracen surged by him only a moment later, with long powerful strides that seemed to lengthen the further he ran and the closer he came to the finish. For the very last stretch, almost a quarter of a mile, Saracen was utterly and magnificently alone.

In the end, the black won the Two Thousand Guineas in a record time and by an unprecedented fourteen lengths.

The crowd went wild, and Susannah blinked back tears as James squeezed her hand, crying, ''We won! My God, how we won!''

''We won!'' The cheer went up throughout the box. Susannah failed to notice whether Sunderly joined in. She had gone to fling her arms around Gussie, who returned the embrace, gasping, ''What a marvelous horse! Truly a marvelous animal! Truly! I have never seen such a performance.''

O'Neill did not come to the box to accept his congratulations. He sent word with a justly prideful Murdoch that he was being mobbed in the stableyard and wished only to escape the well-wishers by taking his winning mount home. He would, Murdoch said, toast his co-victor at Ridley.

''If he cannot come to us, then we shall go to him!'' Lady Augusta exclaimed, rising. ''To Ridley!''

The cry was taken up, and it seemed to Susannah that half of Newmarket came that night to Ridley for the most gala celebration in memory.

Susannah did take the time to visit the stables. The grooms deserved commendation, and if she hoped she might find O'Neill there, she was not wildly surprised to learn he had departed a little before.

Billy Whitlow was awaiting her, however, a cheeky grin splitting his face and his hand outstretched. He had not guessed the number of lengths by which Saracen would win. No one had, but he had come closest of all those who had wagered, guessing Saracen would defeat Archer by nine lengths. They were three guineas Susannah did not regret surrendering.

Soon after Susannah departed, the stablehands took themselves off to the Rutland Arms in Newmarket, for it was Lady Augusta's custom to stand them a round for every Ridley horse that won. They'd never been spotted as many drinks as they were that evening, but however riotous the mood at the Rutland Arms, the atmosphere at Ridley seemed scarcely less so. Champagne flowed more freely than water, but then, water did not flow at all that night.

Only Susannah drank sparingly. O'Neill had come, had toasted Lady Augusta, Murdoch, Saracen, and even himself, but he had slipped away only a little after, without speaking to her.

As she recalled it, their first really amiable exchange had been about Saracen. He knew she understood how much the victory meant to him. But he had not lifted his glass to her, had not inclined his head in her direction, had not even flicked her a glance.

Perhaps she ought not to have cared. He was only a temporary head trainer, after all. Certainly she ought not to have been surprised. He'd done much the same after Barley Boy's win.

She did care, though. And she had not steeled herself sufficiently against Connor's coldness.

She was hurt, and angry, and most inexplicably of all, felt abandoned.

When Sunderly asked her to walk out onto the terrace with him sometime after midnight, Susannah was glad to go. The noise and unrelenting gaiety within the house had begun to take a toll. She'd a headache, and she was hot, and her smile came with increasing effort.

For a little, Susannah stood forgetful of her companion. The air, though soft and warm, was cooler than in the house, and had the advantage of being scented by the roses in the garden. She was breathing deeply of it, scarcely listening to Sunderly, when he turned abruptly and seized her hands in his.

"The week has been so short. I can scarce believe that I must leave tomorrow."

The amiable, companionable man she'd regarded almost as a brother seemed a stranger. Sunderly was gazing down at her as if he would compel her to return his feelings.

"The time has passed quickly." Susannah tried for a light tone, thinking some of Sunderly's depth of feeling might have to do with the amount of champagne that had been served up. His grip on her hands did not loosen, however.

"You'll miss me, I hope, when I am in far-off Scotland?"

His voice was almost husky, and Susannah redoubled her effort to be light. "When you are in far-off Scotland, sir, I doubt you'll think of anything but fish. I won't blame you, though, and even wish you the finest catch ever."

Sunderly had in fact imbibed more than was usual for him, and though he had the sense that somehow Susannah had turned his sentiments about, he was not up to thinking how. "I shall think of you the entire time, Lady Susannah. You are so very beautiful. I do so want you to be mine!"

Pulling her closer to him, he leaned down and kissed her.

Susannah realized Sunderly's intention the moment his eyes fastened on her lips. Her first instinct was to bolt, but she stopped herself, deciding quite calculatedly it would be for the best if she tested his embrace. Perhaps . . . perhaps something unexpected would happen.

The unexpected did occur. Susannah had expected to feel unmoved or perhaps only a little moved. She was, instead, ever so slightly but certainly repulsed.

She knew Sunderly did not deserve such a reaction. He was certainly not a bad man. He was attractive and well-mannered, and he admired her. But Susannah had no control over the way her mouth stiffened beneath his, and she shrank away, pulling her lips from his reach, placing her hands upon his chest to hold him off.

"I . . ."

She knew he meant to say he loved her, and she said quickly, to stave off the worst, "Someone comes, my lord. Please, I do not care to be found like this."

Susannah had not, in fact, heard anyone, but providence, perhaps deciding to take a hand in her affairs, brought to them, in the moment's taut, uncertain silence that fell between her and her companion, the sound of footsteps upon the gravel in the garden below. When Susannah pulled back again, Sunderly released her.

But he looked as if at any moment he might catch her up in his arms again. Quietly, smoothly, Susannah said, "I am grateful you did not think to compromise me, my lord."

She had appealed to his better nature and found it. Sunderly grimaced unsteadily. "I would never do such a thing. You must know it!"

"I am glad to know it. But now I wish you to take me in, my lord. I have left my grandmother's guests long enough."

Poor Sunderly. He did not want to end the *tête-à-tête*. But when Susannah moved to go inside alone, his manners obliged him to catch up with her and escort her where she wished to be.

"Mary! I did not think to find you here, when I gave you the night off."

Susannah stared in considerable surprise at her maid. Mary's head drooped. "I'd naught else to do, my lady."

"Naught else? I thought . . . ." Susannah caught herself. She had thought Mary interested in one of the grooms, and had assumed the girl would go to the Rutland Arms with him. But that drooping head proclaimed a lovers' quarrel, and Susannah let the matter drop. "Well, whatever the reason, I am glad you are here. I am so weary I might have gone to bed fully dressed."

And she was that weary. She could feel her head droop in exact imitation of Mary's, yet when the girl left her, Susannah lay wide awake in her bed.

Sunderly's kiss came back to her. She'd learned one thing with certainty: she would not accept his offer of marriage. No matter the battle she would have with her father, she would not marry a man whose embrace made her stiffen.

Never. She knew how a kiss could be. She knew what desire was. She had felt it.

"Damn!"

She shot up from her bed. Thoughts she did not wish to entertain hovered just at the edge of her mind, and suddenly her room seemed too confining and too stuffy. Hard upon the notion to escape came the decision where to go.

Susannah was actually smiling as she hurried to her wardrobe and dragged out a muslin she could slip on by herself. A linen towel lay neatly folded by the washbowl. Picking it up, she remembered to collect her comb as well.

She only needed her shoes to slip quietly out of the house. A few revelers could still be heard singing lustily in the music room, for Susannah had retired before Gussie and the staunchest of the regulars. As she hurried through the gardens, though, the boisterous laughter faded away, and she was surrounded by the calmer sounds of the night.

A full, luminous moon lit her path. It shone through the trees in the woods, and it illuminated her pool. Wading into it, Susannah laughed suddenly and splashed moonbeams over herself. The air was warm, but the water was warmer, and felt deliciously satiny slipping over her.

Susannah had come to avoid thinking of O'Neill. The memory of his kiss and how differently she had responded to it from Sunderly's had sent her running from the house.

Foolish girl, she chided herself. Where easier to think of him than in her velvety pool, though it was not the sun upon her, but the silvery, shimmering light of the moon?

He had been just there. Her eyes sighted the spot in the shadows, where he had stood stock-still, his eyes fixed upon her.

Susannah shivered, though she was not cold. How set his expression had been. She might have thought him angry with her, but for the unmistakable interest blazing in his eyes.

She'd not seen that warmth again, or anything near it, except for that moment when she had come slowly to her senses after her tumble from Delilah. His concern had been fleeting, however. Almost in the next breath, though she was hurt and aching, he'd deliberately unnerved her, mentioning the pool while Sunderly stood listening to the exchange.

When Susannah rose from her pool after a while, she still thought of Connor. Since her return from Deerbourne, when he had not been cool and biting, he'd been hot and short-tempered. He seemed a man . . . not unmoved. The thought startled her. She stopped in the act of combing her hair. Not unmoved . . . angered, perhaps?

But what had she done to anger him? She resumed her ministrations to her hair, then slowly slipped on her chemise and dress. How could she have vexed or disturbed him, when she had not even been at Ridley, and the last time he had seen her, it would be putting it mildly to say he had looked at her with naught but approval?

He looked at other women with approval and did not subsequently bite their heads off. At least he did not seem to have cut up at Lady Marissa.

Why only her?

Linen towel and comb in hand, Susannah wandered out of the woods. Ridley lay to her right, several rooms still ablaze with light. Without giving herself time to think, she turned left.

In fact the trainer's cottage was closer than Ridley from where she stood. Dragging the comb through her hair again, Susannah decided she would see if there was a light on in his cottage. If there was . . . A grim smile took the place of a thought. She had better use the light, first, to see if he had company. She would not learn much from O'Neill about his change of mood if Lady Marissa had escaped her admittedly unappealing husband.

Years before, Susannah had planted a moonflower vine along the fence bordering Mulcahey's cottage. Flowering only in the night, its white blossoms were impossibly large and soft and fragrant. Picking one, she breathed deeply of it as she followed the fence back around to the back of the cottage.

There was a light in the kitchen. She could not see in the window, however, even when she went up on tiptoe.

The kitchen door stood open, perhaps to let in the night

air. Susannah approached it slowly. No voices could be heard in the kitchen, but that did not mean the Irishman was alone. At the thought of what O'Neill and another might be doing in silence, Susannah came to her senses.

It was well after midnight. What was she thinking? The light from the kitchen spilled out the door, illuminating her, and she turned quickly, before he came to see her there, but even as she did, O'Neill appeared.

Glancing out his door into the night, he caught her movement and called out roughly, "Who's there?"

18

SUSANNAH almost took to her heels. She did not, only because she feared Connor would give chase, and as anxious as she was to duck away, she could not imagine being caught running from him.

"I say who's there?" Connor demanded, emerging from the cottage. He could make out a person's shape, but could not see who it was until she turned fully into the light. "What the devil?"

Susannah smiled slightly. "No one so august, only I. I was . . . out, and I thought if you were up I would congratulate you on Saracen's win."

He stared down at her. Her hair was loose, flowing down her back. He'd only to reach out to touch its silkiness.

"You were out?"

"Yes." Susannah thought better of saying where she had been. "I picked you a flower for your victory." She held out the moonflower. Connor looked very tall, for he stood on the kitchen step above her. She could not read his expression, the light was behind him, but she did not think he was smiling. Nor did he take the flower. "It's not much," she conceded, "but I thought it almost as beautiful as Saracen's run."

Slowly, reluctantly it seemed, Connor reached for the flower. Before he took it, however, a loud hissing sound broke the quiet of the night. Answering the imperative summons, he turned back into the cottage, and Susannah trailed after him. She considered laying the flower upon the table and leaving, but then Connor glanced back over his shoulder and caught her, standing uncertainly, her hand upon a chair.

"Blast!" He let go the iron kettle he'd lifted without thinking because he'd been mesmerized by the sight of her there in his doorway. He had never considered she would follow him inside.

Susannah came forward at once, concern on her face. "Did you burn yourself?"

"No, I only cried out for your amusement." Connor glared at her, then at his burning hand. Idiot, he castigated himself. She's only a woman, you bloody fool.

As the only treatment Connor seemed inclined to administer to himself was that to be achieved by waving his hand to and fro, Susannah asked if he had anything cold on hand.

"A cold cellar? At the trainer's cottage?"

She made allowance for the biting irony in his tone. He hurt. "Butter, then?" she tried with forebearance.

"There may be some left from dinner in the box there."

Connor gestured with a thrust of his chin to a closed box on the counter. Inside it Susannah found a very small pat of butter beside a half-slice of the bread Mrs. Barnes, who cooked for him, had made to go with his dinner.

"It's not much, but it should do. I'll need your hand," she added when Connor remained by the stove, observing her through narrowed eyes. "The butter is effective only if it is on the burn, you see."

Something flickered in his eyes, but was gone before Susannah could read it. With a half-shrug he held out his hand. There was a puffy red line across his palm. Susannah used the linen towel she'd taken to the pool to apply the balm.

Connor watched her cradle his larger hand in hers. The bones of her hand were slender and very fine, and her skin was soft and silky.

Eventually he took note of the linen towel Susannah used. He'd seen one like it in her basket that day at the pool. When

Connor looked again at her hair and saw the damp tendrils curling onto her neck, his jaw tightened.

She had been swimming. At night, only just a little ago, before she came to him, she'd been in her pool. He could imagine with dangerous ease how she had looked, her skin gleaming pearly in the moonlight.

Susannah turned slightly to claim the last of the butter. Because she was still a little damp, the thin muslin of her dress did not flow with her, but clung to her, outlining her body.

Connor jerked his hand from Susannah's grasp, startling her. She looked up in surprise, her slanted eyes widening. They were very dark, and gleamed like liquid in the candlelight.

"I'll get a bandage."

Connor abruptly strode from the room, leaving Susannah to study the empty door. No answers to the mystery of his mood were forthcoming, however. She knew only that, standing alone in his cottage, she felt almost empty, she so missed the closeness they had had.

With a sigh of frustration she turned away, and, her eye lighting upon the iron kettle he'd used to boil water, Susannah determinedly busied herself with preparing the tea Connor had been in the process of making when she interrupted him.

She recognized the porcelain pot nearby. It was John Mulcahey's, as were all the things in the cottage. Idly, pouring the hot water into it, she wondered what sort of things Connor owned. Was his teapot chipped like Mulcahey's? Did he own one, even, and teacups? He must. He must have a home. It would be a real house, she decided, not a cottage, though why she thought that, she could not have said. He seemed perfectly at ease in Mulcahey's cottage.

A few moments later, Connor pulled up short in the kitchen doorway. Had he really hoped she would leave unannounced, facing quietly into the night from which she'd emerged, leaving him, if not in peace, then untempted? Or had he hoped he would find her exactly as she was, preparing his tea, wearing a simple muslin, her honey-gold hair loose and heavy upon her slender back?

In the rustic surroundings of Mulcahey's cottage, occupied at the homely task, she shone the finer, the lovelier. She made him ache for her.

It was not Susannah's fault she'd been born English and a member of the hated country's detested aristocracy, but quite unreasonably, all the anger and frustration Connor might more properly have felt toward fate, he turned upon her.

Damn the golden Sassenach witch for coming! Did she think he was made of stone? he growled to himself even as she, sensing him behind her, turned to hold out a steaming cup. "Your tea, sir."

But Connor was not to be appeased by lightly proffered offerings. Quite the opposite. "I find I've lost my taste for tea, my lady." His mouth twisted in a mocking smile. Susannah stiffened. Slowly, eyes on his, she set the unwanted cup aside upon the counter. Connor ignored it, his eyes boring into her. "I'd much rather get to the congratulations you came to give me. You did say you came to congratulate me, did you not, Lady Susannah?"

Wary of his mood now, she nodded slowly. "Yes. I thought Saracen was magnificent."

"Ah, well, I am glad you confirmed that. I was, just for a moment, you understand, halfway to believing you came to my house alone and in the middle of the night for the same reason half a dozen other women have."

Susannah's chin shot up. Connor was smiling, but it was not a pleasant smile, and his blue eyes raked her with such a look she felt he was stripping her bare. "What do you mean?" she snapped, angry for many reasons, but most of all because he had equated her with "half a dozen" other women.

"I thought you'd come for sport," Connor explained ever so reasonably. "You know: having found her viscount's kisses too bland by half, the fine lady decides to try the hired help's embrace—again."

"That is enough!"

"Is it?" he inquired nastily as they began a strange dance. When Susannah took a step away from him and toward the

door, Connor took a step forward, toward her. He gained
ground easily, of course. "Is it enough, my lady? I thought
honesty sterling. But can it be you did not admit your motive
for creeping up to my door in the middle of the night—
alone—even to your priggish English aristocratic self?"

"I had nothing to admit to myself! I came to congratulate
you, as I said."

Connor was so very close that to look up at him, Susannah
had to arch her neck severely. Behind her she could feel the
open doorway and the night, but unsettled as she was, she
did not think to run. Her focus remained upon the tall, dark,
handsome man with anger, and something else besides,
glittering in his eyes.

"Congratulations keep, my lady. You might have given
me flowers from my own garden anytime tomorrow in broad
daylight with dozens of people properly in attendance."

"How was I to know I would see you then or at any time?"
Susannah flung back. "You have avoided me all week or
been bitter as a wounded bear when purest chance threw us
together. I thought we were friends!"

"Friends!" The word seemed to goad Connor beyond all
control. Pouncing like a cat, he caught Susannah up in his
arms. "You know bloody well you came here tonight to be
more than friends."

Susannah cried out and pushed at his chest, but the outcome
of their engagement was never in doubt. Connor was far
stronger than she. And it must be said, Susannah could not
fight him in earnest. She'd not the time, perhaps. For his
mouth was upon hers so very soon.

At first Connor's kiss was a hard one. Susannah was, if
truth be told, paying for more than appearing at his cottage
still damp from her swim. He had seen her on the terrace
with Sunderly, kissing the viscount. He had seen her pull
away, too, but nonetheless, his emotions were in a roil. He
knew he ought to wish her pleasure of another's embrace.
His conscience told him he could not want the life of a nun
for her, and yet he'd been, first, so infuriated by the sight
of her in another man's arms, he'd have ripped the viscount
from her had she not pulled herself. Then, when she rejected

Sunderly, Connor had felt such a fierce gladness that he'd ended by being doubly furious with himself.

Susannah was subject to emotion as well. And she, too, had her reasons to be angry. He'd stung her deeply. She was no candidate to play his temporary bedmate!

How dare hs insinuate she was! How dare he drag her into his arms! How dare he scorn her as he did! He was not so indifferent to her. Susannah had not Connor's experience of desire, perhaps, but she recognized his desire for her. He mocked her for wanting him, yet his arms were taut beneath her hands, his grip upon her almost painful, and his kiss fierce.

A surge of fury sent Susannah arching into Connor, returning his kiss with an intensity to match his. She would make him admit she was different from the women trooping to his house. She would make him admit he wanted her!

They battled in their kiss, and laid bare, before they knew it, their desire. Susannah felt as if she'd caught fire. Or was melting. Her anger might never have been, so completely had she forgotten it. Her arms twined about Connor's neck and her fingers dived into his thick black hair.

And Connor caught Susannah to him with a groan, lifting her up, molding her against him, demanding all the sweet heat she could give and returning what he took. When he felt her tremble beneath him, he was almost lost.

Almost. His mind leaping ahead to what would happen next, Connor stopped short. Wrenching his mouth from Susannah's, he forced to his mind the facts: he was an Irishman opposed to the English; an Irishman glad to live beyond the Pale. Susannah Somerset was of the English ruling class that had plundered Ireland for so long. His people must see her as the enemy. Her people . . . He did not know how they would view him but it was of no matter.

She was also achingly beautiful. Her parted lips looked almost bruised from his kiss, her cheeks were flushed, and her eyes had gone dark and hot and liquid.

Connor did not have to school his features to grimness, he felt so grim just then, he might have been a biblical judge.

"You've a choice, Susannah. You may stay here and

become the mistress of an Irish horse trainer, perhaps getting
a brat by him, or you may go now, wiser, perhaps, and
certainly unscatched.''

Connor watched Susannah's eyes fly wide and heard her
sharp intake of breath as she registered the consequence of
the fiery passion between them. He forced an image of her
heavy with child to his mind and thrust her away from him.
Perhaps she'd called up the same image, for she did not
protest, only stared at him, the color draining from her face.

But she did not leave.

''Go! Dammit!'' His control close to snapping, Connor
took her arm and thrust her out the door. ''I don't want you
here!''

Susannah reacted then. Her hand flew to her mouth to stifle
a cry that seemed to Connor to be welling up in his own
throat. Then she whirled and ran into the night.

19

"I DON'T WANT you here!" drumming in her ears, Susannah ran until she could run no further. Her side ached so, she sank down upon an iron bench, allowing her head to fall forward into her hands as she caught her breath.

Why had she run so hard? He'd not been chasing her. Oh, no, they had reversed roles. It was she who had run him to ground in his cottage in the middle of the night—alone; he'd added that more than once.

Susannah groaned. She really hadn't realized how much she had wanted to fall into his arms again. Or she hadn't admitted the desire to herself until he had forced her to it.

Ah, but that was the wrong word. He'd not used force. There had been no need. His merest touch had turned her to liquid, warm, pulsing, yielding liquid.

Another moan escaped her, and hearing the pitiful sound, Susannah bit her lip. She had never been one to wail so. To calm her unsteady nerves, she lifted her head, inhaling deeply of the night air.

At least she knew one thing. She knew why Philip Mountjoy had gone from merely holding an exceedingly mild interest for her to half-repulsing her. She had fallen in love with another while she had not been paying attention.

Susannah clenched her hands into fists. She wanted him too. She'd have stayed with him, had he wanted her in return. But he had not.

No, that was not precisely what the Irishman had said. "I do not want you here" were his exact words.

Susannah lifted her hair from her neck. The air felt cool on her overheated skin. "I do not want you here." Her mouth quirked faintly. Might he want her elsewhere, then? She made a low, choked sound, something between a laugh and a groan.

Then it occurred to her to question whether Connor wanted her exclusively. Naive, Susannah was not. Connor was a man who attracted women as easily as a sweet attracts flies. Perhaps he had put her from him, sent her flying off into the night, although he must have known she was as near to putty as she could be and still stand, because he wanted another that night.

Susannah let the unwelcome thought lie heavy in her mind a little. Then she tossed her head. She was not vain particularly, but she did not think it was of another woman Connor had been thinking. She remembered too vividly the raggedness of his breathing after he'd released her lips. And she remembered his eyes. He had wanted her too; had wanted her at least as much as she had wanted him.

Had he sent her off to protect himself? It suddenly came to her to wonder. He had been very close to committing the unthinkable: making love to his employer's granddaughter.

Gussie would tolerate a great deal, but never that. Were he to compromise Susannah, the dowager Duchess of Beaufort would get him banned from England, closing the future opened to him with Saracen's victory.

Would he care?

She knew, even as she asked it, that he would not. O'Neill would take what he wanted, the consequences be damned, and as to being denied England, Susannah could almost hear him laugh at so desirable a consequence.

Then why? Why had he sent her off?

She gave a frustrated moan. She did not know. Perhaps he cared for her too well? Then why the biting, sarcastic manner? She did not know.

And would not know that night. She was too weary to reason her way through such tangled, uncharted territory.

She would think on Connor O'Neill in the morning, when she was fresher.

Standing, Susannah took in at last where she was. She had run further than she realized, reaching her grandmother's rolling lawns. The woods were behind her, and for some reason, she turned to look at them. As she did, a large shape separated itself from the darkness of the trees.

Within moments the shape resolved itself into a horse. Susannah frowned, for it was exceedingly strange that a horse be loose. Then the horse stepped out of the shadows, and she saw it carried a burden.

A man, Susannah realized, was lying prone upon the horse.

Her feet reacted more quickly than her mind. Susannah was already hurrying across the lawn when it came to her that only an injured man would lie so upon a mount.

She could make out few details of the man but that he lay with his head upon the horse's neck and his hand entwined in its mane. He'd lost hold of the reins. They trailed the ground, but it did not matter, the horse stood still.

"Sir?" she called as she approached, but it was the horse responded, lifting its head. "Sir?" Susannah repeated, so close now she could make out he'd dark hair. When he still did not lift his head, she put her hand on his shoulder.

He jerked awake at that, lifting his head, and though he swayed as if drunk, he whispered hoarsely, "Connor. Take me to Connor, sweeting."

The few words cost the stranger his remaining strength. He collapsed so he rolled a little. Susannah quickly reached with her hand to steady him, only to snatch that hand back.

It had encountered something wet and sticky. By the smell, she knew it to be blood.

At once Susannah sprang into action, catching up the horse's reins and hauling herself up behind the wounded man. Luckily the horse was too tired to protest the added burden.

Above the man now, Susannah could see his wound. There was a hole of the sort a bullet might make on his left side, midway between his shoulder and waist. A dark stain surrounded it. She could not tell if he bled still, nor did she take the time to stop and see. She'd nothing to stanch the flow anyway, having left her linen towel behind with the man this one wanted to see.

For the second time that night she approached Connor's cottage from the rear. A light shone still in his kitchen, for which Susannah was grateful, and she rode directly up to the back door.

"Connor!" she called, urgently but softly, lest someone unfriendly had followed the man before her. "Come quickly!"

At least Connor did not ignore her. At the next moment he appeared in the door, a thunderous scowl on his face.

"What . . . Devil take it!" Connor leapt forward suddenly, seizing the wounded man by the shoulder and lifting him. "Rory!"

"He's been wounded. Here on his back. I cannot tell if he is bleeding still."

Connor followed her gesture and swore. In the light spilling from the kitchen Susannah could see the hole in the man's coat more clearly. Studying the stain about it, she decided it was not growing.

"We must get him inside at once!"

"No! Connor . . ." Susannah caught him by the arm when he did not seem to hear her. He froze, looking up at her. "I do not think it would be wise to take him into your house."

"What else shall I do with him? Leave him to bleed to death on the step?"

"We'll take him to Nan's. It is only a little further. And no one will think to look for him there," she added quickly when Connor growled something savage. The simple statement had the effect of arresting his move to lift Rory down. Into the silence Susannah said softly, "Anyway, Nan's an excellent nurse, for all her years, and she has some, ah, admiration for you. She'll be loyal."

Connor raked his hand through his hair. The old woman would be loyal. She knew who he was, though how, he didn't know. He had stopped to visit her several times, and pressed her more than once, but when Nan did not care to be pressed, she turned vague. In response to his questions, she'd only muttered something about having been Lady Augusta's personal maid before she married.

Still, the point was she'd not betray him. "Get down, then." He conceded Susannah her point, but not gracefully. "I'll take him to Nan's. I want you well away from here as soon as possible."

Susannah marked his concern for her even as she shook her head. "Nan's resilient, but I think I ought to be the one to wake her. You would give her a pointless fright. Hurry and close up the cottage while I strike out. "You'll catch us. I cannot go very quickly."

"No."

"Hurry, Connor! We've not time to argue. You'll make much faster progress with me along to help hold him. Truly, if I hear the militia pounding down around us, I promise I shall run for cover. Now, go!"

Connor did not leap to do Susannah's bidding. It went entirely against his grain to involve her. Susannah feared he meant to prevail by lifting her bodily from the horse, when the man before her weighed in with a groan.

"Damn!" There was such frustration in Connor's voice, Susannah bit her lip, but he wasted no more time on argument. Turning abruptly into his cottage, he barked, "Very well! I'll meet you at the gate."

It did not take long to reach Nan's really, but the journey seemed to last an eternity. Susannah felt very exposed on the back of the horse in the moonlight. A troop of militia coming up the lane from the heath would be bound to see them. But worst of all was her anxiety for the man Connor had called Rory. He groaned once or twice and seemed to weaken, for the hand that held so tightly to his horse's mane went limp.

"Where did you find him?" Connor demanded after he'd closed the gate behind them.

"As I crossed the lawn to the house, his horse emerged from the woods. I went to investigate as soon as I realized there was a man lying atop him."

"Of course," Connor bit out, rather dampeningly, all things considered.

Susannah's mouth tightened. "As matters turned out, it was a good thing I did go. You ought to be grateful I am not afraid of my own shadow. He asked for you by name, a fact I don't doubt the militia would be intrigued to learn."

Connor did not, as Susannah believed he ought, thank her. "Fools and children," he muttered instead.

His voice carried quite clearly. "And which do you consider yourself?" Susannah inquired none too sweetly. "God has certainly looked out for you, I'd say."

Connor looked up at her then. His hair had fallen onto his brow, but even so, Susannah could see his handsome face was very bleak. "Me? Oh, I am the greatest fool of all, without a doubt."

"Devil it!" Susannah exclaimed, moved by his expression to defend Connor to himself. "You are the least foolish man I've ever known. I am certain it is he"—she gestured to Rory—"who has gotten you into this situation somehow or other. But you'll see. It will come out right. Nan will take good care of him."

Connor's hand tightened upon the reins he held. She was so fiercely defensive on his behalf, though he had hurt her. So loyal, and brave, and so beautiful. Her dress had ridden up as they plodded along, baring a grand bit of her long leg for his pleasure. He'd have given a great deal to press a kiss to her rounded calf, before he told her she'd mistaken his meaning.

But there was no good to be gained by telling her he'd fallen in love with her. Or explaining he thought himself a fool because he'd leave her as soon as he could without a backward glance.

At the thought, Connor let out a long breath. "Yes," he said, his voice unsteady to his own ears. "I am sure Nan will nurse him well. Ah, thank God." The last was said because Nan's rear door had come into view. "Can you slip down while I hold to Rory?"

Susannah could and did, and realized belatedly that her dress had hiked up on her legs. Connor could not have missed the sight she'd afforded him. He had walked almost even with her bared leg.

"Hurry, lass!" he said into the dark, such concern in his voice that Susannah called herself a fool as she ran up to Nan's back door and knocked softly. Of course, it had been his wounded friend concerned him, not her legs.

Considering the hour Susannah crawled into her bed, she awoke early. Alert at once, she was possessed of an indefinable sense of urgency, and her first thought was that she must get to Nan's as quickly as possible.

Reasoning that if she encountered the militia she would fare best dressed fittingly, Susannah chose one of her most fashionable riding habits, but she doubted her need for haste when she dismounted behind Nan's cottage. Nothing looked amiss. Chickens ran loose in the yard, and the kitchen door was open to let in the morning breeze.

She mounted the steps quietly and found a man seated at the table, facing the door. She stared, for he was Rory. Though he looked pale, otherwise he showed little sign of his injury as he went about the prosaic task of eating what looked to be porridge.

Susannah had never thought to find him up so soon, but then, she'd not been allowed to stay and see how badly he'd been wounded. Nan and Connor had sent her off before she'd even gotten a good look at him.

It surprised Susannah to see how young he was. She had assumed him to be Connor's age, but he did not look much older than she. Her breath caught in her throat when he half-turned, as if listening for a sound from the hallway. His profile explained a great deal. Perfectly chiseled, it could have been an exact, if younger and less mature, copy of Connor's. There were other resemblances as well. The younger man's hair, though not soot black, was dark and thick and wavy. He'd the same high cheekbones as his brother, and equally firm but sensuous mouth.

He looked up suddenly and saw her. Susannah registered that his eyes were not blue, but brown, even as she saw they could spark with a roguish admiration, no matter how weakened his condition.

"Well, well! And who might you be, my beauty?" Rory

grinned slowly, but almost before the words were out, he
took in her fashionable clothes, and his brown eyes widened.
"Never say you are my savior of last night!"

"Lady Susannah Somerset."

It was Connor who spoke. His approach unnoticed by
either Susannah or Rory, he stood in the doorway that led
to Nan's little sitting room. Something tightened in
Susannah's chest at the sight of him. His eyes were veiled
and unreadable, but she did not think he was pleased she'd
come. "My brother, Rory, my lady," he continued in the
same even, slightly ironic tone. "As you can see, the lad
is not at death's door."

Rory grinned merrily, an expression Susannah thought
looked natural to him. "Och! To be sure, it willt ake more
than a single flesh wound to put me anyplace so unpleasant.
And even if I were near death, the sight of so beauteous a
lady would restore me right enough! I say, Connor," he
continued, addressing his brother but not removing his
admiring gaze from Susannah, "you are not going to mind
Liam's opinion, surely. You're mad if you do."

"What does the brat mean?" Liam's rough voice preceded
him into the kitchen. "Sure and you better mind . . ."

The large man's voice trailed off abruptly when he entered
the kitchen and saw who stood there. For a long moment,
as all three men studied their unexpected guest, there was
silence. Rory's regard was entirely approving. Liam's
uncertain, even wary, and Connor's . . . Susannah could not
tell, as usual.

She'd a sudden impulse to do something startling, dance
a jig maybe, to surprise him into betraying some emotion.
It was the most fleeting of impulses. Almost before she
registered it, it evaporated, and she was left, again, with the
tightness in her chest.

"Rory, go on with Liam," Connor released Susannah from
his gaze when he flicked a look at his brother. "I'll join you
shortly."

Rory did not argue, though Susannah suspected he did not
generally obey his brother so readily. He rose swiftly from
his place, but did take the time to bow to her. "It was my

pleasure, Lady Susannah. I thank you very much for the service you did me last night, and I wish you to know I think my brother's a fool.''

''Dammit!'' There was such force in the low oath, Rory took a step backward. Connor's eyes pinned him nonetheless. ''Tell me whose bloody militia you think it was you so narrowly escaped last night before you fling the word 'fool' about.''

Reluctantly, shamefacedly, Rory muttered. ''The Sassenach.''

Connor did not need to tell him to go again. Rory stalked stiffly through the door to the hall, Liam on his heels. Susannah listened to their footsteps recede down the hallway, then the front door of the cottage swing open and shut.

The sound seemed to act as a release upon her. For the first time since she'd stepped into the kitchen, Susannah found her voice. ''You are going,'' she said to the tall, handsome, and just at that moment entirely forbidding man who stood across the small room from her.

Connor did not have to answer. It was this she'd dreaded upon awakening—that with the arrival of Rory, his true business in England was done.

''I wrote a note for you.''

Susannah did not watch Connor extract an envelope from the pocket of the rough workman's jacket he wore. Her eyes were fixed on his face. All the force of personality that normally animated his expression, giving life to his handsomeness, seemed to have settled in the hard, square set of his jaw.

He did not move to hand her the note he'd written. He laid it on the table by him. ''It doesn't say much, certainly not enough. There is no way to say thank you enough.''

''Are you coming back?''

There was no hesitation. ''No.''

Susannah felt as if something inside her fell away. She only remained standing because she'd long practice bearing up to her father when he read her a lecture. Only this was so much worse than any scene with Beaufort had ever been.

As if he hoped to soften the blow with inconsequences,

Connor added, "The meet is over, and Mulcahey will return soon now, and I've left—"

"You came for Rory, didn't you?"

There was the briefest flicker of hesitation, as if, even then, Connor was not certain he could trust her with what was patently obvious. Then, unexpectedly, some of the stiffness drained from him. "Yes, I did. And now I've got him, I must leave before the militia comes. For everyone's sake, it would be best of no O'Neills were to be found at Ridley. Will you deliver this second note to your grandmother?"

Susannah had not seen him take two notes from his pocket, and followed his gesture as he pointed to the table, but her eyes went no further than his hand. He'd long fingers, well-shaped and strong. She could remember how gently they had stroked her.

"Connor." He went very still, and Susannah had to wait a moment before he lifted his eyes from the notes upon the table to look at her. "You are in my debt, are you not?" she asked him.

Wary suddenly, he regarded her in silence before he acknowledged the truth slowly. "I owe you more than I can ever repay, Susannah."

"I've a way you could discharge such an impossible debt tenfold! Take—"

His hand, the hand she'd admired only a moment before, balled into a fist and came crashing down upon the table, cutting her off. There were suddenly harsh white lines by his mouth. "Don't, Susannah." The fierce command was nothing to her. Susannah started to speak, but he cut her off again. "An Irish cottage beyond the Pale of English refinement is no setting for you. We would both grow to loathe the situation. Now I must go."

He turned, prepared, it seemed, to stride out of her life with nothing more than that final unyielding announcement.

"Connor! I won't let you go like this."

Susannah reached him before he had taken a full step, grabbing his arm, her jaw set as hard as his. At another time Connor might have laughed. Lady Susannah Somerset did not catch him back to plead or cajole, but to regard him furiously for denying her.

He did not laugh. He couldn't have, even had he not felt as if something were being torn from him. He could see too easily beneath Susannah's anger. Her eyes were dark with an anguish for which he, and he alone, was responsible.

"God, Susannah, don't do this." He was holding her too now, but whereas Susannah held to him, Connor held her off. "Don't. It can't be. I . . . I am so sorry. I had no intention of causing this."

"But you did, dammit!" she argued. "Now—"

"Now I must go before it gets worse."

He kissed her, against his will it seemed, for he still held her as he bent down, almost bruising her lips with the force of his. Then he was gone, striding down the hall and disappearing out the front door of Nan's cottage without a backward glance.

20

THE MILITIA came later that day. The captain asked Lady Augusta if there had been any unusual activity reported at Ridley the night before, then asked specifically after her trainer, Connor O'Neill.

"But the Irishman is my trainer no longer, Captain. By prearrangement, he left last night, after the finish of the meet. He has stables in Ireland, you see, and only came to help out at Ridley as a favor to an old friend, John Mulcahey."

"And his racehorse, my lady?" the captain asked. "We understand he owned a brilliant racehorse. Did he take the colt?"

"He better not have done!" Lady Augusta exclaimed with vigor. At the captain's surprised look, she smiled smugly. "I bought the colt from him, you see."

Susannah, whose support Lady Augusta had most particularly requested for the interview, only just managed to hide her astonishment. Gussie had bought Saracen? And, more important, had known Connor meant to leave after the meet? Susannah did not believe it. Her grandmother was acting.

And asking a most important question. "Now, I wish to know something, Captain," Lady Augusta exclaimed, allowing her hand to flutter to her throat. "Did my O'Neill commit some crime?"

The soldier smiled to himself at the old lady's use of the

possessive. Really, he thought, she was a grand old thing, and he hurried to assure her that neither she nor her grand-daughter, surely one of the loveliest young women he had ever seen, had been in danger. "Mr. O'Neill committed no crime that we are aware of, my lady. We only wanted to question him in connection with another, younger man, also named O'Neill."

"Well, I am relieved to know I did not harbor someone dangerous, Captain!" Lady Augusta gave him a quite convincingly relieved smile. "I'd have felt simply awful."

The captain had nothing left to do but thank Lady Augusta for her assistance, such as it had been, and allow his eyes to feast one last time upon Susannah before he departed. The door had no more than closed on him before Lady Augusta flicked a searching look at her granddaughter. "I do wonder what you, Susannah, think of O'Neill's sudden disappearance."

"I?" Susannah detected a slightly ragged edge to her voice and tried to overcome it. "O'Neill never made me privy to his thoughts, Gussie. You did not, then, know he meant to leave? And what of Saracen?" she continued without giving her grandmother time to answer the purely rhetorical question. "Did you really purchase him?"

Lady Augusta laughed. "Of course I have not bought Saracen! O'Neill would never have sold him. But what would you? I did not care to have that captain hanging about Ridley until heaven knows when, waiting for O'Neill to return and claim his nag. I do not care for the good captain well enough to endure his company so long. He was so prim, don't you think?"

For the first time that day, Susannah felt the corners of her mouth soften into something approximating a smile. "I think you are outrageous, Gussie. And very loyal."

"Loyal to those I like," Lady Augusta agreed easily. Then added softly, "And I did like O'Neill very much."

"Yes, well . . ." Susannah rose and occupied herself with smoothing down her skirts. "All this excitement has made me, ah, restless. I think I'll go along and take a walk. Until dinner, Gussie."

It was not the last long walk Susannah would take that summer. Indeed, she felt as if she plodded through the rest of July and August. Swimming reminded her of O'Neill so strongly, she had to ration her visits to her pool. Her garden demanded her attention, but visiting Nan was a trial. Inevitably, it seemed, she would find herself in her nurse's kitchen, where she would equally inevitably end by replaying that last morning over and over, imagining all the different things she might have said.

She ought to have been more persuasive. She would have been had she known how imminent the end was. But it had come so suddenly! She had not thought her wishes through. She had not been prepared with cogent arguments; had not known to plead she would be devastated if he left her.

How could she have known? She had only just come to the realization that she loved him at all a few hours before he took himself away. She had never been in love. How could she have suspected how she would ache for word of him? How she would rail against him for leaving her?

He'd not wanted to leave her. It had not been easy. She had only to recall the look in his eyes. There had been pain in them. But there had been determination too. And it was that that had won out. It came to Susannah that the change in Connor after she returned from Deerbourne had had to do with his decision to leave her behind. Apart from her, he'd decided her country or her class or both were too much for him. And he'd gone, leaving her with so little. She knew not where he lived, what he did, or how he fared. And she would never know. Damn him!

The remainder of Susannah's "last" summer was not memorable. She interested herself in little, though she did rouse herself one afternoon to speak her mind to James, perhaps because his difficulties, too, had to do with love.

She was in the gardens when James came upon her. He sank down by her, and when she returned his greeting only vaguely, her cousin regarded her with some concern.

"You seem a trifle abstracted these days, Susannah."

She shrugged, then cast him a perceptive look of her

own. "Nor do you seem exactly merry yourself, James."

"No." Susannah watched him scratch at the gravel with the toe of his shiny Hessian. "It's Phoebe," he admitted at last, sighing. "She spent hours talking to that naval officer at Major Hornbeck's last night, and said hardly a word to me."

There was a pause; then with more energy than she had shown in a time, Susannah asked, "Do you know what I think, James?"

Her cousin noted the spark lighting her eye and asked half-ruefully, "Do I want to?"

"Perhaps not. But I do believe I shall tell you anyway. Phoebe is not worth your little finger, James." He looked so startled, Susannah actually smiled. "I do mean it. You are my cousin, James, and I hate thinking of the life you will lead with her, regardless how much money she brings to cushion the blows. You deserve better, and may have it, if you only look about you."

"Why, what do you mean?"

"Mary Wardley," Susannah said with finality. "By my reckoning, you have spent as much time chatting with Mary as you have with Phoebe—more, actually—but you have not considered how easy you are in her company, because your mind has been set upon Phoebe." Susannah gave him a sympathetic look. "I know Mary is not so enticing as Phoebe, nor so rich, but Mary is pretty in her own way, has an adequate portion, and will prove the better wife. Just think of this, James: what is the first thing that will go through your mind when you are wedded to Phoebe and she gives you the happy news that she is increasing?"

James flushed and looked away, embarrassed to be speaking of such a thing with a lady, even if she was his cousin. But Susannah was confident he had taken her point. With Phoebe he would never be certain his children were his own unless they favored him.

At the end of August Susannah returned to Deerbourne and the inevitable interview with Beaufort. He was more relaxed than usual. Lady Esther affected him for the better, though she was away in Kent visiting relatives. Still, it was no easy matter to inform him his candidate for her husband would not do.

Susannah was not aware of it, but a certain light with which her father was not unfamiliar lit her eyes as she began her rehearsed speech. It was admirably succinct. "I have decided against Sunderly, Father. He has two things to recommend him: he comes of a good family and he has exquisite manners. Otherwise, he is only an amiable, generally attractive man of mediocre intellect and strength. I do not care to ally myself with so little."

Though Beaufort subjected her to a long moment of study, Susannah did not falter. She did not know precisely what she would do, but she did know she could not marry Sunderly. Her certainty was unmistakable, and in the end, his grace accepted he'd little choice unless he wished to drag his daughter to the altar.

"I see." He conceded the issue of Philip Mountjoy gracefully. Susannah felt almost light-headed to have won so easily, but her father was not entirely done. "We shall speak no more of Sunderly, then, but you cannot deny that you needs must marry someone, Susannah. You have had two Seasons to look about you. I trust that this year you will find someone worthy of you."

Beaufort did not add that he would take a firmer hand in her affairs if she did not find anyone, but Susannah read the threat in his eyes. She did not much blame him. As she wrote to Lady Augusta, "Of course Father wishes to be free of me, that he may devote himself to Lady Esther. I can understand his impatience. He must feel he has lived long enough without her."

Lady Augusta, after reading Susannah's letter, sat down to pen one of her own. Having little use for the truth when it did not serve her purpose, she shamelessly altered the account Susasnnah had given of the interview with her father.

Lady Augusta's letter was addressed to the Earl of Iveagh.

My dearest boy,

I wonder, really I do, if you are astonished to find I know where and how to address my letter to you. I did suspect once or twice that you guessed I knew from the first you were old Iveagh's grandson. Breeding will tell, dear boy, as one who knows horses as well as you must be aware. You are ''my'' Iveagh's spitting image. I use ''my'' loosely, of course, for I was far too young to do more than admire him prodigiously from afar, but admire him I did. You, I am pleased to say, resemble him very, very closely.

Enough of such flattery! I am only writing to inform you that Saracen is very well and that I intend to run him in the fall. I shall not send you your winnings, however. Dear boy, I simply do not trust the mails. You will be obliged to come to Ridley to collect them. Mulcahey has readjusted nicely, though you are missed in the stables. I am told the grooms agree there is no one to equal you. As I said, breeding will tell.

I miss Susannah greatly. She is in London for the Little Season. Happily she prevailed upon Beaufort to accept her decision not to marry the Viscount Sunderly, that bland thing who mucked up her race week. However, Beaufort, who has defied all the laws of good sense and fallen in love at his advanced age, is positively feverish to get Susannah off his hands that he may attend, undistracted, to his inamorata. By his decree Susannah has until Christmas to accept an offer of marriage. If she does not, he will choose a husband for her. I do hope Susannah can find someone she at least likes, for I cannot be optimistic that Beaufort will select anyone of whom I can approve. After all, Sunderly was his choice.

I do hope to see you at the fall meet, my boy. I promise that if you return, I shall offer you accommodations slightly better than those you had in Mulcahey's cottage.

Yours,
Augusta Somerset

Connor read with a half-smile the first paragraphs of the letter. He had thought Lady Augusta suspected who he was, but he had not realized she had known from the first—known and held her peace, amused by the charade, no doubt, and curious to discover his game.

Had she suspected his growing interest in her granddaughter? Undoubtedly. She'd not otherwise have reported so fully on Susannah. It was that part of the letter he read without a smile.

Susannah. Connor missed her more than he had feared. She haunted his dreams. Sometimes they were sweet dreams and did not stop with kissing, but twice they'd been horrifying. She'd bounced off that gig of her cousin's before he could catch her, and he'd awakened in a cold sweat, only to realize he would not, in very truth, ever see her again.

Damn! He had hoped distance from her would help. And certainly there were enough willing Irish lovelies about to divert him from thoughts of a cool English beauty.

Ah, but he had long since ceased to think of her as cool. It was thought of her response that last time he'd held her that plagued his nights. As did the thought that he would not be the man to show her what lay beyond a kiss.

And English? She was undoubtedly that, but was she, then, necessarily his enemy or the enemy of his people? What was an enemy? An English girl who protected him from the militia, then later brought his wounded brother safely to him? Or an Irishman, and a cousin who would betray family and friends for naught but a few English coins?

It had taken two months to discover the identity of the traitor in the Greenboys. Rory had told Connor who among his confederates had argued against believing the warning Connor had passed them through the young man, Roger. There were three who had maintained that Connor either had been fooled by the English when he'd visited the jail or had sent them a false message simply to keep Rory out of danger.

One of the three young men had been English, one Protestant Irish, and one a cousin to Rory and Connor. Dick O'Neill, Rory's age, and a friend, had stayed many times at Glendalough Castle over the years, getting into mischief with his cousins. Yet it was he Liam had seen slipping by the back door into the house of a known English spymaster in Dublin. Liam had been following him for weeks, protesting all the while, for he could not credit Connor would hold a cousin and an Irishman suspect. "Why, Dick would not have seen Rory killed, man! It cannot be he."

It had been. When they took him, Dick had three thousand pounds in his pocket. By Liam's reckoning the traitor had made a thousand for each Irishman he'd caused to die, for two had been killed in Norwich and Seamus Fitzgerald had been hanged after the first ambush.

When Liam returned with the news, Connor's mood, already foul, had turned the darker. Rory left Glendalough altogether, preferring his sister's house, though she'd five children, for his convalescence.

It was Liam, a close cousin and large enough to dare, who finally spoke. He had been at Glendalough a week, the longest he had been with Connor since they'd returned from England, and he'd observed little to his liking.

When, after dinner Connor ordered, as it had become his custom, a bottle of claret, with the certain intention of retreating with it to his study, Liam frowned but had the wisdom not to refer to the bottle.

"What do ye think, Connor, of a man who knows himself to have been wrong and admits it? Do ye think such a one a fool?"

If Connor's mind was fuzzy with the drink he had already consumed, he did not show it. The look he gave Liam was hard as flint. "What bit of wisdom is it you would repent, Liam? Out with it. I've not the patience just now for hypothetical discussions."

"Very well. I was wrong about Lady Susannah Somerset. I'd no way o' knowin' what she meant to ye, Connor. Ye never let on. Ye'll not drink forever. Ye're not the sort to drink a bottle of claret an evening forever, but I've the fear ye'll never do so well as ye might, were she here. Aye, I know," he went on before Connor could do more than lift an ironic brow. "I was hard against her. But I've asked myself this, after the business in Dublin, what's the more important: to be English and a loyal friend or Irish and a bloody traitor? Damn Dick's black, greedy soul, the answer's obvious!"

Connor drained off his glass of claret before he looked back at Liam through heavy, half-lidded eyes. "You'd accept an English duke's daughter as the lady of Glendalough, then,

Liam? Hold her in the same esteem as an Irish lass?''

"Esteem?" Suddenly Liam's broad face split into a grin. "How could I not hold a woman who looks like Lady Susannah in esteem? Aye, Connor. As I say, it's thinkin' I've been doing. She's brave, she's loyal; she can ride any horse that runs, and she's the rarest beauty I ever beheld. If ye cannot make her Irish, man, then you're not half the lad I think ye to be!''

21

IN LONDON, Beaufort at first had reason to be pleased. Susannah came dutifully to town, and after word got about that she did not mean to become the Viscountess Sunderly, she was again surrounded by the gentlemen of the bachelor set. It was only after a little—two weeks, perhaps three— that he began to have misgivings. "Susannah does not behave as an ordinary girl would," he complained to Lady Esther. "She looks through every man who approaches her, no matter how gallant or attractive, as if he were as insubstantial as the air."

Happily for Susannah, Lady Esther was he firm ally. "But Susannah is no ordinary girl, Alistair," the good lady observed, almost with surprise. "My dear, she is rare, and it would never do to rush her into marriage for nothing more than the sake of marrying her off. She would wither on the wine were she joined for life to most of those young men she does, I confess I agree, look right through. You'll see. She will find just the man for her."

The duke was little proof against Lady Esther's wise smile. And he agreed with her in some part. The pups swarming his daughter did all seem bland beside her, lacking half her m ettle or fire or warmth. He did want to see Susannah safely bestowed, as it was right and proper that young ladies marry, but perhaps Lady Esther had mellowed him, his grace admitted half-ruefully, for he found he desired there to be at least the prospect of love between Susannah and her husband.

There was one bright note for Beaufort that fall. It pleased him that James had gotten over his infatuation with Phoebe Limley. Beaufort had not approved of the girl, but he liked very well James's new interest, Miss Mary Wardley.

One night at a ball given by Lady Dorthea St. Clare in Mayfair, he and Susannah were standing together as the couple danced by, Mary smiling sweetly up at James, and Beaufort expressed his approval. "Miss Wardley would be a good match for James. I wonder if his interest in her is serious. Do you know, Susannah?"

As the head of his family, her father had a right to interest himself in James's affairs. Indeed, Susannah rather thought he had a responsibility to do more. "James is seriously interested in Mary and she in him. Unfortunately, Mr. Wardley does not share his daughter's sentiments. He favors Lord Windemere, who may be a roué but has the luck to be a wealthy one. If you truly favor a match between James and Mary, Father, you might consider tipping the balance in James's favor."

Beaufort's brow lifted ever so slightly, but otherwise he made no response to Susannah's suggestion. She did not press him. One did not press his grace, but she smiled to herself when she saw him a little later in conversation with James.

James guessed correctly who it was had inspired his uncle to remark, cool as you please, that he believed a wedding present of twenty thousand pounds would be appropriate if his nephew chose a girl as worthy as Mary Wardley for a wife. James very nearly choked upon his claret. Twenty thousand pounds would undoubtedly turn Mr. Wardley from Windemere.

As soon as Beaufort left him, James went to tell Mary the news, then looked around for Susannah, half of a mind to twirl her around in his arms. He hoped she would laugh. She hadn't seemed to be in a mood to laugh for a long while.

He found her with some of her set, the others trading the latest *on-dits* as they waited for the musicians to return from their interval, while Susannah, as had been true so often that fall, appeared to be only half-listening to the conversation going on around her.

She was beautiful, though, regardless of how abstracted she was. James approved the dark gold of the satin slip she wore. Her eyes seemed the darker and more mysterious in contrast to it, and her hair a deeper, richer gold.

She held herself well. James had always admired Susannah's carriage. It helped that she was slender and had those long legs, but even had she been tiny, no one would have had to inquire which of the ladies in the group was a duke's daughter.

"James!" Susannah saw him, and that rare warmth lit her eyes. She was holding out her hand in greeting when Lady Dinah Farley, one of the young ladies standing near her, looking in the opposite direction, asked of no one in particular, "Whoever is he?"

It was not an unusual question, but something in the girl's voice prompted everyone to follow her gaze.

"Good Lord." James blinked, looked again, and listened thunderstruck as one of the young men, preening because he could answer Lady Dinah's question when no one else could, replied, "The man in the doorway, Lady Dinah? Why, he is the Earl of Iveagh. He's Irish."

James swung about to look at Susannah. The expression on her face confirmed that his eyes had not deceived him. The man standing in the door was not only the Earl of Iveagh but also their grandmother's erstwhile temporary head trainer.

James had not truly doubted his eyes. There could not have been two men who looked precisely like that, with such very black hair and those brilliant blue eyes and that powerful figure. He'd the devil's own air about him too. James thought, half-ruefully, he would like just once to stand in the doorway to a crowded ballroom and create the stir the Irishman caused. It was not merely that O'Neill held himself with authority or that he was so handsome. There was, James had long thought, just the hint of something different, dangerous even, about the Irishman. It was that quality that made the women's eyes spark and the men's brows lift. Almost, James imagined, one looked to see if there was a glint of gold at his ear. Not that he looked rough as a pirate. Far from it. James could not imagine, observing Iveagh's aristocratic features now, how it was he'd not guessed the man was more than a horse trainer.

"Why have I never seen him before?" Lady Dinah inquired of Mr. Rupert Chambers, the young man who had identified the Earl of Iveagh.

Mr. Chambers was delighted to be asked, and answered with the greatest authority, "Iveagh rarely comes to England. I know of him only because, when I visited my cousin in Dublin, Iveagh came to discuss sheep with Mortimer."

"Sheep?" Lady Dinah sounded as if she could not stretch her imagination sufficiently to place sheep at the feet of the tall, handsome, supremely assured man in the doorway.

Mr. Chambers understood and chuckled. "Yes, sheep. Mortimer's an expert on a breed—do not, I pray, ask which—that Iveagh raises. But he's no shepherd, of course." No one had to ask whether Mr. Chambers referred to Iveagh or his cousin Mortimer. "He's head of the O'Neill family. Mortimer says it is one of the oldest families in Ireland. They were once the high kings of Ireland, or the ard-ri, as Mortimer told me they were called in the old language."

"It sounds as if your cousin has become half Irish, Rupe," drawled a young man who, perhaps, resented that another man could command such attention as the Earl of Iveagh did merely by appearing in the doorway.

Luckily Mr. Chambers was not thin-skinned. "Actually Mortimer is Anglo-Irish," he admitted cheerfully. "And no matter how much his awe of Iveagh may have prejudiced him, you cannot but agree the earl looks as if his ancestors were once kings."

"Indeed he does!" Lady Dinah agreed on a sigh, at which the other young ladies giggled in agreement.

Only Susannah stood staring across the room in absolute silence. She did not stand deaf, however. She had heard every word said.

Connor O'Neill, horse trainer, sheep farmer, the O'Neill, the Earl of Iveagh.

She realized Gussie must have known, but did not pursue the line of thought. There were other, more pressing considerations to absorb her. An earl! She had a furious desire to stalk up to the latter-day ard-ri and fling her glass of champagne into his oh-so handsome face. He would not look so assured then, with wine dripping from that flashing smile with which he was making putty of his hostess, Lady St. Clare.

The nearly savage pleasure the image gave Susannah was followed in the next moment by a stab of emotion so intense, she trembled. Dear heaven, if he opened his arms to her, she would fling herself into them, and thank God he'd come back for her. Deserter, liar, infuriating man—he might be all those, but she had come alive at the sight of him.

To James it seemed as if the musicians were privy to the drama unfolding, for they provided the cue that heralded the next act. At the instant one of the men struck a tuning chord with his bow, Iveagh's eyes met Susannah's.

James caught his breath at the change in the earl's expression. If he had wondered why the Irishman should make one of his rare visits to London, he had his answer. And if he had ever, if only briefly, entertained the suspicion that there had been something between his grandmother's trainer and Susannah, he had the answer to that as well. No man locked gazes with a mere acquaintance.

James glanced then at Susannah, and felt, oddly, a thrill of pride. She was up to that fierce look and to the Earl of Iveagh as well. Even as the other guests at the ball began to look from one to the other of them, Susannah did not drop her gaze. Chin regally high, she held the earl's eyes. Only a faint line of color rising in her cheeks hinted at the emotion she felt as she waited for the earl to come to her.

And come he did, striding across the floor, his intent gaze never wavering. James did not fail to note that Lady St. Clare's guests parted for the Irishman as readily as had the motley crowd at Newmarket.

When he reached Susannah, Connor stood for just a

moment as if drinking in the sight of her; then he bowed
as formally as he ought. "Lady Susannah, it is the rarest
pleasure to see you again."

"Lord Iveagh." Susannah allowed her knowledge of his
title to sink in. It pleased her when Connor's brow lifted,
but when his mouth began to quirk, she was moved to
continue coolly, "Seeing you is . . . a stunning surprise.
I cannot but wonder how the cottage you left beyond the Pale
will fare without you."

The contrast between Connor's black hair and blue eyes
was always remarkable, but it seemed as if his eyes became
an even lighter, bolder blue. "Castle, actually." Susannah
had not the means to keep him from smiling at her, and
though it was a faint, ironic smile, she had been right to fear
its power. "I didn't wish to seem to boast, you see. It's quite
a self-sufficient place, really, and after a careful inventory
of it, I have decided it is a proper setting for . . . anyone.
Ah, there is the music. I trust you have been approved for
the waltz?"

"I have, yes. In my first Season, my lord. A very good
thing, too, as I gave this waltz to Lord Bagley at the beginning
of the evening."

James heard an avid "Oh!" escape Lady Dinah, and
glancing about, he realized everyone within earshot was
following the interchange between Susannah and Iveagh.
He could not be offended, for he too was gawking, fascin-
ated. It was seldom one beheld such drama, and between
two actors so well-matched.

Susannah's cool parry of an invitation to waltz before the
invitation was even made may have startled Lady Dinah, but
Connor appeared to take it in stride. "I shall speak with Lord
Bagley and ask him to give me the dance."

"That would be very rude, my lord," Susannah returned,
equally composedly. "Lord Bagley has quite looked forward
to our waltz."

"If eagerness is the standard by which you choose your
partners, my lady, there is no contest at all." He gave her
a gleaming, triumphant pirate's smile. "I have traveled

hundreds of miles to dance the waltz with you, and even braved enemy territory, my lady. And I'll not be denied.''

The last was said entirely pleasantly, but no one listening misunderstood. ''You are very sure of yourself, Lord Iveagh,'' Susannah returned, her eyebrows flicking upward.

''In relation to Lord Bagley, my lady, I am entirely certain of myself.''

For the first time, Susannah averted her gaze from Connor's, allowing her lashes to shield her eyes. She strongly suspected they might be gleaming. Her entire being felt aglow, but she was not yet prepared to have Connor know he could be quite as certain of her as he could of himself in a contest with Lord Bagley.

''Susannah,'' Connor said, his voice dropping, that only she might hear it. Low like that, and rough too, it sent a warmth streaking through her veins. ''Come, I'll go on my knees to you, but only in private.''

That brought her head up, shimmering dark eyes and all. ''Will you do so then, my lord?''

Connor's expression was as grave as Susannah's, but the look in his eyes made her knees go weak. ''You may be certain of it, my lady.''

Lord Bagley never thought of again, Susannah laid her hand in Connor's.

''James?'' It was Beaufort. James swallowed nervously. His uncle unnerved him at the best of times. ''Who the devil is that with Susannah, and how the devil does she know him as well as it seems she does?''

James reminded himself to whom he owed the twenty thousand pounds that would make Mary Wardley, her adequate purse and sweet person, his. ''Ah, well, your grace, the gentleman with Susannah is the Earl of Iveagh. He's a horseman. They met at Newmarket this summer.''

James held his breath. He felt dizzyingly, dangerously noble. He was in Susannah's debt. He knew it. But, oh, what if Beaufort should divine somehow that, while his nephew had told nothing but the truth, he had omitted so much as to lie like a cur.

Silently he tried the truth: Oh, that is the Earl of Iveagh. He and Susannah met, when he served Gussie as her head trainer this summer.

The truth, in this instance, seemed so incomprehensible, James gritted his teeth and prayed for help.

It arrived quite unexpectedly in the form of Sir Charles Arbuthnot, a man of some importance in the government. As he approached Beaufort, his eyes, like Beaufort's and James's, were upon the striking couple dancing the waltz with such grace.

"I did not know your daughter was acquainted with Iveagh, Beaufort. Does she know him well?"

"It would seem so," the duke murmured.

Sir Charles apparently found nothing odd in the equivocal reply. He nodded abruptly. "Splendid! Really, that is splendid!"

"Do you think so, Arbuthnot?" Beaufort inquired, never taking his eyes from his daughter.

"Yes, yes! You see, he is the man with whom we must have good relations if we are to have any control of the west of Ireland. He's the only real power in that part, because the native Irish regard him almost as a king, and because he has great wealth."

"Wealth?" It was the first real interest Beaufort had betrayed. "I thought all the native Irish were poor as aborigines."

"Not Iveagh's branch of the O'Neill's." Sir Charles shook his head. "They've been cannier than the rest, or more godless, perhaps. Unlike most of their compatriots, they've never shrunk from having the eldest son of the family baptized a Protestant. As a consequence, the penal laws have never affected them, and they have passed down their lands from father to eldest son as we do, keeping them intact, and adding to their holdings as they wished—both privileges denied those who remain papists, as you know. It would be a great consolation to know someone as pliant as your daughter had influence over him."

At that the ghost of a smile lit Beaufort's gray eyes. "I wonder if you have ever met Susannah, Arbuthnot?"

"Why, yes. Lady Susannah and I discussed the meet at Newmarket at great length not long ago."

"Ah" was all Beaufort said to Sir Charles, but when the man took his leave, the duke could not forbear giving James a wry look. "Arbuthnot is a formidable diplomat, but I wonder if it would ever occur to you, James, to describe Susannah as pliant?"

James grinned. "She is exceedingly beautiful, though, your grace, and never more than when she is speaking of horses."

"Hmm." Beaufort said nothing more, only looked out to the floor where Susannah danced with an Irish earl whom James had characterized as a horseman.

Susannah was entirely unaware of the interest she and Connor excited. The only eyes she saw or cared about were his.

When Connor put his arm about her waist, she felt a tremor go through her. He felt it too, and when he saw the knowledge that he could affect her so register in his eyes as a gleam of triumph, Susannah returned him a look that was not friendly.

"You put me through hell, Connor O'Neill."

"I know." There was no triumph now in his eyes. "If it is any consolation, I was in the same hell."

"Why did you change your mind?"

"I couldn't face a lifetime feeling like that."

Connor tried a smile, but the result was closer to a grimace. It appeased Susannah, that grim, even ragged look, but it did not still all her doubts. "You no longer blame me for being English, then?"

Connor winced a little at the harshness of her tone. He wished so very much he had not hurt her. "I never blamed you, Susannah. It is difficult to explain, for you are scarcely aware of the Irish here in England, while we are so terribly, awfully aware of you. I once fought English rule in Ireland with arms, Susannah. True, I am not so foolish or bitter now, and I see hope for peaceful progress, but old habits of thinking die hard. As the Earl of Iveagh, I thought it would be a betrayal of my people to marry into one of the most powerful families among those oppressing them."

It was Susannah's turn to flinch. Her family was powerful,

and for centuries the English had unconscionably oppressed the Irish. ''But you have changed your mind?'' she asked, her voice sounding a good deal smaller than it had.

He smiled down into her uncertain eyes. ''With Liam's help I came to see it was an individual I wished to marry, not her countrymen. And that my people would understand.''

''Liam?''

Connor's smile became rueful. ''You can guess how foul-tempered I was, if Liam came to argue for you. I do believe he feared I would turn into a drunken sot without you. Rory, as you know, called me a fool from the first.'' Connor paused a moment, and when he spoke again, there was a harder edge to his voice. ''My little brother was more accurate than he knew. It was also not an Englishman who betrayed him. It was not only an Irishman but my own cousin. Susannah, like any man, I want loyalty and steadfastness in those around me, and as it turns out, I found more of both those qualities in a certain English lady than in anyone else I've ever met.''

''I ought to turn my nose up at you, you took so long to come to your senses,'' Susannah returned, but her eyes were alight.

''It's such an elegant nose, I'd not be minding kissing it back down.'' Connor gave her the lazy grin that had haunted a good many of Susannah's dreams, while his eyes conveyed that there was a great deal more he would not mind kissing. Susannah felt a surge of warmth, and Connor, seeing the effect of that surge upon her cheeks, laughed as he pulled her tighter to him.

It was Connor who sobered slightly after they had danced, lost in each other, for a little. ''Susannah, I want you to consider carefully the life I am offering you. We'll not live in a cottage, it's true, but I return a great deal of my wealth to my land. With so many dependent upon me, I will never live like this.'' He looked around the sumptuous ballroom filled with elegant, fashionable people. ''It will not be a glittering life, but for the occasional visits you'll make to London.''

Susannah noted that he did not promise to accompany her on those visits, but did not protest. Later they would see what sort of accommodations they could make between them about England. "Will you be there, Connor, in Connacht? If so, I will be content as I have not been since you left me. For all the pleasure I derived from the entertainments I've attended this fall, I may as well have been sleeping. Do you understand? You are the breath of life to me."

Connor's hand tightened almost painfully upon her waist. "Dear God, Susannah, I want to sweep you up in my arms and carry you out of here. But I must be certain you can accept there will be times when your loyalties are strained."

"As your wife, my loyalties will be with you, Connor." Susannah allowed the simple remark to stand a moment, then added, frowning, "But even were I not married to you, I could not approve the repression and cruelty my countrymen have visited upon yours. Such barbarous behavior only creates wounds that fester and eventually cause the greatest harm to everyone—as I intend to make clear to anyone who will listen."

Connor would have kissed her there on the dance floor, but that the music ended and he was reminded where they were. "Good Lord, I cannot bear this, Susannah." There was no mistaking the rough edge to his voice. "It is agony to hold you and yet not hold you. Before I cause some disastrous scene, I must go. I'll call upon your father tomorrow, and we'll be married as soon as he will agree to holding the ceremony."

Reminded of her father, Susannah gave Connor an anxious look. "You will be tactful with Beaufort, Connor? I am his only daughter, and he is a very proud man."

Connor did not have the opportunity to reassure her, for Beaufort had his own idea when he would meet the man who'd awakened Susannah. Seeing her father appear suddenly before them, Susannah muttered beneath her breath, "Oh, Lord," and Connor had the time only to squeeze her hand before she performed the introductions.

"Father, I should like to present the Earl of Iveagh. Lord Iveagh, my father, the Duke of Beaufort."

"Your grace." Connor's bow was faultless.

"Lord Iveagh."

The two men studied each other a moment in silence. Connor was taller, younger, and more fit, but there was nothing negligible about the Duke of Beaufort. Connor saw where Susannah had gotten her cool assurance. The duke dared scrutinize him as Connor had not been scrutinized since he wore short coats.

Rebellion flickered in him, only to die as suddenly as it had arisen. This man had the right to weigh him. More, he'd the duty. He was Susannah's father, after all, and Connor was only a stranger to him.

Quite unexpectedly Connor experienced a spurt of sympathy for the duke. He would be a father too one day, and would suffer the same plight. The subsequent thought, that any man who came for his daughter had better be prepared, almost made Connor smile.

"I should take it as an honor, sir, if you would see me tomorrow at an hour convenient to you."

Susannah let out her breath slowly. She had feared how Connor would request the interview with her father. They were both proud men, but Connor had surprised her. He had made his request as if he did, indeed, understand how difficult the business of giving a daughter away would be.

Beaufort marked the Irish earl's tone as well. This was no pup begging an audience, but neither did he swagger in to demand Susannah. Of course, he'd no need to demand, the duke mused wryly. Susannah was his.

That Susannah loved Iveagh was obvious. She could scarce look away from him, and there was such a glow in her lovely eyes, her father's heart tightened just a little.

Beaufort bowed to the inevitable with grace. He would never douse that light in Susannah's eyes unless he had cause to believe the man she'd set her heart upon was a scoundrel, something the Earl of Iveagh obviously was not.

Damn him, there was even a sympathetic light in his Irish eyes. Beaufort's mouth quirked.

"Come at one, why don't you, Lord Iveagh, and stay for luncheon after our interview."

Connor had not expected such an open hand. His eyes

registered his surprise; then slowly he smiled. "I should be very pleased to stay for luncheon, sir."

Susannah thought she might cry, which was an absurd way indeed to react when she was so very, very happy. She smiled instead, brilliantly.

James, seeing that smile from a little distance away, felt his breath catch in his throat. He had never seen Susannah look so. Never, though he had seen her smile with purest delight many times. Little wonder that O'Neill could not drag his eyes from her. Lord, she was incandescent.

Connor did take his leave soon after. He had two reasons for going. Not only would it be hellish to stand aside and watch Susannah do the polite with other gentlemen, as he would be obliged to do, but he had a disinclination to encounter anyone who had known him as Lady Augusta's trainer. Though Beaufort had been accepting of an Irish earl, Connor doubted he would be so approving of an Irish earl who had masqueraded as a horse trainer.

Susannah agreed. "Yes, you won him over tonight, but I wouldn't care to test him so soon. Let us wait until after the announcement of our betrothal has appeared in the papers before you go about in public. How pleased Gussie will be to hear our news. She will be in alt!"

"I know." Connor laughed. "She was another reason I came. She wrote to warn me your father had decreed you must choose a husband by Christmas. I did not fear Sunderly half so much as some unknown prospect, and I left Connacht two days later."

Susannah stared, speechless a moment, and then she laughed aloud. "Oh, Gussie! You wonderful wretch. Lord, but was there ever such a grandmother?"

Connor understood at once. "There was no such decree?"

Susannah shook her head, still laughing. "Of course not. You've met him. Can you imagine Beaufort dragging me to my wedding?"

Connor began to laugh as well. "Lord, there really never was such a grandmother! I'll go up tomorrow, after our luncheon, to salute her for her stratagem."

"And I'll go too! I wouldn't miss Gussie hearing the news of our betrothal for the world. Oh, and Connor . . ." Susannah sounded so beside herself, he smiled. "The fall meet starts the day after. Shall we watch Saracen win again?"

A new gleam lit his eyes. "Aye, but it would be my pleasure to celebrate his win a little differently this time."

"Oh, aye, my lord." Susannah's eyes were soft as velvet. "Quite, quite differently."